THE GIRL . . .

A golden-haired, big-eyed beauty named Susan, haunted by the memory of the man who wooed her, married her, and widowed her in the space of a month

THE AGENT . . .

Peter Munro, who lost his cover and his espionage job the same night Susan lost her husband, but whose restless mind and gnawing fear still kept him "looking behind the curtains"

THE MISSION . . .

A deceptively easy assignment: tour guide for an obsessed woman who wants to see the spot where the Communists shot her husband. Munro has been around long enough to know when something nasty is in the works. But even he can't foresee the twists, the betrayals, the shocks waiting for him on the other side of that border. . . .

THE MAN ON THE BRIDGE

Ian Stuart Black

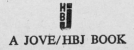

A JOVE/HBJ BOOK

First Jove/HBJ edition published October 1977

Library of Congress Catalog Card Number: 76-5368

Printed in the United States of America

Jove/HBJ books are published by Jove Publications, Inc. (Har-
court Brace Jovanovich) 757 Third Avenue, New York, N.Y.
10017

Written for Isobel, Moray,
Alison and Alan

1

Peter Munro had two recurrent dreams, and they were both concerned with bridges.

In the first, and most alarming, he was coming through a village at night, down an alley-way between crude stone houses. He knew that a short distance ahead lay the bridge. A few steps in front another man led the way. Both kept close to the walls, in the shadows thrown by the moonlight. The man in front turned and gave a sign of triumph. Munro saw he was grinning. In retrospect, this warmed his heart, as well as awoke his pity—as indeed did most of his memories of Stephan Aroso.

"We're there," whispered Stephan. "Another hundred yards." The air was chill with the light wind that blew from the snow tops of the Macedonian hills, not far away as the cranes flew. The village itself was high in those hills; one of the highest, stone walls reflecting the first cold of the year.

Stephan reached the end of the alley-way, and Munro saw him hesitate. This was a moment of decision for both of them. Around that corner was life or death. Not a metaphor in this case. Real life . . . real death. And it was for Stephan to put it to the test.

It was typical of the man to joke at that moment. A boxer's handshake above his head—a gesture of hope or triumph—then he peered cautiously into the main street. It seemed a long wait to Munro, but when Stephan looked back his grin was broader, and he stepped out into the road. He had a theatrical way of expressing himself, throwing his arms wide. Munro thanked God he had the sense to stay silent. He moved on to join him.

7

The village was gaunt and empty, as though it had begun its winter sleep.

They could see the bridge at the foot of the road, and it was unguarded and intact.

There lay freedom. It seemed incredible that no one barred their way. A story-book ending to the great escape.

Afterwards Munro regretted that they hadn't made a run for it, and crossed the bridge to the safety of the country on the other side. It was no distance at all! They could have danced across it in their relief. Stephan was a fine dancer. Munro had seen him join in the local dances on the open hillsides, after the harvest, in a dance only for men; a dance which traditionally the women should not have seen. But the women stayed to watch nowadays—at least the younger ones, although the older generation still held up an arm as if to cover their faces with the veils they no longer wore. And they all marveled at the young stranger who knew their dance and who outstripped their own young men in its execution.

There were some jealous looks, a flickering of hands to knife-belts during the eating and drinking that followed. Then they sang, and Stephan destroyed all enmity when he sang a song that was no longer permitted by the authorities, a song their fathers had sung, and their grandfathers, all about killing Turks, and killing Romanians, and killing Slavs, and killing one another for that matter. And he sang it in a dialect that set the village chanting a drunken roar of approval—and the old men kissed him. And Stephan kissed them back.

It had been worth the effort and danger, to get to Stephan, to warn him that he was no longer safe, and to lead him to routes away from the police zones. Stephan was a key man. Whereas Munro knew himself to be a pawn, a piece that was moved but never moved of his own accord. Stephan was creative. His imagination seemed to be the generator which powered their organization. His flair, contacts, the risks he took, the things he did, these were the basis on which they had achieved success in a hostile world.

But Munro had a right to congratulate himself. It was he

8

who had organized this escape. No one else could have crossed the right frontiers at the right moment. It had been his hard work, the careful plotting of pieces, that had made the route possible. He had done the hack work. He had made it pay off. For all his charm and panache, Stephan Aroso would have been a dead man by now if it had not been for Munro.

The way ahead was clear. Munro saw Stephan move off, holding a mocking finger up for silence. A quick grin and a whisper "Who plays spies?" It was an answer to Munro's old complaint. Stephan treated his work as though it were a game, something dramatic, exciting, full of the romance the public attached to it. Whereas Munro knew it had none. It was mostly a matter of keeping records, office work, of passively consulting computers. As routine a matter as the Board of Trade. Less exciting than the buying and selling that Munro used to do in Eastern Europe.

They began to cross the bridge, keeping a few steps apart. Half way over—it was only a matter of yards—there was a call from behind.

Munro spun around. There was a man behind them, at the end of the bridge.

"Go ahead," said Stephan. "It's only a fellow from the village."

Munro went on. He reached the end of the bridge before he looked back. Stephan was speaking to the man on the other side. Munro couldn't hear; besides he didn't understand the dialect in these hills.

Then someone shouted. It seemed to come from one of the houses. The man at the end of the bridge had become two men. He was three. He was five!

"Run for it, Stephan," he shouted. Stephan turned and ran.

The men had guns. They started after Stephan. Then they stopped. Someone gave an order. Stephan still ran, still smiling, an incredulous smile, as if asking how he could have been stupid enough to be caught by a trick like that. He was still smiling when the firing started. The first shot must have hit him, for he went down and hung on to the wall of the bridge. They still shot at him. He seemed to be trying to climb over the side. Munro broke into a run, shouting, swearing at the gunmen, waving them back. Later he was amazed to think of his behavior, fighting to get to Stephan's body long after he could see the red stain over his jacket, fighting like a madman as they dragged him back into the village. He could see them swinging Stephan's body into a truck that drove from nowhere on to the bridge. It must have been carefully prepared.

They must have known they were coming. They could have stopped them at any time. But they had chosen to let them go so far, and then they had shot Stephan. Munro was still struggling as he watched the truck drive through the village, bumping over the uneven track. They must have tired of trying to hold him, for he got the butt-end of a heavy rifle, and he went down on the stone floor. That was the first fantasy, or day-dream, or recollection. It always stopped there.

And the second fantasy took place at a second bridge. Not much longer than the first, but it was down on the coast road with a railway close at hand and a customs post at each end. This time it was in the morning. The sun came and went as clouds blew in over the Adriatic, for in spite of its blue seas, squalls blow up sharply.

This vision returned to Munro sometimes between sleeping and waking. It was occasionally the tail-end of a dream. In it he would be waiting to cross the bridge, and he would be shaken with alarm in case the occasion was a trick. He couldn't see why it should be a trick. But at this stage of his life he no longer depended on reasons. So many things had happened to shake his belief in cause and effect. Events were arbitrary. They happened because the interrogator wanted them to happen, because the defending officer said they had happened, because the prosecutor had a confession—in some foreign language—that said the events had happened. The judges knew the events. The small public audience knew. Official newspapers knew. Everyone knew the way things happened—except Munro. He was no longer sure of his ability to reason. It took him a long time to recover that assurance. Light, noise and darkness can so

10

fill a man's brain that there is no room for anything else—certainly not for assurance.

This second fantasy had something of a nightmare about it, for this time he had something to hope for. He was going away. He was to be allowed to cross the bridge. Not yet. No. But some time . . . when the signal was given.

But he missed the signal! The very thing he feared most. He missed the signal when they were ready on the other side. Another man was walking towards him. Now they wouldn't let him go! They would get back their own man and still keep him. The exchange was a trick. He would never get away.

One of the officers reached out from behind him and gave him a shove. Another said, "He wants to stay with us. He is applying for political asylum." But nobody laughed. "Go now," said the officer.

Munro had tossed aside his cigarette. He crossed the bridge.

Sometimes the two memories merged into dreams in which he and Stephan both ran for safety. Or in which the officer held him back and he never got away. Sometimes he would keep his eyes shut for he feared to open them. It was only gradually that he convinced himself he was safe. He was in Shaw's Hotel. He was in the safest, most gentle, law-abiding corner of the earth. He was hidden away amongst the harmless elderly, spinning out their years in a south coast holiday town in England.

The lady who ran Shaw's Hotel was Mrs. Shaw, but there was no sign of a Mr. Shaw. She had a quick smile for Munro and a bright look in her eye. It wasn't all that often someone so intriguing booked in for the winter months. He was a young man against the background of retired army officers and their wives that were her guests. One of his cases was covered with bits of old labels from foreign countries. She had made out quite a number. They were in their native languages, Turkish, Slavonic, Greek.

Another thing about Munro intrigued Mrs. Shaw. She guessed he had been very ill. He was like a man with a

11

sun-tan which had faded, leaving a pallid, worn color, and a look of strain in his eyes. She noticed he sometimes used a stick when he walked. She judged that he had been close to death, and she was right.

She met him in the hall. "Oh, Mr. Munro. Someone's been looking for you."

That puzzled him. He had had no visitors in the months he'd been there.

"Who was it?" Anything strange threatened him—anything out of the way.

"A man about thirty. Well dressed. An official I thought."

"Did he say what it was about?"

"He said he would call back."

There was a small bar just off the dining-room. Munro had a couple of drinks while he waited, glancing into the street from where he sat. Later he waited on a chair by his window. His room was at the back of the hotel.

As a residue of old habits, he pulled his flat briefcase from a drawer, opened it and looked at the beautifully-made false compartment. It was empty now, but at one time it had concealed a tiny Italian revolver. It had been designed for a woman, indeed for a woman with a small hand, and his friends had laughed at him for his faith in anything so delicate. He remembered that it had inlay on the barrel and marquetry on the butt. It was more of an ornament than a weapon. But he had killed three men with it in his time, perhaps four. He wasn't sure of the fourth because the occasion was at night and the man had disappeared.

He felt now he would like that gun again. Even a small and pretty weapon. At short range it was effective. He measured with his eye the distance to the door. Seven paces at most. The gun would have been more than adequate for Eastbourne.

Munro was used to waiting, to sitting like that, for he had lived a long time in more restricted quarters. He didn't know what he feared. But fear has no name. Someone was going to come and to knock at that door and that someone meant—what?

He tried to list the possibilities. The worst that could happen was they would kill him this time.

The brief sun dipped into the Channel, and no one came. He reminded himself of an old trick. Often they said he was going to die—and they let him live.

A check arrived for Munro on the first of every month. It was all the money he had. He paid for his hotel and had a small amount left over. He could afford his drinks bill and something for newspapers. He hadn't bought any clothes since he'd been back in England. He had a raincoat he'd picked up in Germany. He didn't smoke. In fact the only time in his life he had smoked was when he was under arrest. The tobacco had been home-grown in the grounds of the prison and wasn't properly dried or cleaned, but he had been grateful for it. He had reminded himself at the time that Balkan tobacco was once very chic. The last cigarette he had smoked, he had stubbed out almost as he lit it—on that famous occasion, on the bridge. One man at one end. One man at the other. Twenty yards between them. Just before he passed the man who was going to freedom in his own country, he knew he was a poor exchange for the professional they were giving for him. He resented the blackmail. But he was trembling, filled with gratitude, as he walked by.

He had never smoked since. This may not have had any significance, but it saved him money.

The envelope containing the check lay in the hall. It was all the mail Munro received. Inside was the usual slip of paper indicating the amount payable, sending the compliments of the British Travelers Interest Fund. For the first time there was a line of writing at the foot of the slip. It read "Hope to see you in near future" and it was signed CC. Munro tore the paper into tiny pieces as though they might contaminate him.

He pushed the check into his pocket and went out.

The main shopping street lay at right angles to the sea, running inland to the railway station. Munro had fallen into a pattern for his evening walk. He went to the sea, then along to the main street. He turned down that and walked as far as the shops. Last-minute customers hurried by, office workers, young families; a relief after the gentility of his hotel. He bought a London paper. It made him feel less cut off. After all, London was only sixty miles away. There were moments in the homeward bustle when he could almost relax. Then a face was reflected in a shop window, or a figure across the road, and the sense of safety had gone.

Rain blew in from the sea, making the street lights glisten. Munro stopped to shelter above the beach. Cars splashed past. The street quickly cleared of the few people who had been out. Only Munro appeared to enjoy the solitude.

He could see the waves breaking on the sand. Out in the Channel were the faint lights of a ship. It hardly made progress, just a light, coming and going in the darkness. He stood watching.

Over the years he had developed a special awareness. Sometimes he was able to pick up faint sounds; sometimes a tiny object told him a whole story. Sometimes he was suddenly alert. In the past he would have thrown himself on the ground, taking cover. But here, in Eastbourne, there could be no danger.

Munro turned to look through the glass panel of the shelter. Across the road a car was standing by the curb, just out of a circle of light thrown by a street lamp. There was someone beside it. A girl. As he turned, she got in and drove away. In that brief moment he'd seen a small round face, thoughtful, serious. Long fair hair; a brown coat, a fur collar.

The automatic device in Munro's brain recorded her. He couldn't be sure she had been watching him. She too might have been watching the ship at sea. Of one thing he was certain, he'd never seen her before.

The rain vanished as quickly as it had come. Munro moved on. Each evening, the same walk; four sides of a square. A compulsion, a duty even.

The most important thing for a prisoner is to keep moving. It was all too easy to stop taking exercise, but then it was a short step to give up everything—willpower, identity,

14

resolve. Munro forced himself to walk twice a day—in the morning and before dinner. The cell had been six foot by four, with a small barred window eight feet from the ground. He had exercised every day, had swung his arms upwards and outwards, had done kneebending until he had leg muscles like a footballer, and shadowboxed until his jailers had thought he had gone mad. After that, he remembered with satisfaction, they had taken him out into the sunshine each day and had walked him up and down in a courtyard from where he could see distant snow-tipped mountains, and small birds flying. When he had gone back to his cell he had started singing.

The walk over, he headed back to the hotel. Mrs. Shaw was waiting. There had been a telephone call for him.

"He didn't leave a name."

A mysterious caller, a phone call. Such tactics didn't disturb him. They were dealing with a man who had been in the hands of experts, professionals who knew how to unhinge the mind, and reduce a man to a three-year-old.

"It was a long-distance call. London, I think," said Mrs. Shaw.

He sat in the bar after dinner. He drank slowly and very little. One ear turned to the phone in the hall. Mrs. Shaw joined him. "You have been busy today," she said. "It makes a nice change, we have so many retired people."

Munro was careful what he said. "Yes. I've had one or two things to think about."

She must know he did nothing. She opened a cupboard behind the bar. "I've got some of the whiskey you liked." She dropped her voice as though it were a secret. "I wonder if you'd like one with me."

She was going out of her way to be pleasant to him. He wondered what she wanted. At one time he would have wondered whom she was working for. It never occurred to him that she might find him attractive. He had opted out of relationships with women, as out of much else in life, and he had done it under bright lights, in moments of humiliation, naked before interrogators; for they were behind bright lights, asking questions, shouting if his answers changed. "You said you had seen the accused at his home.

Now you say 'outside' his home. Why do you say that?"

"I beg your pardon," he said. Mrs. Shaw was speaking. "I didn't catch that?"

He leaned against the bar, holding the glass, hardly drinking at all. Distant, brooding—his dark good looks clouded. Black hair curling slightly.

"I hope you are happy here?" "Oh yes. Very."

The truth was that he *wasn't* there. At the edge of the sea, as he moved through the streets, walked the chalk hills, he wasn't there. His body was; but some part of him, a vital part, perhaps *the* most vital part, had gone.

Christopher Cecil usually introduced himself, adding, "No relation to the famous family," but by doing so some of the association managed to rub off on to him. He had a fairly exclusive background as it was. Old school friends held positions in Government or Opposition. Cousins were merchant bankers; father dabbled in property. But neither politics nor finance attracted Christopher Cecil. Well, not exactly politics. Although he did settle for something along those lines.

Munro detested him. But there was no point in refusing to meet.

"There's a gentleman to see you," said Mrs. Shaw. Munro had just returned from his routine walk.

"The same one?" he wanted to know.

"A different one. In the lounge. Very charming." Cecil was known to be charming. It was one of his assets, and he made use of it.

He turned from the bar as Munro came in, a warm smile of welcome, an outstretched arm. Munro didn't respond, but Cecil appeared not to notice. He shook hands and put the other arm around Munro's shoulder.

"Well, how are you, dear fellow? How are you? How nice to see you. What's it to be? A whiskey, of course. How have you been keeping? Better, I hope. I trust you got my note?"

Munro imagined he was referring to the one line on the slip with his check.

Mrs. Shaw had hurried behind the bar.

16

"What is it?" Munro looked grimly at Cecil.

"Nothing special, dear fellow. Had to be down in this part of the world. Caxton said to look you up."

"Who?"

"Caxton. You remember. John Caxton. Sir Johnny. Runs our little outfit."

"I don't know him."

"Of course you don't. He's had promotion since your day. You knew Freddy. Upper House, you know."

Munro detested the way Cecil talked, detested his manner, his assumptions, his familiarity with things fashionable. And he also detested the pretense Cecil made that Munro was part of that world. The tone of his voice suggested London was a club for a few, and that Cecil was one of those few.

"Why are you here?" There was cold hostility in Munro's voice. Mrs. Shaw was quite taken aback. The stranger was so friendly, so pleased to see Munro.

"Auld acquaintance," said Cecil heartily. "Soda? Water?"

Munro thought twice about drinking with him, then decided any gesture was pointless. Cecil had a job to do. For all his air of authority, he was only a cog in a wheel.

"You don't want to see me about anything?"

"My God." laughed Cecil, "you take some convincing. Always were a great one for checking and double-checking. Get a yarn past Peter Munro, I used to say, and you could have it signed in the Kremlin. Great to see you again, dear fellow. Nice to note the effects have worn off."

"What the hell are you talking about?"

"Seen a doctor lately?"

"No."

"There you are. Must be getting better. Don't need a doctor."

"You must have had some reason for coming here."

A shrug from Cecil. "Nothing urgent. Matter of admin. It seemed to us you must be a little short of cash. Cost of living goes up. The fixed income buys less." He cleared his voice like someone speaking at a meeting. "The British Travelers Interest Fund want to be fair. The point is,

17

we've been reviewing pensions. Yours included. Interested?"

"You're a bloody liar," said Munro.

"True. But the money's there. Sir John thought we should talk about it."

"Who?"

"You . . . me . . . Sir John."

"Is he here?"

"No."

"Where is he then?"

"In his office."

"So what are you up to?"

"Nice choice of phrasing," said Cecil. "We thought you'd like to discuss upping your monthly check."

"I'd rather starve," said Munro. He was being manipulated again. He didn't know how, but he sensed it.

"I can always give you a five per cent increase," said Cecil thoughtfully, "I've got authority for that. But in your case we thought it should be more. Fifteen per cent. Twenty. I can't sign for that lot, as you know. I'm a minion. But we felt you'd had the heavy end of the stick. Ridiculous for you to be tucked away in a place like this. Shabby deal. After all, the whole department knows how much we owe to you."

Munro didn't believe a word. He said nothing.

"Very good whiskey. And she's a sweet girl behind the bar. No wonder you stay here, dear fellow." He had dropped back into his previous act. The interview was over—the essentials, anyway.

"Think it over," said Cecil. "I'm not going back till tonight. Do you eat here?"

"Yes."

"Every evening?"

"Yes."

Cecil looked around the room. "Care for a change tonight?"

"I don't particularly want to eat with you," said Munro. It was as if the pawns were being maneuvered into position. He guessed he couldn't prevent it. Nevertheless, he wouldn't assist.

18

"I quite understand," said Cecil. For a moment it seemed as if he did. Then he saw Mrs. Shaw at the bar. "One more round of that excellent blend," he smiled—sensitive mouth, beautiful white teeth. "And for yourself, if I may be so bold."

Munro thought how easily the man could adapt his behavior, assuming the genteel vulgarity of this place.

As Cecil left he put it clearly on the line. "We expect to see you later, Munro. The meeting's fixed for Thursday morning at the office: lunch with Sir John. Just the three of us."

So they wanted Munro to go to see them. He couldn't think why. His work with them was over. It could only be about money. Cecil hadn't said it, but they *could* stop his money. A disturbing thought. He was convalescing, Munro told himself. He needed peace and quite. For that he needed money. He would have to go—if just to insure the amount they gave him.

2

John Caxton had his office in a featureless block behind the old War Office in Whitehall. Indeed, the entire department of the British Travelers Interest Fund had its offices there. The buildings had been built in Victorian times and were a maze of wide corridors. The heating had been improved, Munro noticed.

He had arrived at Charing Cross station. It was a short walk from there.

Munro signed a form in the reception hall, aware that the woman at the desk recognized him. It was some time now since his picture had been in the newspapers, but they don't forget easily in this corner of the city.

An usher took him through passages he'd walked before. Not that he had been a regular visitor to the head office. That would have been foolish. But he'd been there on a couple of occasions.

Sir John Caxton was waiting, while Cecil hovered in the background.

"Come in, my dear chap. Pleased to meet you at last." It sounded as if Sir John had been trying for years to get in touch with Munro. What could have been the obstacle, he wondered? "You and Cecil have known each other a long time?"

They shook hands. Caxton was a short, slim man in his fifties, bald, with a long, pleasant face. He smiled continuously. His handshake was firm. Caxton gave an impression of being direct.

"Sorry to drag you from Eastbourne. Still, this is business and we must have some formality. You probably know more about the Travelers than I do?" He made it sound a question. Munro waited. He had learned to let the other man speak.

"Ours is a semi-official institution in a way. Government cash, but administered by us."

"Us?" said Munro.

"You know. The department. It's a way of spending money which we don't have to account for to auditors. Well, we couldn't, could we? Half of it goes on blackmail, bribes, women, contacts. It wouldn't fit into the books. Some of the things you authorized yourself. I've been looking through the records. Fascinating—but not for publication. I found one or two of yours that absolutely shook me. Where are they? I made a note."

He was flicking through a couple of files on his desk.

"Here we are. 'Payment for boys and sheep. Had to be dollars. Head man won't accept pounds, local money or salt' . . ." Sir John laughed. "Now why did you say 'salt'?"

"I suppose I thought it was funny," said Munro. He remembered the incident. The money had got him out of trouble that day. They had betrayed him three days later.

"And this," grinned Sir John, turning the pages, " 'payment eleven pounds ten pence for the murder of railway official.' Why eleven pounds ten?"

"It was the current rate for the job," Munro told him.

"You can see why we have to do it all under the cover of the Travelers," said Sir John. "Couldn't have them chatting over *that* in committee."

He paused for a moment.

"How's the pretty lady in the hotel?" asked Cecil. Munro didn't bother to reply.

"The thing is this," said Sir John, "we'd like to put your money up by half."

"Half!" That surprised Munro. He was more wary than ever. "Cecil said twenty per cent."

"Did he? I'd like to double it. You see, I know the sort of thing you've been through. In another part of the world, of course. But that's by the way. I want you to be easy in your mind, while you get a chance to get back your equilibrium, so to speak."

Munro wondered if he had done the man an injustice.

Could they be on the level? Was he genuinely concerned?

"The thing is, we might have to explain in principle why we've ignored official recommendations. You know, we've got outsiders on the committee. Chancellor of some university, a surgeon, a couple of legal men. They like explanations. If we fix your money this way—the way I want to—then they'll require a reason. But don't worry about it. I think we've dreamed up one."

"A reason to pay me more money?"

"That's right."

It was becoming clearer to Munro.

"What's this reason?" He spoke almost gently, a trick he'd developed, when something threatened.

"We thought that if we said you were back on the active list—in an advisory capacity—something like that, then they would accept the new pay structure.

"I see. You'd say I'm working for you again."

"That should do it," Cecil chimed in cheerfully. "You're back on the pay-roll."

"That wouldn't fool anyone," said Munro.

They looked at him sharply. Had he thought of something that had escaped them? It was hardly possible. They had been going over this proposition together for a month.

"Why not?" asked Sir John.

"What good could I be to you now? I'm finished. Everyone knows who I am."

"Not everyone," said Sir John.

"Who doesn't?" said Munro. "Where could you send me?"

There was a moment's pause. It seemed to Munro it was a special silence; then Sir John said, "We had thought of sending you back to the same place."

He couldn't believe his ears. "What!"

"Your old hunting-ground."

He was almost too dazed to speak.

"Do you mean Greece?"

"That's right," said Sir John, "Greece. The Albanian-Greek frontier. That area."

"No one knows it like you," said Cecil.

Did neither of them understand what had happened?

22

"I think you must be mad," said Munro quietly.

"We don't mean *cross* the frontier. Just stay around in that area."

"What for?" Munro looked from one to the other. They were asking him to step back into a nightmare.

"It's just an arrangement to justify this money . . ."

Munro didn't let Cecil finish. "For Christ's sake," he said, "how stupid do you take me for? You brought up the money to get me here. You want me to go back—God knows why—so you twist the situation till it works for you. I don't need the money. I don't have to do anything."

"It's a matter of policy," said Sir John. "The Travelers comes up for review periodically. People don't stay on the pension scheme forever."

"I thought you'd say that some time," said Munro.

"My dear fellow, it's not a threat. We'll drop the whole matter if you like."

Munro sat for a moment wondering at their simplicity.

"What could I do for you?" he asked. "Wherever I went someone would be watching. I'm the man who had his picture in the papers. Splashed across the front page during the trial, then at the exchange. Less than a year ago! Oh yes, they've forgotten in London. But out there! In that part of Europe! I wouldn't stand a dog's chance."

"We didn't want you to do anything like that," said Sir John. "We know the business too well. But there was something you could have done."

"What?"

"As you don't want to go back under any conditions, we'll just forget it. Besides, we might find someone else."

"There *is* no one else," said Cecil sharply.

Sir John lifted his hands, a gesture of mild resignation. He got up. The meeting was over.

"I'll show you out," said Cecil.

"Don't bother. I know the way."

"It's a stupid regulation we have. No strangers are allowed unaccompanied in the building."

Cecil walked beside Munro through the corridors. He seemed to bear him no ill-will.

"I know you aren't too fond of my company, old fellow,"

he said, "but let's not make an issue out of that. We had arranged to have lunch together at Foresters. Got a table for four. Sir Johnny won't be there now, but that could still be a pleasant threesome. They have a nice claret . . ."

"Three?" enquired Munro.

"Oh. Yes. Now, let's see . . . I suppose in these circumstances only the two of us."

"Who was the third?"

"Like Sir Johnny said, no point going into that."

They had arrived back in the reception hall. "I'll hand in the slip you signed," said Cecil pleasantly. "And if you feel like being in the bar at Foresters at one o'clock, I'll be there. Seems a pity to come all that way and not have lunch on the old firm."

They were crossing to the main door when Cecil recognized someone at the reception desk. He gave a quick smile in that direction and opened the door for Munro. Munro glanced towards the desk as he did so. There was a girl there, writing out one of the slips. She must have been a visitor. She had a small round face and she looked across at them with large, troubled eyes. She clicked like a snapshot in his brain. Long fair hair to her shoulders. A brown coat, a fur collar, fur-topped boots; it was the girl who had watched him in the rain at Eastbourne. He got a much clearer picture of her now: no tricks of lamplight and rain. Fair skin flushed as if she had arrived in from the cold that swept down Whitehall from Trafalgar Square. She had seen them cross the hall, and looked up, suddenly expectant. Cecil gave a tiny shake of the head and the girl stayed where she was, otherwise Munro got the impression she might have joined them.

Cecil hurried him to the door.

"Goodbye, old fellow. Duty calls. See you at lunch." He more or less stood between Munro and the girl as he ushered him out.

The wind blew along the Embankment. Traffic drove at speed. Munro looked into the dirty water of the Thames. This river would pour into the sea, fragment and flow. It would sweep east, west. It would be spray on the rocks along the Channel, at Eastbourne; wash the shores of the

Adriatic, the Ionian Sea. Water was universal, neutral. What was Thames today could be Nile tomorrow, and the marshy basins of Albania next spring. The thought fed his feeling of impermanence. Nothing was solid. Nothing substantial.

He wondered about the girl. He'd seen her at Eastbourne, then again here. That was no coincidence.

He walked aimlessly until it was one o'clock. Then he took a taxi to Foresters.

Cecil was in the bar. He greeted him like an old friend. "How very nice of you to come. Shows you bear no ill-will. Well, as you know we don't have control over our own fate, do we? At the mercy of circumstances like everyone else. Otherwise we'd never get mixed up in some of these affairs that come our way."

Munro marveled at the man. So consistently bland. Nothing got under his skin. Or if it did, he didn't show it, retaining his manner, his patronizing friendliness.

"Sir John regrets and all that. He took it badly, you know. Didn't expect you to be so outraged. Of course he hasn't been in the business like you and me. Not the same side of it. I tried to explain, I said you had a right to be outraged. You felt we'd let you down over the whole affair. No one gets over being condemned to death *that* quickly. And no one spoke up for you: I reminded him of that. You were left utterly alone. It must have been like being deserted at birth. Then we expect you to go back to the same part of the globe—well—nearly the same part, and revive all those nightmare experiences. 'He must think we're mad,' I told Sir John, 'really mad.' Same again, Edward." He turned, still in full flow, and called across to the barman. Munro couldn't help but admire him.

They had a table reserved. It was for four, but a word from Cecil and two places were swiftly swept away.

"Always an excellent menu here," said Cecil. He presented it to Munro.

"Who was the girl?" asked Munro.

"So you noticed," said Cecil. "You *are* quick."

"Who was she?"

"Least said," said Cecil.

"So she's part of the intrigue?"

"Well . . ."

"Don't be so bloody mysterious."

"She's pretty, don't you think?" said Cecil.

Munro had the snapshot in his mind. "Very pretty. More than that, she looked what used to be called a nice girl. Not mixed up with you, is she?"

"My dear fellow! That's straight out of the thirties! Of course, we get mixed up with some of the nice ones too. Part of the image. Come on, Munro, you remember. You were one of the nice ones yourself."

The waiter came and Cecil suggested the meal. Munro hadn't recovered his interest in food since his stint on prison cooking. He had dreamed of dishes while he had starved in those days, but when he came out, the flavor had gone from food as it had from sunshine, moonlight, friendship, women, and the other good things of life. He did however drink much more. He drank now. It didn't affect him, except to give him an equilibrium. The meal was undoubtedly good.

"Turbot," Cecil informed him, pointing a fork at his dish. "It's the sauce that's so good. Basically a bechamel with oysters, shrimps, bits of lobster and one or two other things. Simple really. Anyone could do it."

Foresters was a converted Georgian house with a bar on the ground floor. Waiters squeezed past each other on the stairs with packed trays. They were all very adept and fairly slim. About half-way through the meal, Munro began to wonder why they'd been so anxious for him to lunch. Then he looked up and noticed a girl's legs coming down the stairs. He saw she had beautiful legs before he recognized the coat, and the fur-topped boots. Cecil saw him stop eating and turned to see the girl. She was with Sir John, heading for the door.

"Ah yes," said Cecil. "We thought it best for Johnny to take her upstairs. Couldn't exactly cancel it, you know." Cecil rose slightly and Sir John waved. The girl smiled; then she saw Munro. The smile vanished. She flushed with anger, and turned away.

Munro was taken aback, as they disappeared. "What the

hell was that about?" He was angry, as though she had insulted him.

"Search me," said Cecil. "God knows what Sir John's
been telling her."

Munro pushed his chair back and followed them out. A
taxi had just driven away.

"What's the matter, old fellow?" Cecil enquired.

"What have you bastards been up to?" asked Munro.

It was no good trying to pacify him, Cecil understood.
"Not so loud, old fellow. Come back to the office, and we'll
explain things."

He had to go back. Munro knew that. It was his own
decision. Yet at the same time he guessed he was going
according to plan. Was it arranged? Could Cecil be *that*
astute? Or Sir John? You bait a trap with a live animal.
The female calls in the dark and the males move into gun
range. Was that what was happening?

"All right," he said.

"I am glad," Cecil beamed. "Let's see how things tick
along."

They had coffee. At least Cecil did, glancing at his
watch. Munro drank some more whiskey. Then they got a
taxi back to the Travelers, and Sir John was there to greet
them, as if he had expected Munro.

"Glad you decided to reconsider," said Sir John.

"He's not exactly doing that," said Cecil quickly. "He
had a brief glimpse of the lady, and he wants to know what
dirty trick we're plotting." He turned to Munro. "That's it,
isn't it?"

Munro nodded.

Sir John went on. "Well, I suppose we did jump the gun.
We assumed you'd fall in with the scheme, so we fixed up
the next step. The meeting."

"That was the lady we were going to take to lunch," said
Cecil. They were beginning to sound like a music-hall turn.

"The point was, as we told you, we hoped you'd be prepared to take a trip to Greece. Well, to be honest—back to
the frontier area."

"What for?" asked Munro.

Sir John shot Cecil a glance. Cecil gave a little nod.

27

"It's a simple matter. The girl you saw wants to go there. She wants to visit those places. She wants, for example, to take a look at the bridge."

Munro looked at them blankly. "The bridge?"

"The bridge you nearly got over. Where Stephan Aroso was shot."

The girl wanted to see the bridge where Stephan died? Where the men had sprayed him with bullets as he tried to climb the parapet? The scene came back. He felt his skin prickle. They wanted him to take the pretty, big-eyed blonde out to the scene of that murder? He couldn't be sure he had understood.

"You want me to take her on a tour? To where we . . ." He looked from Sir John to Cecil. Neither appeared to see anything bizarre in this request. Running conducted tours to the place of death? This was one step further than the eye-witness story in the Sunday papers. Not just "I was There" but "Let Me Take You With Me." What next? Charter flights to scenes of torture?

He couldn't reconcile his impression of the girl with this project.

"Look. Are you sending her? Have you some reason to need her in that part of the world?"

"It's her own idea?"

"Who is she?"

They hesitated a couple of seconds this time. But there was no withholding the rest of the situation. Cecil gave a wry smile. "We thought you would have guessed by now. You're usually so quick."

Nothing came to Munro's mind.

"She's Mrs. Aroso," said Sir John.

That startled Munro. Old suspicions welled up in abundance.

"Mrs. Aroso? Stephan's wife?" he mocked them. "Come on! Who are you kidding? I worked with Stephan, I knew him better than any of you. He never had a wife."

"We were a little surprised, too," said Sir John. He reached down and pulled open a drawer in his desk. He pushed a passport across to Munro.

Munro opened it, and looked at the photo. It was the girl. "For God's sake," he said, "do you expect me to fall for this one. I've had seven passports out of this office myself. You could have rigged this."

"True," said Sir John. "But it's harder to rig the records at Somerset House."

"I'll check," said Munro.

"That sounds like the old Munro talking," Cecil smiled.

Munro fingered the passport thoughtfully. He used to believe he could sense a phony. But this one felt right. He looked at the date of birth and worked out her age. She'd be twenty-three. She was five feet four inches tall. Her hair was put down as fair, her eyes brown—yes, that was what he had thought—and her place of birth was London. First name, Susan. There were a couple of entry dates stamped on an inside page. Both were in Paris. He did a quick calculation. It was just before Stephan had made his last trip to Albania. They saw him looking at the entries.

"Yes," said Sir John, "they had a couple of weeks in Paris. We've checked that. You see, we were as suspicious as you. They were married that morning in Kensington. That was the honeymoon. Stephan came back and reported to us next day. Cecil saw him for a briefing in Wigmore Street. They used the same dentist, with the waiting-room as their point of contact. I think you saw him next in Athens . . ."

"Piraeus," said Munro.

"Then he got into trouble. You know. The whole Albanian episode. And you got him out."

"I got him out?" questioned Munro.

"Nearly out," said Sir John. "Although technically I think you really got him out. Once you were on that bridge you were no longer on Albanian soil."

"They forgot the rules," said Munro grimly.

"Thing is," added Sir John, "that was all she had of married life. The honeymoon. Didn't see him after that."

"How long had she known him?" asked Munro.

"It was a whirlwind affair," said Sir John. "You know what Aroso was like. No more than a couple of months.

He proposed the day he met her. And every other day after that."

Cecil put the passport back in the drawer. "Our Stephan was always the nineteenth-century romantic. Panache before all else. He goes to prove this theory that Munro is so boring about: you know, about things not being what we think. Stephan was play-acting all the time. Dramatized everything. It was *The Prisoner of Zenda* that brought him into this business. He never looked at the sordid side. One great dramatic presentation."

"I think it's very dangerous to use a man like that," said Sir John quietly. He was criticizing his predecessor.

"H'm. Well . . ." said Cecil, "he *was* absolutely brilliant. Look at the languages he spoke. The dialects. He had the whole thing taped in the southern Balkans. Built it from nothing. No one else could have done that . . . and he created the Aroso code." He glanced towards Munro and added, "Which we still use, by the way."

"It was foolish to make him such a key man. Look what happens when he is killed. We have a complete vacuum in that area." Sir John looked thoughtfully at Munro. "You are the only other person with his knowledge."

"I was an amateur," said Munro drily. He knew it now. For all the training they had given him, for all he had picked up during the time he was associated with Travelers, he was no professional as Stephan had been. "Besides," he added, "anything I knew went out of date once they got hold of me. And I've learned my lessons. I'm too old to be caught again. Besides, the money didn't cover what I lost in my own business." He was bitter about that.

"Oh, yes," said Cecil. "How is the china trade?"

"I wouldn't know," said Munro. "You killed it for me."

"Porcelain, wasn't it?" asked Sir John. They were doing the music-hall act again. Munro hated it.

"Forget it," he said coldly, "my contacts have gone. They wouldn't let me near Dresden. They think you planted me in the job years ago, and had me standing by."

"That wasn't the case?" asked Sir John.

"You should do your homework," Munro told him. "Read my files."

30

Cecil chipped in. "Munro had a nice business in East Germany, buying porcelain and importing it. We got him to go a little further. He went in for antiques as well, figures mostly. Eighteenth century. He gave good prices. Antiques are hard to come by—the best, that is. Munro had to travel around. He did that for a year before we asked his help."

"I see," Sir John was thoughtful. "So in that sense they were right. We did have him standing by."

"If you have any ideas . . ." Munro began angrily.

"We haven't," Sir John interrupted. "We had one proposition for you. This trip to Greece."

The phone on his desk rang, and Sir John picked it up.

"All right. Put her through," he said. Then he handed the phone to Cecil and added, "You'd better take it."

Cecil took it and said hurriedly. "Did they say . . ." Then someone spoke on the other end, and he talked into the phone. "Hello. Cecil here . . . Yes, I'm sorry about that. It didn't go according to plan. No, I don't think you can blame him. It's a very painful business . . . Of course not. It's nothing to do with your reasons. We didn't tell him . . . Nobody thinks you're stupid or anything . . . Leave it with us. Newspapers can do such damage . . . Leaving tonight?" He seemed startled. He covered the mouthpiece and hissed at Sir John. "She's going to Ireland tonight. She's got this journalist friend in Dublin."

"Christ," said Sir John.

Cecil turned in desperation to Munro, his hand still over the phone. "Would you like to see Mrs. Aroso this evening?"

Munro's pulse beat a little faster. "What for?" he asked.

"For heaven's sake, man," said Cecil sharply, "you were Stephan's best friend. There are lots of things you could tell her."

"Like what?" said Munro.

"She doesn't think her husband's dead," said Cecil grimly.

Munro could only look at him blankly. The bridge had been splattered with blood. He'd seen the body as they took

31

it past. The jacket, the shirt were red. The stretcher dripped.

The blonde girl must be out of her mind.

Munro nodded slowly. "I'll see her," he said.

3

Susan Aroso was flying out to Dublin that evening. Cecil drove Munro to the airport. "She's a rather odd lady," he said brightly. "I wouldn't be surprised if you decided to have nothing to do with her."

Munro never accepted anything Cecil said at face value. He used words to achieve ends, not to convey information.

The departure hall was crowded. Cecil had arranged to meet beside one of the air-line offices. She wasn't there. Cecil spent an anxious time looking for her. "I'll bet she's gone through to the departure lounge," he said.

"They don't call the flight for half an hour," Munro told him.

"She's like that," said Cecil. "Gets overwhelmed, or something. Runs for safety."

"What from?"

"In this case, you."

They looked around for another minute.

"You think she's gone?" asked Munro.

"There she is," said Cecil. She was waiting beside another air-line office.

She saw them coming, and her chin went up. She was not friendly. Her cheeks flushed as Cecil introduced Munro. "This is Mr. Munro, Mrs. Aroso. As you know he was a great friend of Stephan's. He was the man who nearly got himself shot trying to help him."

"Yes, I know," she said. The thought seemed to make her relent, for she reached out a hand. "It's kind of you to spare me your time, Mr. Munro."

Her hand was very small. There was a quality about her, evoking instincts of protection. Munro had felt incapable of

33

looking after himself since the days of his interrogations. Now he had a desire to protect her, to keep her from a threatening world. The wide eyes were warm, but insecure. To have your husband shot to pieces after a honeymoon must be a disturbing experience, difficult to get over.

"There must be quieter places than this," said Cecil. Later Munro guessed Cecil had arranged everything, he got them into the VIP's lounge so quickly.

The waiter was deferential. "Which flight are you taking?" He would let them know when it was called. The drinks came quickly.

Cecil did most of the talking. "So glad I've got you two together at last. You're the only people who really knew Stephan."

Munro found it was hard to keep two lines of thought going simultaneously, watching for the motive in all Cecil did and at the same time being so very conscious of the girl. She had been Stephan's wife! Not for long, but that didn't alter facts. She had been closer to Stephan than he had. All the time, on that last expedition, Stephan had never mentioned her—had given no indication he was married. It was hard to believe that Stephan, who had been with him in so many shared dangers, had said nothing about a wife. Munro thought he had known everything about the man. What else had Stephan kept back?

"I didn't know Stephan was married," he said.

The girl nodded; a timid movement, very uncertain. "So I am told," she said. She flashed a quick look at Cecil. She didn't seem to know what she was permitted to say. Or was she looking for approval? Assurance?

"Where was this?" Munro asked.

"The ceremony? We didn't have a wedding in church. At a registry in Kensington."

"It was all very quick," said Munro.

"He didn't tell you what he was doing?" asked Cecil.

"No. He had to go to Greece, or Bulgaria."

"You didn't know his job?" Munro suspected she did. But Munro suspected everything.

"He said he was in Security. I knew what languages he spoke. Six," she added with a touch of pride. "When he

34

told me where he had been—those places near the Black Sea—then I guessed."

"He told you before you married him?" asked Munro.

"No. After. Why?"

"Would you have married him if he had told you before?"

"Why not?" She looked surprised.

"If you had known he was a spy?"

The thought seemed to strike her as fresh. "Yes," she said, "I suppose he was a spy."

"What else?" said Munro coldly.

"Security?" She looked at him questioningly.

"What do you think that is?" said Munro. His voice was dry. He didn't want any illusions, no blurred edges. "Security. Spies. It's the same."

"Then you're a spy?" the girl said.

"That's right," Munro said. "I used to buy and sell little china figures to stick on the mantelpiece. I was quick off the mark when East-West trade opened." He laughed without amusement. "Then my country needed me. Or someone like me. The Travelers needed me. And Mr. Cecil got in touch."

"Are they spies?" she asked. "I mean, the Travelers."

"I don't think there's any need . . ." began Cecil.

"Let's begin the way we intend to go on," said Munro grimly. He enjoyed Cecil's discomfort. "As Stephan's wife, she has a right to know." He turned to the girl. "It's a clumsy device to hide an operation that our opposite numbers from Peking to Tiranë know all about. But it does serve to shelter the British public and the saintly minded ruling classes from the fact that we spend a lot of money on as dirty a business as any in Madrid or Moscow."

"Please," said Cecil. "We haven't a lot of time before Mrs. Aroso goes. Do you think we could discuss her idea of going to Greece?"

"Was it your idea?" asked Munro sharply.

The girl looked startled. "Yes," she said. "I wanted to see where Stephan had been. Where they said he died. I wanted to see the village."

"You can't see that," said Munro, "it's on the wrong side of the frontier."

"Then I could see the bridge."

"What in God's name for?" He was almost angry.

She hesitated. "I don't think I shall ever believe he is really dead until I see it. There should always be a funeral. I want to throw my handful of earth on the coffin. Do you see? Until I do, he isn't really dead."

Munro took a deep breath. He had wanted to tell her something—just how dead Stephan was. But he found himself unable to say the words.

"You think I am foolish?" she said. He had no thoughts about that. She went on. "Sometimes I think I *am* foolish. That was why I took so long to make up my mind. Now I must go. Just to forget Stephan . . . Well, it hurts me. This pilgrimage, I owe it to him. You understand?"

Munro wasn't sure he did understand, but he nodded. "It's a long way," he said. "It won't be pleasant."

"I'm not thinking of it as a holiday," she said. Munro felt rebuked.

The waiter appeared in their alcove. "Your flight has just been called," he said. Cecil began to get up.

"If you don't mind," she said, looking at him, "I don't wish to catch that plane."

Cecil didn't understand. "I think it's too late to transfer."

"I don't think I shall go at all," she said.

Munro gave the girl a quick look. She avoided his glance. But he couldn't deny the demand she made, nor the commitment.

"You're staying in London?" Cecil wanted to get the situation straight. He hated it when he didn't understand what was going on.

She just said, "Yes." Then she quickly looked across at Munro and away again. There was a startled, almost fearful look in that glance, as if she had a secret she didn't want him to guess, and at the same time a secret she wanted to share.

Munro was still working it out.

"Right," said Cecil briskly, "I'll run you both back to town."

36

She had an apartment in a tall block of flats close to Marble Arch.

"Do you have any time to talk?" she said. She looked at Cecil as she spoke, but included both men.

"I'm afraid I'm involved this evening," said Cecil.

She hesitated for a second as she left the car. She didn't say anymore, but she looked around. Munro got out with her. "I have time," he said.

Cecil drove off. It was hard to guess whether this was as he had expected—or even what he had wanted. They took an elevator up several floors, and finished with a startling view over the city. She saw him looking around the apartment.

"I packed very quickly," she said. "It's a mess."

"Why were you going to Ireland?"

"I have a friend. A journalist. I thought he might give me advice."

"You don't think you need advice now?"

"What do you mean?" She didn't follow.

"You aren't going to Ireland now."

She understood. "No. I think I don't need him."

"What did you want his advice about?"

"If the Travelers couldn't help me, I thought he might. I didn't want to go alone. Will you have a drink?"

"Thank you. What have you decided?"

"If the Travelers cannot help . . ." She looked at him, wide eyes suddenly wider . . . "If you don't go . . . no one else can do anything for me."

"You don't go?"

"No, I still go—by myself." Then she remembered and poured out the drink.

"When are you planning to start?"

"As soon as possible."

"Is it urgent? Isn't it just a sentimental journey?" She didn't answer.

"How well did you know Stephan?" she asked.

"We worked together for three years."

She was surprised. "You must have known him very well."

"I thought I did."

37

"Thought?"

"I didn't know he was married."

"Surely it is safest not to know too much about one another in your profession?"

"Correct. But Stephan disregarded most of the rules. He was a great one for the big gesture. It would have been like him to say casually, "My wife was telling me the other day . . ." But you didn't get a mention even as a joke."

"He made jokes all the time," she said, remembering. "He was always laughing—always smiling."

That reminded Munro of something. "When he came running back over the bridge he was smiling," he told her.

"You mean when they shot at him?"

"Yes." He hesitated—remembering the moment. "Even after they shot him. Still smiling. Holding the parapet smiling."

There was a silence. Neither could guess that particular joke.

"Cecil says you think he's still alive."

"Yes."

"Why."

"I dream about him." She was perfectly serious.

"Does that surprise you?" asked Munro.

"He's so vivid. At one end of the bridge, speaking to me."

"What bridge?"

"The one in the photographs."

"Did Sir John show you those?"

"Yes. They said that was where he died."

"Look. If you have seen photos, and your husband got shot in this—well . . . this bloody fashion—of course you'll have dreams about him."

"They are vivid."

"I wouldn't set too much hope on dreams."

"They say the same."

"Sir John?"

She nodded. "Sir John. Mr. Cecil. They tried to make me give up the whole idea. They were not going to help."

"Why did they change their minds?"

"I said I would go to this newspaper friend. I would naturally have to tell him about Stephan and what he did. Sir John wanted me to say nothing about the Travelers. I was angry with them. I promised nothing. Then they spoke about you."

"What did they say?"

"That you were his friend. You had been there."

"Did they say I would take you?"

"Not exactly. But they said no one else could tell me what happened. They gave me the newspaper reports where you said you and Stephan had not been spies."

"Didn't they give you the confessions I made in Albania?"

"They gave me those too."

"I said Stephan and I were spies in that."

"I thought that was forced out of you."

Munro remembered drily how it had been forced. "It was," he admitted, "but it was also true."

"You denied it at the press conference in London . . ."

"Of course I denied it when I got home. That's part of the play."

"The play?" She lifted her eyebrows.

"It's a play," said Munro. "I must tell you about it some day."

He finished his drink and sat, letting his intuitions go to work. She was motionless, silent, very self-contained. He liked that about her.

It looked like this to Munro; the girl had gone to Sir John and tried to get his help to trace Stephan's last days. Sir John would have tried to discourage that. He wanted to admit no connections with Stephan. "Let the dead past bury its dead," was the motto over the Travelers door. But the girl had not been easily brushed aside. She had friends who might use her information in the press. A Dublin journalist could make a meal of the hypocrisy of English diplomacy. And what the hell is the British Bully doing in poor helpless Albania, small and peace-loving as Ireland itself? No wonder Sir John and his side-kick had had second thoughts.

And Peter Munro had been their second thought.

"What did they tell you about me?"

"Quite a lot," she said. "They said that you had a breakdown after the exchange, and blamed them for not helping you at your trial. That you had lost weight. That you were not like you used to be."

"Did you make any sense of that?"

"You must have had a terrible time." She looked at Munro with compassion. "I think you were tortured."

"They didn't exactly touch me," said Munro slowly. He was breaking out in a sweat. The old sweat. But there was nothing to be afraid of now. It was irrational; a memory. He controlled his voice. "This isn't the first time you've seen me," he said.

"No," she said, "I drove to Eastbourne."

"Why?"

"I thought we were going on a journey together."

"I see. And what did you think when you saw me?"

The look of compassion came back. "I thought you were very brave," she said, "and very sad."

He recalled how sad he had been by the sea, in the rain. "I promise nothing," he told her. He got up to go.

"I understand," she said.

Munro went around to the Travelers the following morning. He had no appointment, but had no difficulty seeing Sir John. This gave him some idea how high in their priorities he and Cecil held this project. They greeted him cheerfully.

"Charming girl, don't you think?" said Sir John.

"I don't know who you think you're fooling," said Munro, "but I have been playing these games for years."

They looked surprised. "I thought you two were getting along famously," said Cecil.

"I've nothing against the girl," said Munro drily, "she doesn't know she's being taken for a ride."

"I'm not with you," said Sir John.

"Oh, come on!" Munro was annoyed that they should think him so simple. "You aren't setting up this expedition out of the goodness of your hearts. You wouldn't lift a finger if it didn't do something for you. You're using her, and you want to use me."

"How could we use you, old fellow?" Cecil made that sound as if Munro didn't amount to a row of beans.

"You make me tired," said Munro. "You're still playing spies in a world that's covered by satellites. Anything any government wants to know they can find out from computers. You go on with this fatuous set-up to justify your existence. Why don't you shut up shop, and leave ordinary people alone?"

"Mrs. Aroso, you mean?"

"Her too."

"She came to us. Or didn't she tell you?"

"She told me. What she doesn't know is that you're going to make use of her."

"We are?" Cecil was amused.

"I don't know how," said Munro, "but I know the way your minds tick. You've some cloak-and-dagger tomfoolery going on, and you think she can help. You think I can help, or you wouldn't have called me in."

"What for?" asked Cecil.

"I'll work it out," Munro assured him.

"You suggest we have some work for you to do back in your old territory?" said Sir John.

"What else?" said Munro.

"You didn't believe Mrs. Aroso?"

"What do you mean?"

"I imagine she told you her ridiculous dreams. Her desire to see where Stephan Aroso died. This irrational need she has to go to the damn place?"

"She told me that."

"But you didn't believe her?"

"I didn't say that. She wants to go . . . never mind how stupid her reasons. You see this as the moment to get *me* back there. So you jump at the chance. You pretend to go along with her; you send me with her."

"But in God's name, old fellow," Cecil's voice rose above his usual controlled level, "whatever for? Give us a good reason to send you back to Greece and we *might* jump at it. But in my opinion you aren't any good to anyone. As an agent, you're done."

Munro wondered why Cecil was so angry. Nothing ever

41

shook Cecil. Now he was shouting—well, nearly shouting.

"So let's not waste any more time." Munro left the office. This time he made his own way back to the entrance hall, and went out himself, breaking all regulations.

He realized how much he had done in two days when he got out into the street. The column in Trafalgar Square swayed a little, and Munro was glad he had his stick. He walked slowly up to Piccadilly while he got his breath back. He had an idea of phoning the girl, or going around to explain his decision. Then he decided it was not his problem. He took a taxi to his hotel.

"Message for you, Mr. Munro," the porter told him.

He thought it was from Cecil, but the message slip read "Please phone Group-Captain Brenner" and it gave a number. Munro phoned from his room.

A woman's voice answered. "Annex here." Munro explained who he was. "I'll put you through to the Group-Captain, sir."

There was a clicking on the line. Another girl's voice was heard.

Then a man came on the line. "Ah! Is that you, Mr. Munro? I'm Group-Captain Brenner. Sorry to bother you like this. I suppose Caxton told you I'd be in touch?"

"He didn't mention it. What's the trouble?"

"No trouble," came the voice. "We wondered if we could have a brief chat. It won't take ten minutes. We could have a staff car at your hotel in a couple of minutes."

"Who is that?" asked Munro.

"Didn't they tell you?" The voice sounded surprised. "I'm Group-Captain Brenner. We're Special Security."

"Look," Munro was getting irritated, "I don't have to waste any more time on this business."

"Believe me, I quite understand," said the Group-Captain, "you'd be doing us a great favor. We always seem to get our lines crossed with Sir John and his outfit. He never explains what he's doing or what help he wants us to give. We're just around the corner, off Baker Street. We could pick you up in thirty seconds . . ." The Group-Captain sounded as if Sir John was a troublesome man to work with.

"Right," said Munro. "I'll be outside the hotel."

A black car driven by an RAF sergeant pulled up almost immediately.

"Mr. Munro?" He was very brisk. He had Munro outside an office block in less than the estimated two minutes. "You'll find the Group-Captain on the second floor, sir. Things are in a bit of a mess. We're an overflow unit. We haven't settled in properly. I'll just park this thing. Stupid place to give us for offices, sir. No place for cars."

He gave Munro the feeling that he would have run things much better if he'd been put in charge. Munro went up two flights of stairs. The lift was out of order. He rested on the first floor. On the second floor, a very pretty WAAF met him. "Mr. Munro?" she asked. "The Group-Captain is waiting for you. This way."

She led Munro along a corridor which they were still decorating, and into an office.

The Group-Captain rose to shake his hand gratefully. "Glad you could make it," he said. "We have to pick up the pieces after the Travelers, you know. Not always easy. And they expect help. You know, flying their people here, there, and everywhere. That's really the point of this exercise. We understand it's immediate, yet they haven't had the common decency to tell us what range they want, or when we're taking you."

"You're not," said Munro.

The Group-Captain's jaw hung open for a second. "Not? But Caxton led me to suppose . . ."

"Forget it," said Munro. "He should have checked the passenger list 'cause I'm not on it."

"Good gracious me," said the Group-Captain, "I *have* made a bloomer."

"Not you," said Munro, "they did. I only told them this morning."

"So you're not doing anything for them," said the Group-Captain thoughtfully.

"No," said Munro. "Is that it?" He was ready to go.

"Of course," said the Group-Captain. He was still a little taken aback. "As a matter of interest, what did they have lined up?"

"I've no idea," said Munro. It was his old instinct of not saying too much, that was at work. "But the trip was Greece."

"Oh, we knew that," said the Group-Captain. He was about to say something else when he changed his mind. He shook Munro's hand warmly again and showed him out. The pretty WAAF took him to the end of the corridor. At the bottom of the stairs the staff car was waiting. They seemed a very efficient unit, in spite of the decoration and the general air of having just moved into the place.

The sergeant had him back at his hotel in a flash. Munro was already crossing the entrance hall before he realized he was walking without his stick. He'd left it in the offices. The staff car was driving away. He called after it, but the sergeant didn't hear. It was a damn nuisance, thought Munro. The hotel bar was on the ground floor. He went in and steadied himself with a couple of drinks.

They paged his name about half an hour later, but he was convinced it was Cecil or Sir John, so he didn't take the call. He was thinking of leaving the bar when his name was called again. He was wanted on the phone. It was indeed Cecil. "Trying to get hold of you earlier," said Cecil.

"What about," asked Munro, "Group-Captain Brenner?"

There was a moment's silence at the other end of the phone.

"Who?" said Cecil.

Munro repeated the name. "You should know," he added, "Special Security. That place they've got off Baker Street."

"Could you give me the exact address?" said Cecil.

"No. Why?"

"What was this about?" Cecil wanted to know.

Munro had a feeling he was walking in ice. "Let me ask the questions," he said. "Do you know anyone called Brenner in a branch called Special Security? I think it has a code name—Annex."

"I don't," said Cecil.

"Does your boss?"

There was a moment's silence. Munro could hear him speaking to someone in the background. Then Cecil came back on the phone. "No, he doesn't. Would you like to explain . . ."

Munro put the phone down and headed for the door.

It couldn't have been much more than an hour and a half since he had been driven in the staff car to the offices. Less than that since he had left. There had been a scene of busy activity with decorators, at least one WAAF, the Group-Captain himself, and one or two other people. Munro went up the stairs quickly, ignoring his spasm of fatigue. He knew what he was going to find before he went in. The offices were empty. All the notices, calendars and other details were off the wall. The desk in the office had been pushed back against the wall. The decorations were as they had been as he had gone past them. There was nothing there to suggest it was the place he had visited, except his stick against the wall.

He didn't feel he had any obligation to Cecil or Sir John but he found himself calling a taxi outside the offices and giving the Travelers address. He sat in the taxi and dissected himself coldly. He must have been stupid to fall for that one. Very stupid, or out of practice. Perhaps a little of both.

Sir John was clearly pleased to see him. "What was this you were telling Cecil?" he asked. "Wait, I'll send for him."

Cecil joined them.

"I thought you'd like to know," said Munro, "whatever you are doing, you have an interested audience. So interested, they went to the bother of hiring an office this morning, giving it a bit of service veneer, and picking me up in a car."

"Who were they?"

"Quite a convincing act as a Service Intelligence type who does your flying for you, driver, WAAF officer, and the like. All to find out what I was doing for you."

"You didn't tell him?" Sir John was anxious.

"I did," said Munro, "I said I was doing nothing for you."

"Good boy," said Cecil. He turned to Sir John. "There

45

you are," he said proudly. "They don't train them like Munro anymore."

Munro snarled. "I said that because I *was* doing nothing."

"Was," Cecil was quick to notice. He knew Munro, sensed the change.

Munro frowned. He was working on an insoluble problem.

"You came around here pretty quick," added Cecil.

"Why should anyone be interested in this trip?" said Munro.

"It's beyond me," said Cecil.

"You're a lying bastard," said Munro.

Cecil seemed to take that as a compliment.

"I gather the girl intends to go by herself."

"If she has to," said Sir John.

Munro sighed. "Can't we have a little mutual trust. Tell me, is our friend the bogus Group-Captain interested in this Greek trip only if I go along. Or is he involved anyhow. I mean, does Stephan's wife get a share of his attention?"

"Now that's hard to know," said Cecil slowly. Munro could see he was trying to work out which answer would be most to his advantage. "I suppose they must be interested anyhow; though why, I cannot for the life of me understand."

"It's never your life that's involved, "Munro told him. "You're always cozily tucked up here in London when someone gets hurt."

Cecil pretended that was another nice thing Munro had said, but it was beginning to get under his skin. He wanted to insult Munro in return, but he dared not. He felt Munro was poised to take the bait. The only thing to do was wait. Munro walked up and down the office. Cecil prayed that Sir John would say nothing. Munro would construe anything as cause for suspicion—even if someone just said, "Good-day."

"There's something about that girl that worries me," said Munro. They looked at him blankly. He went on, "Something about her I don't trust." That *really* surprised them.

46

Sir John gave a small dinner party that evening. It was in his apartment with his wife as hostess. Munro calculated that he had arranged it this way in order to make it a social occasion. But Munro wasn't fooled, and his manners were only marginally influenced by the fact that Lady Caxton was present.

"Of course I've heard of you," said Lady Caxton. She smiled pleasantly as she welcomed Munro. She had black hair on top of her head in a style that reminded him of royalty. The other guests were already there, Cecil and the girl.

"And you know Mrs. Aroso?"

"Some of the details," said Munro drily, as he nodded briefly.

They had drinks before dinner. Sir John had champagne in an ice-bucket.

"So it's a celebration," said Munro.

"Any excuse," smiled Cecil.

"Some excuses are better than others," said Munro. "For instance, do you know what we're celebrating tonight?" He turned to Lady Caxton.

"I understand you and Mrs. Aroso are leaving for Greece," she said blandly.

"That's right," Munro nodded. "So what is there to celebrate? I don't know Sir John well, but I do know Cecil. He wouldn't celebrate his golden wedding unless the occasion were being used as a cover to get a truck-load of coded candles out of China."

Lady Caxton thought that was very funny. She laughed. Even the girl smiled. "You are very hard on Mr. Cecil," she said.

"Good clean fun," said Munro grimly. "Old buddies, Cecil and me. Through thick and thin. Never lets you down."

Lady Caxton understood the implication. "That's hardly fair," she said. "Mr. Cecil did get you out."

Munro nodded. "I apologize. He got me out. Eighteen months later."

Sir John cleared his throat. "Well, my dear. Got something nice for us to eat?"

Munro sat through the meal guessing the girl opposite

47

disapproved of him. This didn't upset him. If she was going on a long trip—and a dangerous one—it was as well she learned the facts. Besides, Munro had little appetite. And it was better not to drink too much. So he spoke.

"I haven't had a chance to tell Mrs. Aroso what to expect. This is as good a time as any. Before witnesses." He indicated the others. "I'll take her. I've agreed, and that's it. I know there is more to this jaunt than meets the eye. But it puzzles me. It really does."

"What does?" Lady Caxton raised her brows politely.

"What function can we fulfil?" said Munro thoughtfully. "What can we do, especially when we don't know what they want us to do? Time was, I used to get a briefing. I've had three weeks learning names, places, codes and all that rubbish. Three weeks, then I had it by heart. But this time I know nothing. Except that I'm some use to them."

"Very useful, my dear Munro," said Sir John. "I feel we owe Mrs. Aroso at least this consideration. If you can't help us to pay a small part of a large debt, then no one can."

"Thank you," said the girl.

"Don't thank them," said Munro.

"May I fill your glass?" said Sir John. He seemed uneasy at the way Munro worried at the problem.

"We could be decoys," said Munro thoughtfully.

"Decoys?" The girl frowned.

"We're going to be damn conspicuous on the Albanian border," Munro told her. "My old jailers are going to ask why the hell Peter Munro has turned up. And while everyone is taking a good look at us and wondering what bloody daft mission we're on, guess what? Something important is happening elsewhere."

"That's a very good theory," said Sir John. "Why didn't you mention it before? We could have done something with it."

"Don't get caught up in Munro's thinking," said Cecil. "He has a brain that ticks over with wheels within wheels within wheels."

"Indeed?" said Lady Caxton with some admiration.

"I have learned to look behind the curtains," said Munro.

"I should hate to be so suspicious," said the girl. He felt there was nothing useful he could say to her.

After that they spoke about Greece and how beautiful it was, and how they hoped she would enjoy her trip— although of course they realized this was really a belated homage to Stephan.

"You will find Munro very good company," Cecil assured her. "He'll look after you, if it's the last thing he does." Later Munro wondered how literally Cecil had meant that. He spoke no more of his suspicions, nor of his bitterness. In fact he ended by quite enjoying the evening. But he remained convinced: it *had* been a celebration.

The following morning Cecil handed him a sum of money. It was a large amount. "I haven't given you a check, in case you don't have time to put it through your account," Cecil told him. "You've probably got one or two things to tidy up before you go. If you get back to London the day after tomorrow, that will be plenty of time. We've booked you for the flight that evening."

It was typical of him to assume so much. In just two days' time they expected Munro to fly off to Greece for an indefinite period. They took him for granted—as they had always done. He wondered if he should be bloody-minded and say he wouldn't be ready. But it didn't seem worth the bother.

"We'll have everything fixed by the time you get back," Cecil assured him. "You know, hotels, schedules. You might even enjoy it this time."

That comment worried Munro more than most.

Going back to Eastbourne was stepping into the past. He'd been away only a couple of days; now it seemed an alien world. He walked along the sea-front, sat in the shelter, looked out over the Channel. Safe, and friendly. It had served to shelter him during an autumn and winter of sadness. The sadness still clung, but was now diluted by other emotions; by curiosity, by puzzled interest in Stephan's

49

wife. He looked across the road to where he had seen her first. A small figure, partly hidden by her car.

Mrs. Shaw was delighted to see him, and dismayed to learn he was going away.

"I don't know how long I shall be," he told her, "but I'd like to store my things."

She was pleased to do that. It showed he intended coming back.

Munro didn't require the two days Cecil had given him. He had no affairs to put in order. He thought of writing a will, but he had nothing to leave and no one to leave it to, since his wife had written him off while he was lying in an Albanian jail. She had taken what was once theirs, changed her name, and set up house with a man in Bristol. Munro had wondered why she didn't divorce him. Perhaps she wasn't sure if his being arrested in Albania was grounds for divorce. Anyhow, he felt she was right to leave him. There was no point being married to a man whom one saw only on fleeting visits, a man who had allowed himself to get involved in the antiquated and destructive profession of espionage.

Cecil was waiting for him in Sir John's office the morning he was to fly.

"Where exactly are we going?" he asked.

"To Athens," Sir John told him, "you'll have transport from there."

"Where to?" Munro let them know he was not disinterested. "I might need fur-lined boots if we're mountaineering."

"It's all laid on," said Cecil. "We did a shopping list for you. Went to the tailors you used to use. Got a light-weight for you. One or two other things. All on the bill." He peered at Munro closely. "You seem to have lost a bit of weight, old fellow. I hope they fit."

If they wanted to run his life, then let them. "This time I want a gun," he told them.

"You know the policy on that one," said Cecil.

"You know where to stuff your bloody policy," Munro said.

"You won't get a gun into the country," said Sir John

thoughtfully. "If you decide you want one later, get it there."

Munro noticed that they were no longer denying he was on some sort of an assignment. They admitted nothing, but by implication they were going along with him. He knew it was no good asking what it was. But he wasn't going to go unprotected.

"I want my little revolver," he said, "the Italian one that fits into this briefcase." They were going to protest, so he added, "Or I don't go."

They gave it to him. He fitted it into the case.

"There are still people, especially in that part of the world, who remember me," he reminded them.

"Of course," agreed Sir John. "Particularly when you are known to be in northern Greece."

"You've thought about that?" Munro asked drily.

"We have given it more thought than you suppose," said Sir John. "But as you said, we have one thing in our favor."

"We have?" Munro couldn't think what that was.

"Everyone will know you can't be working for us again. You will be left alone."

"Think so?"

"Well, they'll be very confused. It would be like sending the Scarlet Pimpernel openly to revolutionary France."

"God help us," said Munro.

"My point is, with your history no one will think you're back to spy."

"What about Mrs. Aroso?"

"Yes, we thought of that. It seemed to be asking for trouble if she went openly as herself. Sure to arouse a ghoulish interest in the press."

"We've got a way around that," chipped in Cecil. "We haven't got any cover for you, but we have for her."

"She isn't going as Stephan's widow?" Munro was trying to work out the implications. His instincts were tugging his nervous system.

"No," said Sir John. "To avoid unpleasant publicity she will be using her name before marriage. Susan Marsh."

"But what excuse does she have to go to that area then?"

If they had constructed a jigsaw puzzle, Munro hadn't yet put it together.

"She is working on a thesis for her Ph.D. She is writing a paper on modern poets, and she is specializing on an English poet who lives there."

Munro didn't need anyone to tell him who Sir John meant. He knew Leo Rhodes. He had stayed with him in his mountain villa, overlooking the road north.

"So that was why you called me in," he said. "You knew the old man and I were friends."

"We could have got her to see Rhodes without your help," said Sir John sharply. "What we couldn't do without you is show her exactly how and where they murdered her husband." He gave a good exhibition of indignation, but Munro wasn't impressed.

So the girl was going out under an assumed name—her maiden name—and she was to pretend to collect material from Leo Rhodes to write some book. This would bring them close to the frontier, and Munro could show her the places used by himself and Stephan. He could take her to one side of the bridge, for that matter. It made quite a story.

They had kept back this aspect of the assignment until the last stage. Munro didn't have all the time he needed to think it out.

He was on the plane, with the girl sitting beside him looking through the port window as they crossed the coast of England, and he wondered if it was Eastbourne below. The last white splash of chalk cliff disappeared under fluffy clouds.

A new problem presented itself. If she was not traveling as Mrs. Aroso, what was his supposed function? If she was not his dead friend's widow, then who was she? And why was he traveling with her? He could see that Sir John and Cecil hadn't foreseen that one. For once they had slipped up.

He told the girl. "They've made a mess of it already," he said. "They send us out together, and the only way we could do this is if you are known to be Stephan's widow.

That's the only way it would work. They destroyed that relationship and didn't work out another."

She looked at him a little shocked. "They didn't tell you?" Big eyes looked bigger.

His mind went blank. "No."

"But they worked out a story to cover the whole journey," she said, "so we could go to these places."

Just before she told him he guessed, and he goggled at her.

"We're engaged," she said.

4

Munro had expected some attention at Athens airport. After all, it was not so long ago that he had been headlines in their newspapers. An editorial had accused him of abusing Greek hospitality, and it was right. When Britain had agreed to their spy-for-a-spy, the exchange had taken place at another frontier, so Munro had not returned through Greece. Technically, the last time he had been in Greece was when he had run across the bridge. For a few seconds he had stood on Greek soil before he went back to help Stephan. However, no one at the airport recognized him. He was relieved that the public had a short memory.

The girl was enthralled by what she saw, prepared to like everything. He realized how little he knew about her.

"Haven't you been to Greece?" he asked.

She shook her head. Her eyes wandered over the crowd. It was still early morning. They took a taxi into the city: rooms had been booked from London.

"They never looked after me like this before," Munro told her. "It must be the company."

Sir John's department had worked out an efficient schedule. They both had a list of times and places, and a number of tickets attached. Their program was plotted from hour to hour. Munro read his aloud in the vestibule of the hotel. He was outraged.

"Three hours rest at hotel! How do they know? We may not be tired."

"We should do what they say." She was nervous in case he disobeyed instructions.

"They've put down the names of the restaurants we eat at!"

"Perhaps it's important," she suggested.

"They must be out of their minds. I know this town better than they do."

"Maybe it's changed."

Munro looked down the list. It was harmless enough, but the attempt to pull strings from London annoyed him. They were shown to rooms looking towards the Acropolis. The great extrusion of rock seemed like a fortress. On the flat top they could see the ruins that brought the world to this capital. She had not been prepared for this sudden glory. It took her breath away.

Munro looked over the rooftops to the rock. "The one in the center is the Parthenon. Over there you can see the Propylaea, and that one is the Erechtheum. Or is it the other way around?" He was surprised to find himself acting as a guide. He felt something of a holiday atmosphere.

"I know a place for breakfast," he told her.

"We are to rest," she reminded him.

"You don't pay any attention to that."

But she insisted, reprovingly, like a school prefect in charge of an outing. Munro was beginning to appreciate what he'd taken on.

She consulted her schedule. "After that we are to have drinks at a place called the Sphinx. Do you know it?"

Munro recalled it vaguely with distaste.

"I shall change before we go," she said. "It's much warmer than it was in London."

The Sphinx was specially designated for the tourist trade. The music that jangled through the bar came from the sound-track of a Greek film. The spits over the kitchen fires were a mock-up of a village feast. The wine was resinated. Munro looked around with disapproval.

"Isn't this nice?" said the girl.

He didn't bother to contradict her.

He hadn't ceased to wonder why Sir John and his department were organizing their time, but felt some amused admiration at the detail that must have gone into their preparations.

The girl saw him smiling, and got a glimpse of what he

must once have been like. He spoke with some contempt about the place, but she liked it. "What's this meat?" she asked.

"It'll be terrible in a place like this," he promised her.

She had the schedule with her. "We have to eat here." It was worse than a conducted tour.

"Suppose we go some place else?"

"We must do as they say." She was stubborn about that. "Let's get it over."

There were a number of Germans already in the restaurant, and a few Americans. But it was too early in the year for many tourists.

They took a table near the door. A fat man came puffing in from the street. He stopped, and peered in the dim light, fanning himself with a newspaper. He saw Munro a few feet away, and appeared both startled and relieved. He began to smile, then he checked himself, and moved off towards the bar.

"I thought he recognized you," said the girl.

Munro shrugged his shoulders. That wouldn't surprise him. The meal was better than he had supposed. Perhaps the Travelers were sending back more accurate reports than of old. Not that he was expecting to eat well in Greece: outside Athens a decent meal was hard to find.

He was going to order coffee.

"I am sorry," said the girl, "I have no time."

This was a surprise. He pulled his paper from his pocket. "What's the hurry?" he asked. "We're here—and I quote— 'for the afternoon.' "

"No," she shook her head. "I have to see a publication at the British Council. An essay on poetry."

Munro thought she'd made a mistake. She showed him her schedule.

"This is different!"

"Didn't you know?"

"Of course not." Munro was annoyed. "Who gave you this?"

"Mr. Cecil. I have to see what material they have on Leo Rhodes."

56

Munro couldn't get over it. "They gave you a different schedule to the one they gave me?"

"Only slightly different. This visit, and one to the English library."

Munro let her go. He hoped to God they were not going to play spies and code-words much longer. He paid his bill and crossed to leave. The fat man moved very quickly for someone of his bulk. He left the bar and caught Munro by the arm before he was through the door. Munro reacted with speed acquired by long training. He had the fat man's arm in a lock which lifted him on to his toes.

"Mr. Munro. Good gracious me. I wish only to talk." The man was in pain. Munro let him go.

"My goodness." He rubbed his arm. "You are too quick, you did not give me time to introduce myself." He was about five foot six and very wide. "I am Yanni," he explained.

It meant nothing to Munro. "Excuse me," he said, "I was just going."

Yanni was about to clutch his arm again, but thought better of it. "Mr. Munro," he said, "you are to stay with me . . ." He looked at Munro and added, "For the afternoon."

Munro moved away before he realized the implication. Yanni called after him. "You must stick to the schedule." Munro came back. It was like being involved in a farce.

"Schedule?"

"Of course." Yanni was pulling papers from his pocket.

"Who the hell are you?" said Munro.

"Your contact," said Yanni. He was pleased to be able to say that.

Munro considered collecting his bag and flying back to London. "I don't have a contact," he said coldly, "I don't need one."

Yanni was dismayed. "Of course you need a contact," he said. "You are Peter Munro, the spy. Everyone knows you." He spoke with pride.

Munro caught sight of himself in a wall-mirror behind the bar. His face was expressionless. In this moment of incredibility he was reassured to see how little he gave away.

Yanni was still talking, nervously at first, then with growing confidence. "I am sorry to be rude, Mr. Munro. I did not expect you to leave. I thought you would be here for the afternoon. Then I could approach you as Sir John said."

Munro felt exposed. The man was openly making a connection between him and the Travelers.

"There is no need to be alarmed, Mr. Munro," said Yanni, "there is no one here of any importance." He indicated the restaurant. God knows who might have been there, thought Munro. He had a built-in sense of alarm.

"Where exactly do you fit in?" he asked.

Yanni had large eyes in a round friendly face, and a gentle expression often found in Mediterranean races. "As I tell you, I am your contact. I have instructions to meet you."

Munro was still angry. "Did they never tell you that the first thing a contact must learn is to avoid attracting attention?"

"What for?" asked Yanni, spreading his arms. "Everyone knows me. I am in no danger. I am an agent for British Intelligence."

"They know that too?" asked Munro.

"Naturally." Yanni was proud. "I have been working for Sir John, and before him for Mr. Cecil, for many years." He expanded the gesture to include Munro. "I was working for them when you were here last. Of course, in those days no one knew you. No one. Except Stephan Aroso of course."

"Look, Mr. Yanni," said Munro.

Yanni interrupted. "I'm sorry. These are times you would like to forget." He indicated the bar. "Have a drink," he said, "we have things to discuss."

"I have nothing to discuss with you, Mr. Yanni," said Munro and he went out.

Yanni hurried after him. "Not *Mr.* Yanni, just Yanni. It is a code-name," he called.

Munro stopped. "Get lost, Yanni."

"I can't." Yanni was dismayed.

"Get lost," snarled Munro, "or I'll call one of your police." Yanni stopped in his tracks. A car pulled to a halt beside them. There were two men inside. The man nearest him wound down the window. "Mr. Munro?" This wasn't a question: he knew who Munro was.

"What is it?" asked Munro.

"Will you be kind enough to come with us?"

Munro felt a wave of insecurity. He was being set up like an Aunt Sally. What kind of fool had he been to come back? "I'm sorry," he said. "I'm here on holiday."

"Mr. Munro." One of the men flicked open a wallet. Munro glanced at the card. He didn't read it but he knew what it was. The man was from political security.

"I must get in touch with my consul," said Munro. He knew he didn't mean that.

"Go with them," said Yanni urgently.

Munro knew it was useless to protest. "Where are we going?"

"Not far," said the man.

He opened the car door. Munro got in. Yanni started to follow. The man in the car barked something at him in Greek, and slammed the door.

"I must come," said Yanni loudly. "It is something to do with me."

"You are nothing," shouted the man contemptuously in English. They drove off. Munro saw Yanni on the edge of the sidewalk, a deeply insulted man.

They went through the center of Athens faster than the rest of the traffic: then they were out among villas behind high walls. They stopped at one. A man in uniform at the gate let them in without checking. They stopped at the side door: Munro wondered if he didn't rate the main entrance. Or was he being slipped in unofficially? The man from the car went in, signaling for Munro to follow. They went a few steps along a passage. Munro noted the mosaic floor-ing, a pattern of stars and geometrical designs. These were the details he had once been trained to notice. Now the faculty was operating again—though he told himself he didn't need to make notes; he did not need to count steps from door to door. But he had made a mental map of the

59

streets the car had driven along. Why? He was no longer a spy.

The man knocked on a door. Someone replied. The man signed to Munro to go in. There was a civilian at a desk opposite, with a tall man in army uniform. They had been looking at something on the desk, but now they stared at Munro. Both seemed surprised.

The civilian spoke good English. "Please sit down, Mr. Munro. We will not keep you long." Munro sat. There was no point protesting at this stage. He wanted to find out what this was about. The civilian shuffled through a few papers on his desk.

"You arrived in Greece today?"

Munro nodded.

"From London?"

"Correct." The less he said, the more he might learn.

There was a pause. "We know, of course, who you are, Mr. Munro," said the civilian.

Munro shrugged. "Why not?" he said.

"We knew you were coming here."

"Oh?"

"You had bookings in your hotel."

"Of course."

"And there is Ioannis Soüstäs."

"Who?" That surprised Munro.

"Yanni," said the civilian.

"He has nothing to do with me."

"Do you deny you employ Yanni?" The civilian seemed to think he was on to something.

Munro looked at him coldly. "I am too poor to employ anyone," he said.

"Your Intelligence in London?" he suggested.

"Just for the record," said Munro softly, "I got caught. Remember?"

"What do you say, Mr. Munro?" asked the civilian. He was not sure he had understood.

"Look, I don't know who you are but I can guess. If it's your business to check on me, all well and good. But you know who I am, so I don't see much point in asking questions."

60

They were surprisingly tolerant, even sympathetic. "You are going to see Professor Rhodes?" said the civilian.

"Correct," said Munro. He was surprised to find he was sweating.

"Professor Rhodes is an old friend of yours?" This was part statement, part question.

Munro nodded. "I used to go and see him when I was here. He was accepted by your people."

The civilian nodded. "We respect Professor Rhodes," he said. "A great poet. Like your Byron. The Professor is a wise man. He has lived in our country thirty years. He never mixes with politics."

"Now that *is* wise," said Munro dryly.

"You must not be angry," said the civilian. "It is our business to investigate special people who come to our country. And you cannot say you are not a special person."

"Not anymore," said Munro. He felt tired. It was almost sad that he wasn't special. Special meant that you were in possession of certain knowledge; you were meeting someone—or they were meeting you. You didn't know who. It was the unpredictable game. And it was a game; or rather, it had been a game, until the moment of death, Stephan's death. Now he felt like an old man looking back on his youth. Yes, it had been a great game while it lasted— even though people had died along the route. That was what it meant to be special . . . Munro sat in the cool, sparsely furnished offices of what he took to be a branch of Greek Intelligence, and he suffered pangs of regret he didn't think possible.

"Why do you come back?" asked the Greek officer.

"Don't you know?" asked Munro.

"Yanni is driving you to see the Professor?"

"Is he indeed?" Munro was surprised. "That's the first I've heard about it."

The civilian went on. "You go to see Professor Rhodes because he is a great poet?"

"That comes into it," said Munro. He felt no need to give any information.

"There is still one thing that disturbs us," said the civilian, "it is where the Professor lives. He is so far to the north, in a part of Greece with few visitors, less attractions than elsewhere in our country."

"That depends on what you find attractive," said Munro.

"What do you find attractive, Mr. Munro?" asked the officer.

"Not me," said Munro, "we're discussing Professor Rhodes. Maybe he likes to get away from people, live off the beaten track. Solitude is a precious commodity. Soon you won't be able to buy it. Rhodes lives up there in peace, in quiet, in the mountains . . . in emptiness."

The civilian mused over this. "He lives close to the Albanian frontier," he insisted.

Munro wondered if they'd been convinced by his performance. And he wondered why he bothered to sustain the fiction. Why didn't he come out in the open and say, "I'm taking Stephan's widow back to the place he died. A futile pilgrimage." He didn't say that. Something stopped him. The story was to be that he and his fiancée were visiting Rhodes because she was doing a thesis on English poetry. So that was the story he'd stick to.

They seemed to be summing him up. Munro was sure they had found out all they wanted.

"We hope you have a happy stay in Greece," said the civilian. They were dismissing him.

"I always do," said Munro.

The civilian added, "Who is Miss Marsh?"

He wasn't ready for that one.

"Miss Marsh?" Then he felt he shouldn't have called her that. "Susan?"

"Oh, yes. Susan Marsh," said the civilian. He was waiting for an answer.

"We're engaged," said Munro. He felt he said that awkwardly. This was one part of the cover story he had not rehearsed in his mind.

"Engaged to be married?"

"Yes."

Both men smiled. "Our congratulations," said the civilian. There was a knock at the door. Munro turned. The man from the car was showing in Susan. He was startled, suddenly apprehensive.

Susan smiled, very relieved, coming to him quickly. "Darling," she said, "I got a fright! I didn't know where you were." She kissed him. Munro's mind buzzed with the sweetness of the kiss, and with the speed with which she played her part.

Back in the hotel, she explained. "A man came to the library. He said you had been taken by the police. He said I might be some help." Then she added, "I'm very sorry."

"Why?"

"I never thought what it might be like for you back here."

"It's all right," he assured her.

"I never thought you'd be in trouble."

"Am I?" asked Munro.

"You should go back home," she said. "I could see Rhodes myself. If this man Yanni drives me, I can visit the place myself. Perhaps see the village that you came through."

"You can't do that," said Munro. "It's on the other side of the frontier."

"I'll be all right by myself," she said.

"Forget it," said Munro.

They were in her room, and heard someone knocking at the next door. Munro looked into the corridor. A pageboy stood outside his door. "Someone to see you, Mr. Munro," he said. "In the bar."

It was Yanni, smiling broadly as he slid off his stool, welcoming Munro with open arms.

"Back safe, Mr. Munro," he said happily. "I knew there could be no trouble for you. You are above suspicion, as I am myself. They know very well who we are. No one can touch us. Your department is highly respected in Greece. Many times they have been in co-operation. I am only a small man, of course, but even I am of some consideration. It is important to have connections in London. I saw Sir John myself when he was here some weeks ago. We do not have quite the same sort of English gentleman in Athens. We have gentlemen of another sort. Very fine, very old families. But not quite the same, not like Sir John."

Munro could think of nothing to cause such admiration.

But Yanni's delight was infectious. He was proud to be with Munro.

"I am driving you in the morning," he said cheerfully. "It is some distance, and the roads are bad. We must get away first thing. Will you tell your fiancée? By the way, what happened to your last wife?"

"She got a divorce," said Munro quickly.

"England is a very reasonable country," said Yanni, nodding. Munro didn't follow his train of thought. "I suppose," said Yanni, "she got tired of waiting for you when you were in jail with the Albanians?"

"That could have been it." Munro nodded dryly.

"Something for you to drink," said Yanni, pushing a glass towards him, "to seal our partnership. One of the best wines of Greece. Surprising to find it in a place like this." He lifted his glass. "To our future intimacy."

Munro grinned. "Good luck," he said.

Yanni had something important to say. He began a couple of times, but it was difficult. Then he said, "Your fiancée? She does not join us?"

"No," said Munro, "she's tired. She wants to sleep. All that traveling."

Yanni seemed pleased. "Of course," he said, "and more traveling in the morning." He plucked up courage. He leaned across. "Mr. Munro," he said, and his whisper carried along the bar, "you must understand: always different bedrooms. This is not permissive as in London. We are in your Victorian age, here in Greece." He looked anxious.

"Of course," said Munro.

The smile came back to Yanni's face, bigger, wider than before. "Another glass," he said, "a little celebration."

5

It was a sparkling morning.

"I know you are not here for sight-seeing," said Yanni, "but I have allowed a little time to show you the most beautiful city in the world."

He drove them around the splendors of ancient Greece. "Nothing but ruins," he said, "yet people come from all over the world to see them."

He took his hands off the wheel to gesture to left and right. "For my part I don't think much of them. I have seen better ruins in other places. Have you seen Balbeck? Have you been to Petra?" He was concerned to let them know he had traveled, and was not just a provincial Greek.

The girl sat in the back of the car, marveling at the beauty of the city and the morning. Then Yanni accelerated and headed through suburbs. "Grand tour is over," he told them, "now to business. We have a long way."

He proved to be an excellent driver, twisting and turning through the morning traffic, reacting to split-second situations, avoiding schoolchildren, racing at speed by a railroad track, heading for open country, scattering roadside hens, braking sharply, and then, as sharply, getting back into top gear. All the time he talked, a mixture of affection and criticism about his country, the people, the roads, the car, himself.

Munro felt he had no right to complain about the road. It was modern and well built. The sky was a bright, almost colorless, blue; the country smudged with beige, dotted with gold and grays. They raced into the distance; hills presented themselves ever further away; hills of strange shapes, curved like the backs of animals, or pyramids climbing from the early mist. All was ethereal for the first few hours. It was only as they closed in on the high lands that they saw how solid was the line of rocks; how steeply they rose. By the side of the road old women looked after goats; outside a cottage a girl used a spinning-wheel. "They never change," said Yanni proudly. "Stubborn! They won't learn. With a modern machine they could do a year's work in a day. They won't change." They raced on; goats again. "Nothing is worse than goats," Yanni called over his shoulder. "They strip the bark off the trees. The trees die. The soil won't hold water after they die. The soil gets poor. The people can grow little. What happens? After that the land is only fit for goats!"

He said everything with pride. If Greeks were stupid, then they must be the most stupid people in the world. Yanni would accept no half-measures. They hit a bad patch of road. He swore in Greek. "You see," he said, "corruption! Someone has pocketed the money instead of mending the road!"

Munro listened with half an ear, deeply moved as they drove north. Something he had forgotten was coming to life. This was a land he had known and enjoyed. Two years ago he had lived here: two years that spanned a chasm in his life. Everything more than two years ago seemed to have happened to someone else. Now he remembered that it was he who had been a young man in places like this.

They were in and out of fertile plains before the sun was overhead, driving past vineyards and olive groves, shivering in the first touch of spring. Ahead, forests climbed down from the rocky heights. They skirted the base of a precipice. "We use the morning to break the back of the journey," Yanni told them. "The roads get worse. Some are only tracks. True, there is a bus route everywhere in Greece. But those buses are driven only by brave men and fools."

Munro left it to Yanni. They stopped for drinks by the side of the road, in taverns where the wine was from the village, and Yanni drank soft drinks. "It's like ginger beer," he told Munro, "English ginger beer." Munro thought they had stopped making that before the last war; Yanni knew better. "I get it often when I am driving." He was virtuous about this.

After midday they drove into mountainous country. It was bleak and splendid. The girl was entranced by the sheer rocks. "It's like being at the beginning of the world."

"Or at the end of it," called back Yanni.

Chasms fell away from the mountain roads. Sometimes deep below they could see the thin trickle of a stream. "These are fierce rivers in autumn," said Yanni, "but in Greece we lose all the water. And we are short to grow things. You see what I mean. We are not modern people. Modern people would build dams and reservoirs, and then the agriculture of Greece would be the best in the world."

The valleys became narrow gorges; the plains grew smaller. They seemed to have climbed to a great plateau stretching northward. Yanni indicated it with pride. "It is the barrier that protected us from the invaders. It goes like this, range after range, all the way to Albania. Can you wonder no one ever comes here . . . except for Professor Rhodes, of course."

In the plains they had seen modern houses, prosperous and colorful. But in the mountains the villages looked primitive. Mountain houses were little more than stone-built huts, merging into rocky backgrounds. Roads became tracks, loose stones and dusty surface. The car lurched over great holes. Yanni was triumphant. "You see! As I told you!"

It began to get dark. They had seen monasteries and fortifications on the pinnacles of rocks, perched like eagles' nests overlooking the valleys. The whole country was a series of theatrical splendors—jagged, abrupt, barren, and dry. Spring had not yet begun to show. Night came quickly below the high rocks. They wound into a village and headed uphill. A blaze of light shone from the side of a mountain.

"Thanks be to God," said Yanni, "the Professor is home." Susan was amazed. By night the lights seemed to shine from nowhere. The glow hung in a black space.

They had to leave the car for the last part of the journey and climb a flight of steps cut in the rock. Then suddenly they were on a flat terrace, part rock, part soil with an orange tree. A low wall marked the edge of the garden. Ahead was a stone archway. They went under it and the lights shone full on them.

She hadn't expected to find such a villa perched in the mountains. Modern, stone-built like a cottage, but stones cut to make a smooth face. Huge picture windows made it look like a stage set. She felt light-headed, above the rest of the world.

A bell rang, dogs barked, voices called in several languages. The entrance to the villa was thrown open. A servant bowed them in. Rhodes welcomed them in the hall.

"Come in," he called. "Munro, isn't it? I expected you hours ago. What happened? Lose your way round these parts nowadays, eh?" He chuckled. "Thought you must have slowed down as you got near Albania." He chuckled again, welcoming Munro, one hand on his shoulder, the other pumping his arm.

He hadn't noticed Susan, a couple of steps behind: she had time to look at him in the bright light. A tall, white-haired man who stood straight as a soldier; ruddy-faced as if out of a high wind, grinning, boyish—that is, boyish for his eighty-one years. Then he saw Susan and gave her a smiling bow.

"So this is Miss Marsh," he said, and he put out a hand to bring her in.

She got a glimpse of a large, open living room with a number of people at a long table.

"Nina will show you to your room," said Rhodes, and Susan found herself following a tiny girl in black clothes along pinewood corridors. Her room was pinewood and stone. The girl opened cupboards for her as Yanni arrived with a servant and her case.

"The Professor says there is something to eat, but if you are tired he understands, and they will see you in the morning."

"Thank him," said Susan.

A peasant-weave curtain covered the window. She pulled it back. The ground fell away outside: they appeared to be perched on the edge of space. She could hear the sounds of people in the house—a warm, friendly sound. She felt safe. This was strange, because a few miles from here, Stephan and Peter Munro had tried to escape from an unfriendly country. Here, if anywhere, she might have reason to feel uneasy.

Munro didn't sleep until much later, until the early morning, in fact. He sat drinking with his old acquaintance, Rhodes. To have thought of him as a friend would have been an over-statement. Rhodes was too removed from ordinary relationships for that—aloof from the trivialities of life, unaware of them perhaps. His fine head thrown back, square shoulders shaking with laughter, inside that old man was a giant of a boy, an idealist disregarding reality.

It amazed Munro how Rhodes had survived the wars that had swept Greece in his lifetime. He had fought for the partisans; in fact he was part of the legend of those days. He had been there when they had thrown the Italians out and sent them running for their ships. They talked over those times, for some of the men with them that night had come across the Pindos mountains to see Rhodes. It was often like this, the mountain villa an open house for men and women, a place of pilgrimage for people who looked on Rhodes as a great man, taking the place of oracles who had indeed lived not so far away. It was for these reasons that Munro did not question the presence of anyone there that night; otherwise, he might have been more suspicious.

The view was spectacular in the morning sunshine. The mystery of how they were suspended in mid-air was solved. The village was below, steps winding down the rock-face. Rocky outcrops rose like the stubs of old teeth around them. The road they had traveled the night before was white thread disappearing in the valley. Sweeping around them, mountains rolled like waves, one range behind another.

Yanni came struggling up the steps. Susan saw him from the wall of the garden. She had risen when the cockerels crowed.

"Good morning," shouted Yanni, "I have your passes for you."

She had no idea what he was talking about. "Where is Mr. Munro?"

She went into the villa with Yanni. Munro was having coffee. There were other people at the table.

"Now I shall get to know you properly," said Rhodes. He bowed her into a chair.

"I have passes," said Yanni.

Rhodes turned to Munro. "We blame that on you," he said. "Now they have closed roads. The military zone is patrolled between Greece and Albania. They have poor young men above the snow-line; frozen, in little cabins—just to examine your papers and to tell you to put your cameras away."

"What for?" she asked.

"God knows," said Rhodes, "there is nothing to photograph."

"It was always like that," said Munro.

"It's worse now," Rhodes frowned at him, "ever since that silly escapade of yours. All these politics do harm. A town like Florina used to be a prosperous place. Now it is a dead end, an occasional car passing from Yugoslavia or Albania. The hotels there have fallen off, and the food is unpalatable." This seemed to be a grave criticism.

Yanni whispered his stage whisper to Munro. "We must start soon. At a certain point you have to walk."

"Where are you going?" Rhodes wanted to know.

Munro was in two minds. He had to make an effort to remember which story they were presenting. "Susan wants to have a look at the country I was in," he said. There was a silence in the room. People stopped eating.

"I see," said Rhodes. He turned to Susan. "You know what sort of people Peter got mixed up with before?"

For a moment she didn't react to the name "Peter". Then she smiled fondly and put a hand on Munro's arm. "He has me to look after him now."

Munro's admiration increased.

"Then it's different," said Rhodes. "You may go. But when do we start work, young lady?"

"When I get back," she smiled at him. "And I don't consider it work." She played her part well. She was so much the future wife that she could smile and flirt with an old man. She was at ease with Munro, taking his hand as they left the villa.

"Nice work," he said outside.

She smiled. "I started this. I must see it goes properly."

Yanni had the car at the foot of the track. He spread a map over the seat, pointing out the route.

"You stop at the closed road. There is a cabin. I don't know if he lets you take the car further."

"What's the idea?" said Munro. "Aren't you coming?"

"Only two passes," said Yanni. It was obvious he was pleased not to be going.

They drove off.

"Is it dangerous?" she wanted to know.

Munro shrugged. "Why should it be?" At the same time he was aware he was going out on a limb, and the girl wouldn't be able to do much if the situation turned nasty.

"You are worried?" She was observant.

"Ever since I was arrested, since I was a prisoner, I've been—well—watchful."

"I understand," she said. She sounded as if she did. "I'm not surprised after what you went through."

"How do you know what I went through?" he asked.

"I'm beginning to guess."

They drove along the narrow mountain road, over a desolate sea of rock and gorse, winding above ravines, and then climbing over the backs of mountains. It took a long time to cover a few miles. Munro found himself slowing down. He was looking for the turn-off, but he was also aware of his dry mouth and a growing fear. He was a madman to come back, to seek out this melancholy corner with the gray village and the old stone bridge.

"There it is," he said. "Closed road."

It was closed only by a tangle of rusty wire which had been pulled across the track. It didn't cover the road completely; sheep or goats had gone past leaving strands of wool on the wire.

The closed road went off at an angle, and a stone hut marked the junction. A soldier was stamping his feet by the side of the track. He had been expecting them, and took a quick look at their papers and inside the car.

"Camera?" he asked.

Munro shook his head.

The sentry pulled the barricade aside, giving the car space to get through.

"No trouble at all," said Munro. Behind them the sentry was already pulling the barricade into place. Then he hurried into his hut.

Munro frowned. Perhaps it had been too easy. Why should they have a closed road if it was so simple to use it? Why didn't they ask what they wanted. What would have happened if he had said, "To go and see where they shot Stephan Aroso—this is his wife who is pretending to be my fiancée. She wants to see where the killing took place."

Who would have believed him? Put like that, would he have believed himself? He swore softly. They should turn back even now.

"There," she said suddenly. "That's the hill above the village."

"How do you know?" he asked.

"I've seen pictures," she told him.

The track gave out shortly, narrowing to a path wide enough for a donkey-cart. But the car had one set of wheels on the rocky edge. Munro pulled up. He pointed to the ravine. "The village is down there. We'll have to walk."

They set off; air chill, sun a bright, cold ball in the sky. The wilderness fanned out, the ground dipped ahead, went into a fold, and rose again. The rocky plateau stretched forever. It seemed possible to reach out and touch the snow-streaked hills of Albania. It was like being on the edge of the world.

They followed the path around a shoulder of rocks. Now they could see the ravine. The closer they got the deeper it became.

"You were on the other side?" she asked.

Munro nodded. "Not very wide is it?" He left the rest unsaid.

It took an hour to reach the lip of the ravine. The path ran along the edge, following the course of an old river.

"There's no water," she said.

"Not this time of year," Munro told her. "When the snows melt it's a torrent."

It was a deep drop to a bed of loose stones. They came around a twist in the path and the village was right in front of them. They stopped: Munro felt his heart thump. He'd been expecting it, but it still gave him a shock.

"Is that Albania?" she asked. It was so close, so similar. Not like another country.

"Yes," said Munro. His heart was going like mad. He had a fantasy about going into an arena to do battle. But with whom? he asked. His days of battle were over. He was the gladiator who had been vanquished—whose life had been spared. Those men don't come back to fight again.

The very stillness was a threat; the village a trap, waiting to close around him. Sweat went cold on him; he was sticky with fear.

"I can't see the bridge," she said.

He knew he had to go on.

"Come on." He led the way. The bridge was below the village. From now on they would be in full view from the other side. Munro was shaking. "No bloody wonder!" he told himself.

The parapet of the old stone bridge came into view, and then the bridge itself. As he had remembered it! The unreality of this moment bewildered him.

It had a center arch and a half-arch at each end. It was reputed to have been built by the Romans, had certainly been there before the Turks had ruled these mountains. Severe, stony, Munro thought it soulless. But was that because a man he had loved had died there? The memory came back with a rush. He looked at Susan. This was the end of a journey; for her, a pilgrimage. How did she feel?

She quickened her step. The nearer she got, the faster she went. She was almost running. They came down the track to the bridge; pot-holes filled in with rubble, now no longer used. He thought she was going to go headlong across. "Susan!"

She stopped, one hand on the stone wall. "There's no one here," she said, "can't we go on?"

There wasn't a sign of life in the village. Munro wondered if they'd evacuated it, as it was so close to the frontier. Then he saw an old woman in the black dress of the peasants. He remembered it as a village of old people. The younger men went with the sheep and cattle to the winter pastures. The old woman didn't give them a glance.

"It seems all right." Susan stepped on to the cobbled stones. Munro sensed someone was watching. The girl took his hand. He remembered she was supposed to be his fiancée, and they walked along the bridge together.

They were half-way across when he saw the sun glint on something at one of the windows opposite. He saw the barrel of the rifle as it moved. He stood very still.

"What is it?" she asked.

"Nothing." But he held her back.

She turned towards the village. She didn't see anything, but she hadn't been trained to pick out the reflections on a gun barrel.

"There's no one there," she told him. She knew he was on edge. She tried to move on, but he still held her.

"There's a man with a gun on the first floor."

She didn't believe him.

"First house at the end of the bridge. Ideal position. Gives them the clearest view. Leaves no cover on the bridge."

"What do you mean?"

He took her literally. "If they were in the next house, or the next, that would increase the angle. They couldn't fire directly on the bridge. Anyone on it—like you and me— could use the wall as shelter."

"What are you talking about?"

"Gun fire," he said dryly.

He couldn't see the gun anymore, but he knew there was someone there.

"You imagine things," she said, and tried to walk away.

"Stay where you are." He tried not to show alarm, but he kept his hand on her arm.

"You're hurting me," she said.

"Don't move." He let her go. She stood for a moment, uncertain, looking up at the house.

74

"Are you sure?"

He didn't answer but he was sure. They stood watching, but there was no sound and no one moved.

"Whoever it was," she said, "they've gone."

Munro wasn't sure.

"What did you see?" she asked him.

"A reflection."

That didn't convince her. "It could have been anything." She sounded like a mother comforting a child. She looked into the gorge below, walking to the edge of the bridge and looking over. Munro kept glancing from her to the house. Nothing moved. No sound. He began to wonder if he'd made a mistake. He was liable to see devils in shadows.

The girl called to him. "Show me," she said.

He didn't understand her.

"Where were you? I mean, when you crossed. Where was Stephan?" Munro remembered the macabre reason for the mission. It smacked of laying out a corpse to him.

"We came down an alley-way into the village. You can see it." As he pointed, his eye went up to the window again.

"What happened?"

"We got to the road." It was a narrow cobbled track that came from the hills on the other side. Munro remembered coming along it. "There was no one in the village. Stephan was ahead of me. He started to cross, I followed." He stopped.

"Why didn't you cross?"

"We did. A few steps . . ."

She interrupted. "Where to?"

"Where to?" He didn't understand.

"How far? Where were you?"

"Does it matter?"

"Yes. Show me."

He thought she was being hysterical. Her interest was morbid. But she was calm and absorbed.

"We were half-way."

"Both of you?"

"Of course."

This seemed important to her. "You were standing together?"

"A couple of steps apart." He was uneasy at this spate of questions. He tried to remember exactly what had happened. He gave another glance at the village: even the old woman had disappeared.

"I read all the reports," she told him. "Sir John gave them to me one day in his office."

"Why not?" said Munro.

"A man called to you. You said someone appeared at the end of the bridge?"

"Yes." He could visualize the man now. An old peasant in the moonlight.

"Where?"

"There." He pointed at the beginning of the bridge. Every time he pointed he was aware of the end house.

"Do you know where he came from?"

"No. He was near the house."

"Which house?"

"The one I showed you. Where I saw the gun." He looked at the window. "He could have come from there."

"You said in the report he called. What did he say?"

"I don't know. It was some dialect."

"Stephan understood?"

Munro nodded. "He went back to speak to the man."

"What for?"

"God knows . . . he was like that."

"What?"

"Flamboyant. Everything was a gesture." He sounded bitter now.

She was puzzled. "I don't understand. If Stephan was ahead of you . . ."

Munro closed his fists: she was being irritating. "What does it matter? He was ahead. When the man called he went back."

"You mean, he was here? Then he crossed you to go there?"

She showed him what she meant by taking a few steps along the bridge towards the village.

"Don't be a damn fool," he called. "Stay on this side."

"What for? There's nobody here."

She wasn't exactly mocking, but she was amused. Munro could have hit her. He repeated, "Stay where you are," but she ignored him. She crossed to the far end of the bridge, stopped, and began to pace out steps back to the center. He watched her, disbelieving. "What the hell are you doing?"

She kept on counting as she walked, measuring the distance with an unnatural stride. "Fifteen yards," she told him.

He was very angry with her; at the same time afraid. The place alarmed him; familiar, and at the same time strange. Solitude and silence—except for an English girl, measuring distance as she might on a croquet lawn!

"That's about half-way," she called. She began pacing the walk again. Munro looked up at the window. The village seemed shocked, startled, stunned into silence by the affront. Dark windows, wide gaping mouths, gasps of wonder! She went up and down counting. Measuring what?

"Just ask," said Munro. "What do you want to know?"

"You can't have been far away," said Susan.

"I was here." Munro strode to the Greek side of the ravine.

"Thirty steps," said the girl.

"Well?" He saw nothing strange in that. But as he turned, he saw there was someone in the village. An old man had come out of the alley-way. He was peering towards them.

He went back to Susan. "There's a man watching." She was not concerned.

"We're doing nothing." She was kneeling down by the wall of the bridge. Munro watched her. The old man was watching her; Munro heard him say something. He was talking to someone in the house beside him. So there was someone there! The old man suddenly shuffled off at speed.

Susan wasn't alarmed. She repeated, "Thirty steps. In the report you said, 'All this shooting.' "

Her calm unnerved him. "For Christ's sake. There was all that shooting!"

She turned to look at him. It was like a challenge. "He was here, where I am. You were there . . . what did you

77

say?" She seemed to be speaking very loud. " 'They were using automatics.' How is it . . ." she remembered where they were, and added, "Peter . . . how is it, Peter, you didn't get hit?"

Munro could only blink at her. The accusation shook him. "He tried to climb over this wall?" she asked. Munro nodded. "He was too badly hit? You said they still fired."

"They did."

"They must have killed him while he hung there." She touched the wall. "Bullets must have bounced off. It's solid stone."

What the hell was she saying? That he should have been killed too? Because Stephan was dead, he should be dead? Was she *that* unforgiving?

"I'm sorry," said Munro, "I was just a few steps away . . . like you say. I didn't get hurt."

He walked over to the wall. It was a crude mortar, binding stone blocks, chipped and broken in many places. It was impossible to say where the shots had struck.

"Is it so important?" Munro was gentler. One man dies, another lives. One man she had loved. Why couldn't it have been the other way around? Then a man whom no one in particular loved could have been buried in this wilderness instead of Stephan, young, amusing, attractive. Munro had sometimes wished that he had died that night instead of Stephan.

"What else do you remember?" she asked him.

"Stephan went back to talk to this man."

"Can you think why he should? Any reason?"

Munro thought. "Perhaps he thought that the man might be less likely to give the alarm if he spoke to him."

"But if you had both run, you could have been out of Albania. You would have been safe."

"I know," Munro nodded, "it was a trap."

"Why didn't they shoot you both as you went onto the bridge?"

"I don't know."

"Or while you were on the bridge? Why call Stephan back?"

"I don't know."

"Unless they wanted you two apart."

Munro frowned. "What for?"

"Then Stephan could be shot. Not you."

"Why should they give a damn about me?"

She didn't answer.

My God, he thought, now we're getting the full story. This is why she wanted to come out here! She thinks I had a part in killing the man.

"For God's sake! He was my friend." Munro's voice rose. "Just about the only man I had any affection for."

The girl seemed to be thinking about something else.

"Why's there no barricade at the end of the bridge?" she said.

"There's no need," said Munro. "The track ends here. The road's closed on the Greek side."

"You'd think they would have a customs post or something." She was still trying to figure it out.

"There's no traffic," said Munro. "Nomads in spring, nothing else."

"People like you and Stephan?" she asked.

"I think we were the last," he said. "No one would try to use this route again."

She thought about that, moving along the bridge.

He called, "That's another country over there. An outpost of evangelical communism, run by fanatics. They haven't grown old and wise like Moscow. They're the uncontaminated converts."

She understood that he was warning her. "There's no one," she called, and took a couple of steps onto the soil of Albania.

Munro didn't know what he supposed would happen. He never formalized his fears. They were vague and terrible. Munro waited. When nothing happened, something seemed to explode in his head. He raced after the girl. She smiled at him. "You see," she said, "you are in Albania, and quite safe." It was as if a time-bomb had failed to go off. Was it defused? Or was this another trick? Why was he on this side of the ravine anyhow? Hadn't he suffered enough? Did he want to spend the rest of his life in a cell, six foot by four? He was back in the land of nightmares!

Susan saw something. "That must be the alley-way."

He stuck to her like a child with its mother, and cursed her for her madness. They must go back: they were tempting the devil.

He spoke in a whisper. "There could be patrols." She moved to the opening of the alley. Munro joined her. "That's it." He was still whispering.

He thought he could hear someone else whisper. A man's voice, faintly.

There *was* someone in the corner house. And now they were directly below the window. No one could see them from inside unless they put their heads out. More whispers. To Munro the voices sounded bewildered, uncertain. Then the sound of a safety-catch coming off a gun.

"Did you hear?" he whispered.

"What?"

He indicated the house. "Someone with a gun."

She looked at him sympathetically. "It's all right," she assured him.

Munro took her hand in a grip that hurt her. They walked back. It took all his control not to run. He knew their backs presented an easy target. He expected the shot all the way. When he got to the other side, he let her go. He sat on a rock and tried to understand. He saw the men at the window that time, two of them. They weren't peasants. Both had guns. They looked as shaken as Munro felt.

"Look up at the window," he said.

Before she had turned, the men had gone—a simple matter of stepping behind the shutters.

She said nothing. Munro didn't care what she thought. They had been into the mouth of hell and back again.

She took a fountain-pen from her pocket. He thought she was going to make notes.

"We're going," he told her.

"Two minutes," she said. She went back to the bridge, looking down at the fountain-pen, peering into some part of it. Then she slowly swung it around. There was a faint mechanical sound. Munro heard it clearly. He looked towards the village. Did the sound carry?

Susan joined him.

80

"Taking photographs," she explained brightly. "It's a camera. They told me it was forbidden to take photos. Don't you think it looks exactly like a pen?" She put it away with satisfaction.

They walked back to the car. She thanked him for taking her. Munro didn't answer. He was still working out the logic of the morning—if it had any logic.

They drove the car back over the bumpy track. The sentry was waiting for them; he took another look at their passes, and inside the car. Then he waved them onto the road. Munro looked back. The sentry was pulling the blockade over the road as they drove away.

6

Professor Rhodes was waiting for them. He seemed to get some dry amusement out of their expedition. "Visitors come to Greece for its famous ruins, not to go to these poverty-stricken parts. Barren mountains! You two spend your time on that bleak rock! What kept you?"

Yanni had also waited for them. He was alarmed when they were not back by noon.

"I would have hired a car and come to look for you," he said.

The girl was surprised.

"Anything can happen," he said.

"What?"

Yanni shrugged his shoulders. "It's a military area," he said. "I think they have minefields."

"Rubbish," said Rhodes.

But there had been concern during their absence. Yanni had asked local people about the frontier. Had there been incidents? In return, the locals had wondered what two foreigners were doing there. Yanni had not told them. Munro was puzzled that Yanni should be so concerned.

"What was the problem?" he asked.

"I had instructions you would be back at noon. When you were late I thought of sending a cable to London."

"You're out of your mind," said Munro.

"I had instructions." Yanni showed him and he had a note initialed by Sir John. "Return by noon at latest. Or make urgent inquiries."

"I didn't have these instructions," Munro told him. "And if I had done, I'd have torn the bloody thing up. That schedule has come to an end."

"I know," said Yanni. "Mine too. This was the last thing. You should have been back three hours ago."

"We stopped to make tea," Munro snarled at him.

Susan was having the first of her academic discussions with the Professor. Munro had to wait to speak to her.

"Did you know we had a deadline?"

"No."

"Nothing in those instructions they gave you?"

"They've finished," she told him. She showed him her papers. There was nothing to say how long they should stay at the bridge.

"Cecil messed that one up," he said grimly. "We don't want these anymore." Munro tore up the papers, and felt better. London was no longer running their lives. "When do we go?" he asked.

She was vague. "I have some more talks with Professor Rhodes."

"What for? That was just a cover story. You've seen the bridge."

"I can't just hurry away after one day," she told him.

"Why not?"

"It would look strange."

"Who to?"

She looked at him if he were being stupid. "To everyone."

Munro felt there was no sense staying. The mission was over. He had done what he promised. He had every right to get out.

Yanni came up to the villa to see him. He was very pleased with himself.

"I sent off my cable," he said cheerfully. "There is a small post office in the village. They made difficulties. They could not take cables, they said, not for foreign countries. The lines were blocked. They were overworked. There was censorship. Nothing could go through in code."

Yanni had lost him. Munro didn't know what he was talking about.

"What cable? What code?"

Yanni was dashed. "To your office." He had been expecting a word of praise.

"I have no office," said Munro.

"To Sir John. I had to report."

"In code?"

"Of course."

"What did you say?"

"I told them your mission was well done."

That sounded harmless. But Munro saw no reason why even that should be sent.

"What code?"

"The Aroso code," said Yanni.

"They told you to use that!"

"Why not? It is unbreakable."

"What did you say?"

Yanni took a dirty crumple of paper from his pocket, and handed it to Munro.

He read "Dresden 0992."

That sounded like a telephone number, but Munro recognized his name. He was "Dresden." He looked at Yanni angrily.

"Why did you send this?" he asked. "You know what it means? It means "Munro had a successful beginning." You must be a damn fool! I'm not beginning anything, that's *all* I came to do. You understand? Now get out of here. Have the car ready. You drive me back to Athens in the morning."

Yanni was shaken. "I am sorry. This is the message they told me to send."

"Who?"

"Sir John."

"They told you to cable this to London?"

"Yes. As soon as you had visited the bridge." Munro couldn't make sense of that. Why should they care? Why use a top security code?

"It doesn't matter," said Yanni. He was trying to placate Munro. "No one else can understand that message."

Munro knew he was probably right, but perhaps "Dresden" still meant something in this part of Europe. Any Albanians monitoring cables—and they most emphatically did—would remember the name without difficulty. They had called him that on the charge sheets. "Peter Munro, alias Dresden . . ."

"Okay," said Munro. "I don't suppose it matters."

"What about the car?" asked Yanni.

"I'll speak to . . . Susan," he said.

She was taking a walk in the village with the Professor, the servant told him, pleased to talk to Munro in his halting Greek. He went back to the garden and stood at the wall, looking down into the shadows as the sun dropped. He could hear voices long before Rhodes and Susan appeared. She was wearing something white which showed up as they wound in and out of the rocks.

He wondered why Susan was talking so loudly until he heard what she was saying.

"I knew Peter slightly before they arrested him. I didn't know what his job was, but we had mutual friends in London. When they exchanged him for that German spy, I got to know Peter better. I was staying in Eastbourne. That's where he was."

She was letting Munro know the story she had told Rhodes. He would have to go along with it.

"There you are!" said Rhodes, as they got to the top of the path. Susan came and took Munro's arm. She was playing the part automatically now. Munro felt she was enjoying it.

"A very intelligent girl," grumbled Rhodes. "Can't understand what she sees in you." He went into the villa.

"We'd better stay out here a little," she said.

"Why?" Munro was surprised.

"They must expect it of us," she said. He was irritated by the situation.

"Yanni sent a damn fool message to the Travelers," he told her. "In code! Suggesting we haven't finished here."

"I think you can go when you like," she said gently.

He looked at her sharply. "What about you?"

"I'll stay a day or two."

"On your own?"

"Why not?" She gave Munro the feeling she was protecting him, and he hated that.

"What do you want to stay for?"

"I told you. To make it look better. I'd hate the Professor to think we had made use of him."

"But if I go?"

"I'll tell him you aren't well, and you're going home. I'll stay a couple of days."

"Only a couple of days?"

"Yes."

"If that's all right," said Munro, "I'll stay."

She seemed genuinely pleased, but perhaps she was just playing her part in case anyone in the villa was watching.

The atmosphere was transformed that evening, the villa crowded.

"All my friends," Rhodes informed them. "This is open house for anyone who is out of touch with the times." The villa was bright with lights. It was a festival.

Susan changed into an evening gown. She looked startling. "Professor Rhodes asked me if I had brought any pretty clothes."

Munro caught his breath, she was so spectacular. She behaved as though she was contentedly in love, holding his hand, quiet, undemonstrative.

"Charming," said Rhodes, "you will be very happy." He gave a shrug. "Sometimes I think I should have married."

Susan kissed his cheek.

"Do they eat here?" Munro indicated the visitors.

"Why not?" said Rhodes. "There is enough."

Munro was puzzled. "Did you invite them?"

"Some of them," said Rhodes.

He didn't give that a second thought.

Most of the talk was in Greek. About half-way through the evening Munro tired of the noise and good fellowship. Much of it seemed artificial. Rhodes spent his time with a few men he had known a long time, talking about old campaigns. Munro went into the garden. The moon made everything even more theatrical.

"Good evening, Mr. Munro."

He was surprised by a voice at his elbow. It was a dark little man with a short beard. "You were far away," said the man, "beyond those hills perhaps?" He nodded towards the mountains of Albania. It was an accurate guess.

"I don't follow." Munro disliked the man instinctively.

"Don't take offense, Mr. Munro. Everyone knows who you are. You know the other side of these hills very well."

"That's my affair," said Munro.

The stranger smiled. "You don't remember me?"

"No."

"I am Kostes Vilaras. I am a teacher. I was here the night you arrived with your beautiful future wife. Professor Rhodes introduced us."

Munro was off-hand. "I was tired that night. Nothing registered."

"I understand," said Vilaras. "You don't object if I talk to you?"

"Why should I?" asked Munro.

"Professor Rhodes is an old friend of yours?"

"Yes," said Munro.

"I have always had an admiration for him," said Vilaras. Munro wondered what the devil he was trying to tell him. "But he begins to live in the past," said Vilaras.

"I dare say you are right." Munro was deliberately off-hand.

Vilaras continued. "I have not known the Professor personally . . . not long."

"Everyone drops in for a meal," said Munro casually.

The little man did not change his tone. "Why are you here, Mr. Munro?" he said.

Munro suddenly realized that he was wrong to treat this stranger with disdain. He had made a mistake.

"It's the noise," Munro indicated the music in the villa, "I'm not hearing too well."

"I asked why you were here," said Vilaras. "One would have thought last time was enough."

"Every country has its own code of good manners," said Munro gently. "It's not for me to question what is proper in your country. We don't consider it the thing to ask personal questions." He smiled blandly at Vilaras.

"We are not joking," said Vilaras, sharply.

87

"We?" said Munro in surprise. He peered into the darkness as if expecting to see someone there.

Vilaras recovered himself. "You once escaped. Don't expect to do so twice."

"Do you talk Greek, Mr. Vilaras?" asked Munro.

The question took him unawares. "Of course. I am Greek."

"You surprise me," said Munro. "Not Albanian?"

That made him angrier. "I am Greek! One does not need to be a fascist to belong to this country."

"Excuse me," said Munro, "I never talk politics."

Vilaras seemed to lose his head. "What do you mean, you don't talk politics? You work for politics! You are bought and paid by politics! Do you think anyone forgets you?"

"You have the advantage," said Munro, "I don't know what Intelligence you work for."

"None." Vilaras' voice rose. "I'm not interested in money."

"Ideals maybe?" asked Munro.

"I am a school teacher," Vilaras began.

"What school?" asked Munro sharply.

The man hesitated. "None at present," he said, "I have been victimized."

"Exclude me from your problems," said Munro. "I never worked for any country but my own."

"You think not?" said Vilaras. "What are you doing now?"

Munro thought he would find out. "What *am* I doing?" he asked.

Vilaras looked coldly at Munro. "You have no disguises, Mr. Munro," he said. "Whatever you do, you are known. It was foolish to run risks. Foolish to cross the bridge."

"Who told you?" asked Munro softly.

Vilaras didn't answer. "Be wise and go home."

"Nice meeting you," said Munro. He went into the villa.

Munro saw the Professor next morning. "Who was the little man with the beard?"

"A school teacher," said Rhodes. "A dedicated man. He

is opposed to the government, and he tries to organize opposition."

"How?"

"Collecting money. Organizing groups."

"You mean cells?"

"Cells if you like," admitted Rhodes.

The girl was listening. She said "Cells?" and looked at them.

Munro explained. "The man is a communist."

"He calls himself a patriot," interrupted Rhodes.

"This is a dangerous country for communists," went on Munro. "Too many communists lie on its frontiers."

"The people look poor. Perhaps communists would bring them a better life," said Susan.

Munro was dry. "I don't go much on theories. But when men like Vilaras tell me it's time to go home . . ."

The girl looked at him. "What did you say?"

"Told him to mind his own bloody business," said Munro.

That amused her. "Didn't you say you had arranged to go?"

"Have you?" said Rhodes. "I was looking forward to working with Susan."

"There's no hurry," said Munro. The more one pushed him, the more he tended to resist. Vilaras had tried to push him. "He thinks I'm in Intelligence," said Munro. "You'd think an educated man would realize I couldn't be. As he said, everyone knew who I was."

"You went back to your old haunts," said Rhodes thoughtfully.

"That's another thing," said Munro, "he knew we had crossed the bridge."

"Some goat-boy could have told him."

"The cattle aren't back on the hills yet," said Munro. "Someone else must have told him."

"Who knew?" asked Rhodes.

"The men in the village?" Munro shook his head.

Susan said quickly. "Peter thinks there were men in the house. The old guardroom."

89

Rhodes nodded. "Possible," he frowned, "but how could they tell Vilaras?"

Susan answered again. "Perhaps this man Vilaras is working with the Albanians."

Rhodes lifted his hands in a gesture of acceptance. "I don't care what people are as long as they have sympathy for their fellows."

Munro nearly said something, then thought better of it. He walked to the village with Susan. She chatted all the way down the rocky steps.

"Be careful," said Munro, "your voice carries."

But she just laughed. "I'm happy you are going to stay," she said.

"Happy?" said Munro.

She nodded.

"I thought you were here for a funeral?"

Her smile went. "I have been to that," she said.

They went out of the village and along a rough track, at the foot of a cliff. In a niche was a ruined chapel. Munro pointed to it.

"Full of the bones of heroes. Men who died for the freedom Vilaras just talks about. But that lot in the chapel were fighting the Turks. This country has been suffering for two thousand years. What does the school teacher think he's going to achieve, except more dead heroes?"

They walked on, between boulders strewn along the valley. The gorge opened up. A small plain lay ahead, a basin set in the hills, outcrops of rock rising, gaps in the rock revealing mountains beyond. On the top of a peak, another building clung to the rock, growing out of it. The sun touched them. There was a new warmth in the air.

But even in this peace and solitude, questions presented themselves in his mind. Why had she bothered to take photographs at the bridge? Surely that was an unnecessary folly?

She looked up at him. "You're serious."

"No."

"What are you thinking?"

"Nothing." He pushed all the questions away. They were going to leave in a couple of days. Why could he not merely accept the pleasure of the moment? Look on it as a holiday. A very short holiday.

On the way back, when they were in sight of the villa, he took her hand. Rhodes waved down to them from the terrace. Later they sat in the garden, under a fig tree, drinking, while the old man recited some of his own verse. They sat close together, he and the girl with his arm around her. It was very proper; after all they were engaged. If Munro had still been able to recognize happiness, he would have known that at that moment he was a happy man.

7

Yanni came puffing up to the villa early next morning. He was carrying a cable. It had come from London and was addressed to Yanni, but the message was for Munro. It read: "Permission obtained to visit grave stop letter follows."

Munro didn't need to be told what that meant. No one had mentioned the possibility of going to see Stephan's grave. It was on the other side of the frontier. What could be the purpose of such a visit? Who would go? Did they expect him to go? The idea made his head swim.

He showed the cable to Susan. Her eyes shone. "How wonderful!"

Munro blinked at her.

The letter came that afternoon. A man on a motorcycle arrived in the village. Yanni was waiting for him. The letter had been delivered at the British Embassy that morning. On the back of the cycle, strapped to the pillion, the man carried a wreath. It was large, but in good taste. He gave that to Yanni before he drove away.

Munro had an eerie feeling that he was part of someone's dream. The letter—or documents as it turned out to be—wasn't addressed either to himself or to Yanni. It was a semi-official letter to Leo Rhodes. In it Rhodes was requested by Sir John, as a British subject of high standing in that part of Europe, to represent the Crown in the proposed visit to the burial place of the late Stephan Aroso. The occasion had arisen, the letter explained, out of the visit to the area of Aroso's one-time associate, Peter Munro. The Albanian authorities had been contacted, and had given their permission for a party of up to six to meet at the bridge beside the village of Karlovo.

"Is that where we were?" Susan asked.

Munro nodded. He didn't trust himself to speak. Rhodes read the document to them: he took it as some sort of honor bestowed on him.

"A party of six," he said. "Tomorrow at nine in the morning."

Munro waited for Rhodes to react. Surely the old man would wonder why the hell he'd been asked to go? Why should anyone go? Who had made this bizarre request in the first place? Rhodes nodded over the letter. "It's better to have this relationship with the Albanians than none at all," he said. "They are very fine people. Brave, loyal, stubborn. They have a passion for their country. During the war, the great powers were grateful for their courage." He looked gravely at Munro. "I suppose this expedition is on your behalf?"

Munro was going to deny that. If anyone wanted to see where Stephan lay, it must be his wife. But that couldn't be said.

"Does it say where he is buried?" asked Munro when they were alone.

"Some kilometers north of Karlovo."

"Some?" asked Munro. " 'Some' could be a hundred."

"That's all they say." Rhodes handed the papers to Munro. A Ministry heading topped the pages and each sheet had been stamped. It was very impressive, and Rhodes was impressed. "You don't have to do it," Munro told him.

Rhodes looked shocked. "Of course I shall do it! It's good to think I can be of some service to my country, and to another country I admire."

It was impossible to reason with him. The old man moved through life with his head in the clouds. This request appealed to him; it had heroic elements and he didn't question its intention. He was an ambassador, won over by the use of the word "Crown." He was to represent the "Crown." From then on he failed to analyze the project.

His task was to serve with courage and dignity, and that came easily.

"A party of six," mused Rhodes. "That might take some consideration."

"No names mentioned?" said Munro.

"None in the letter."

Invisible hands were plucking Munro, moving him from one square to another. "I made no request for this," he told Rhodes.

Rhodes lifted his white eyebrows. He didn't see any significance in that.

"If I'd wanted to go into Albania, I'd have told them," said Munro.

"They have their own ends," said Rhodes.

"Like what?" asked Munro.

"There may have been questions in the House," said Rhodes thoughtfully. "People like to know that British citizens are not forgotten when abroad."

"For God's sake," said Munro, "the man's dead."

"Even then," said Rhodes, "there are organizations concerned about graves, funerals, religious things. Not that I hold with a lot of their attitudes. But one must play a part when asked . . ." he hesitated. Did he think the "Crown" had named him personally? Did he have some fantasy that this mission had a national—even a human—meaning? It was no good talking to him.

Munro explained to Susan. "They must be out of their minds," he said. "Cecil fiddles about in that office in London. He has no idea what it's like here . . . what he's landing us in."

"What *is* he landing us in?" she asked. She was trying to understand him.

Munro was nervous, drumming fingers on his knuckles. She had no conception of danger.

"You're so bloody innocent," he said. "And the old boy thinks this is a walk to a war memorial."

"Isn't it?"

"It's a trap," said Munro. "If they wanted to manufacture a border incident, this could be it." She was bewildered. "Someone gets shot," said Munro. "Someone disappears. Something happens to someone!" He almost said someone could find himself back in jail, but he didn't.

Nevertheless she guessed, and put her hand on his arm. "You know why they have arranged this?" she said. "For me. It's a chance to see the place. Then I could close the chapter completely. Does that sound heartless to you?"

"No," said Munro, "nor does it sound convincing." He wondered if Cecil and Sir John wanted to get rid of him? Surely there must be easier ways?

Susan was speaking. "There's no need for you to come. Professor Rhodes is looking forward to it. He says we must take an interpreter. He knows someone. That's all that's necessary. We'll go tomorrow, then we can leave for England next day."

"You can't go alone on this with Rhodes!" said Munro. "He's in a bloody dream world."

She was firm. "I'm going," she said. Munro looked at her in despair. She was ringing his death-knell—for if she went, he had to go.

Rhodes had already started to organize, with a collection of maps on his desk. "London have certainly done things the right way this time," he informed them. "They've been in touch with the army. The border patrols know about us. There's some talk of giving us a guard of honor."

Munro tried to visualize that. "Where to?" he asked.

"To the frontier, of course," said Rhodes sharply.

Munro wasn't interested. If they could have had a handful of Greek soldiers to the grave and back, that would have been more to the point. They needed no protection this side of Karlovo.

"I've been drawing up the order of the party," said Rhodes. "They will probably have an official welcome for us. We'll have to walk part of the way: the track out of the village is bad, so we can't take a car. I don't want the British party split up. We must do things in an orderly fashion. Don't forget what we represent."

Munro wondered what they did represent.

"I'll go in front," said Rhodes, "you follow me, Munro, with Susan. Then your man, Yanni, and the interpreter. In that way we will be orderly, restrained and dignified. A mark of respect for our dead countryman, and also to our hosts."

Munro wondered if Rhodes was fooling himself. They were going among a suspicious and backward people, who might take offense at a sideways glance. A country where ignorant mountain tribes were rough and crude—where jealousies flared, family feuded with family.

"Are you going to take a gun?" asked Munro.

"Of course not." Rhodes stared at him. At times he found Munro incomprehensible.

Yanni seldom came up to the villa unless he had business. He had a room at the inn, and he spent his time in the village, accepted by the locals as a friendly and amusing fellow. They were inclined to mistrust strangers from Athens and the south, but Yanni had no big city airs, so they liked him. They didn't understand what he had to do with the Englishman, but they didn't ask. They read newspapers and knew the rumors. Munro was the English spy who had been caught, the man the Albanians were going to execute last year, but changed their minds and exchanged for one of their own men. A senseless world, politics! Problems enough of one's own. Taxes, corruption. So they drank and joked with Yanni in the evenings, but did not discuss his business.

That, of course, was before the wreath arrived. That changed things. It was a large wreath, for an important occasion. They all knew Yanni had to take it to Karlovo and put it on a grave. It was a long time since any of them had been in Karlovo; not since the war, when they had joined the Croats and Slavs and Macedonians and anyone else, to throw out the Italians.

Munro came down to the village that evening to see Yanni. They sat at the back of the inn, and Yanni speculated cheerfully about the journey. "Perhaps they are showing the flag," he suggested.

"What flag?" Munro was skeptical.

"The British flag. After all, they shot one of your citizens and imprisoned another."

"That was according to the rules," said Munro.

"Then why do you think we go?" asked Yanni. He wasn't troubled by the prospect.

Munro flourished on suspicion. He could see no pattern in this journey to Greece, but it was more than a mere retracing of steps.

"That wreath," he said. "A bit odd to put it on the back of a motorcycle."

"He was a good rider," said Yanni.

"Why didn't they give him a car?"

Yanni shrugged. "Is it important?"

"In a car no one would have noticed it . . . You know, Yanni, everything about this is conspicuous."

"One wreath on a motor bike," said Yanni. "What else makes us conspicuous?"

Munro thought a moment. "You do," he said.

Yanni was indignant. "I am ideal for the job," he said. "There is no point trying to smuggle Peter Munro back here. *That* would have attracted attention. So I was open. I say "I am working with Munro, the famous British spy," and all my friends smile. If they take it lightly, then my enemies take it lightly. Also your enemies. It was for this I was so extrovert."

Munro may have been listening, but he said, "And on the bridge Susan was conspicuous."

Yanni said, "The great danger in our job is getting a persecution feeling—like everyone is looking for you. Or another feeling of being important and people noticing you. Two bad feelings."

"There are worse," Munro told him; "When you *don't* notice people are looking for you."

"Mr. Munro," Yanni gave a wail, "who can be looking for you, when everyone knows where you are?"

That was something Munro couldn't answer.

Long before nine o'clock next day Munro heard Rhodes moving about singing tunelessly. "They are waiting," he called to Munro. It was early, but there was no point delaying.

The sky was faint white-blue. A late spring was racing

up the mountain sides, bringing sudden splashes of pastel color.

Munro debated whether or not to take his gun. He decided not to. If there were trouble, one gun was not enough. And it was possible they would search him.

A car was parked at the front of the steps. Munro followed Susan and Rhodes.

Yanni waited with another man. Munro was surprised to see it was Vilaras. "What's he doing?" asked Munro.

"I am your interpreter," said Vilaras. He bowed a brief "good morning" to Susan.

"You speak Albanian?" asked Munro.

"Many dialects," said the little man. "None perfectly, but sufficient to be understood."

"So that's what you teach at school," said Munro.

Vilaras shook his head. "Not languages, Mr. Munro. I teach another thing. Call it sociology. Human freedom. Man's struggle against man."

"Who's winning?" asked Munro, as he got into the car.

They set off. Yanni drove slowly, with his eye on the clock. It was safest to stick to the timetable. After all, no one was in a hurry to cross into Albania, except Rhodes who leaned forward. "Got the flowers?" he asked Yanni.

"In the back," called Yanni.

Rhodes nodded with approval. He was enjoying himself. The stone hut at the head of the closed road came into sight.

"Well, well," murmured Munro, "there's a turn-out." The wooden barrier was no longer guarded by merely one sentry. Four men flapped their arms in the mountain air. A ragged little bunch, at a loss until they heard the car. Two more men came out of the hut, one an officer. He shouted to the men as the car pulled up. They began to pull back the barrier. The officer nodded in recognition to Rhodes, asking for papers in Greek.

Rhodes took the letter from his pocket and handed the officer a sheet. This satisfied him. He looked at the people in the car, bowed briefly to Susan, then stepped back. Yanni drove on.

"The track gets worse," he said, "soon we have to leave the car."

"Very good." Rhodes was crisp and brisk.

They parked the car where Munro had left it before.

"We don't want to look a mess like those sentries," said Rhodes. "I suggest we march."

They set off, a little body of men . . . and a woman . . . over the mountain track; headed by a white-haired man, like a general in front of his army; followed by Munro, with Susan holding his hand. Behind them, puffing, Yanni carrying the wreath, and Vilaras, taking short, trotting steps to keep up.

Munro thought they were indeed showing the flag as Yanni had suggested: the true flag of his country in this day and age, its glory gone and in its place the travesty . . . an old man, believing in God knows what, and a pretty girl with a bizarre sense of mourning that had come two years too late. Behind them two foreigners made up this "British" contingent. Well, that was a fair proportion, Munro decided. The greatness he had inherited from his father, and his father from his grandfather, had been based on a power that relied probably on about two-thirds alien support.

Yanni did not realize that the admiration he had was for a country that had vanished during Munro's own generation, and that history has a time-lag when it comes to discarding images. The other Greek, Vilaras, with his smiling eyes—revealing pinpoints of his astute and uncommitted brain—had a clearer picture of the crumbling reality of the flag he followed at that moment. Besides, thought Munro as he marched after his straight-backed leader, was Vilaras a Greek? A man who spoke Albanian in many dialects, could he be a Greek? Perhaps born in Greece—but with another loyalty, in a fast-changing world. These things passed through Munro's head as he walked towards Karlovo; for, as they say a man's past floats before him as he drowns, so Munro's mind free-floated as he went down this track.

He grinned. Susan pressed his hand. "We must look pretty odd."

"There's no one here to see us," she said.

"There is," he said. "Ask Rhodes. The gods live in these hills."

Soon they were above the ravine and a few moments later they saw the village. Rhodes led the little party at the same steady speed towards the bridge.

Munro expected some military order, like "Right turn" or "Squad halt," but they showed no sign of slowing down.

"Karlovo," said Vilaras from behind.

They came level with the village. It was no longer deserted. On the Albanian side a small crowd had collected, about a dozen people. Men, mostly. Rhodes' white head bobbed up and down, solid as a man on a monument. Indeed, he was a man on a monument, removed that much from his fellows.

But Munro was grateful to him, aware that no one else could have taken the village with the same assurance. It needed a plaster-cast knight to impress the reception party. Rhodes had been right. Their hosts were taken aback at the sight of the five people marching down the mountain side, then swinging onto the bridge and striding towards them.

So Munro crossed into Albania for the second time in a few days.

The British had long had a reputation for being eccentrics. Rhodes and his friends were supplying material for the legend. Yanni had dropped back a step or two, running with sweat as he peered over his wreath.

"Why are there soldiers?" whispered Susan.

"Are they soldiers?" said Munro.

"They have guns," said Susan.

The waiting men were mostly armed, but Munro had taken this for granted. "It's the custom," he assured her. "Officials carry guns."

They were now over the bridge. Munro came to a halt. "Dear Albanian soil," he said. His voice was remarkably steady.

Rhodes advanced and lifted his clenched fist in salute. He called something—an old slogan? It had its effect. Clenched fists rose in response. The slogan was called back: an operatic moment. How right Cecil and Sir John had been!

For a moment the old man was lost to sight, surrounded by the reception party. Munro and the others were forgotten. The Albanians had found an old friend. Previously taciturn gray-uniformed men were smiling—surprised, tentative smiles, as if they could hardly believe he was one of themselves. But they knew him—knew his reputation. The man who had fought alongside their fathers; the man who had, in fact, led their fathers on occasion—although that fact had been left out of their revised official history.

Rhodes made his way out of the crowd, bringing an officer. "Major Pec," he informed the others, "in charge of the proceedings. He has been sent from Tiranë specially." He introduced Susan and the others in turn.

Pec bowed to each. He spoke English. "May I welcome you to my country," he said. "I have had instructions from my government to conduct you to the burial ground. Please follow." He was an intelligent and good-looking young man.

Pec turned back to his own party. They were well rehearsed, and moved off through the village. The Albanians stayed in no sort of formation and some fell in around Rhodes. He was cut off from the rest of his party. Munro and Susan found themselves flanked by observant strangers. A little way behind, Yanni followed, with the wreath; Vilaras had been swallowed up in the crowd. Munro waited for Yanni. He offered to help him, but Yanni would have none of it. "I am proud to carry it," he said. "He was a brave man." It was timely to remember they were in fact a funeral party. They left the village behind.

It was much more primitive than the Greek side of the frontier. Pec and another officer led the way. Every now and again he looked back to the rear of the procession—for that was what it had become. A man in a blue civilian suit brought up the rear. Munro knew the type—self-contained, expressionless, cold-eyed. He'd seen such men before. They had asked him questions, not so long ago. He thought about warning Susan that the KGB were there, then he decided against it. Besides the man wouldn't be KGB—he was probably Peking-trained and hated the Russians. She was still holding his hand. "Fascinating, isn't it," she said.

Munro shook his head. "No. I'm counting the steps like the babes in the wood," he said, "so we know our way back."

She smiled. "There won't be any difficulty."

God, thought Munro, I wish I had her innocence. But he just nodded, and kept a sidelong look-out for the civilian in the blue suit.

They moved through a few miserable trees, along a path. The procession became a long, thin line. Then they came out into a small clearing, in the center a crumbling building, part chapel, part mosque, part stronghold. They came to a stop; Pec and Rhodes joined Munro.

"This is the place," said Pec. "It has been holy land for many religions."

Susan looked around. "I see no burial ground."

Pec pointed. "Over here." He took them to the end of the clearing. There were signs of old graves.

"Please bring your friends this way," said Pec. He moved to a lower terrace. Rhodes followed. Munro handed Susan down the slope; Yanni labored after them. Suddenly Vilaras reappeared. A handful of Albanian officials came with him; the others stayed by the chapel, with the cold-eyed civilian.

"This is the grave." Pec pointed to a newly erected gravestone. Rhodes nodded, and looked around as if inspecting its upkeep. Then he remembered that Munro had been the dead man's friend. "Ah! Munro," he said, "this concerns you." He indicated the blank stone on the ground. "The grave," he said. Munro brought Susan forward to let her see the dreary plot of ground, as meaningless as any other on the bleak hillside.

She was very thoughtful. It seemed to Munro she was going to say something, but she stopped.

"We appreciate the trouble your authorities have taken," said Rhodes, as though he were addressing a meeting. "It was right to know the whereabouts of our dead countryman. Even after death it is important to honor one's fellows."

102

That was as good a reason as any for all this palaver, thought Munro. He was ready to go, but Rhodes was still orating. "It's a sign of good fellowship when men can cross frontiers to share each other's rites," said Rhodes. "The people gathered here have more in common than they have differences. It is time the rulers of the world learned this."

Munro watched Pec to see if he was ready to put an end to this belated burial service, but Pec was in no hurry. They were giving the old boy his head. Rhodes seemed to have finished. Yanni pushed his way to the stone.

"This one?" he asked Pec in English.

Pec nodded.

Yanni laid the wreath gently on the stone. Then he stood back, and it was time to go. Munro turned away.

Susan was standing beside him silently. When she spoke it was somehow startling. "Does this mean he is buried here?" she asked.

Everyone looked at her. She was pointing at the big stone. Rhodes was irritated. The Albanians had been proper; the British should be equally circumspect.

"Of course he lies here," he said sharply. He frowned at Munro, as if he were to blame.

Susan was puzzled. "Are you sure?" she said. She wasn't talking to Rhodes, but was looking at Major Pec. There was an uneasy movement among the officials.

"Are you accusing us of something?" Pec asked.

She shook her head. "Of course not. I just want to know if you are sure about this grave."

"Of course I am sure," he said. Munro thought he was shaken. The question upset him. But he couldn't think why Susan had asked it. Nevertheless, he didn't like Pec's manner. He decided to throw in his own twopenny worth.

"What is it?" he asked loudly. "Don't you think it looks like a grave?"

"Oh yes, it's a grave," said Susan, still looking at the stone. Something about it baffled her.

"What's the fuss?" said Rhodes angrily. He would tell Munro to take the girl back to London. She didn't know how to behave.

"I am just surprised at the . . . well, the size, and the fact that there is a grave."

Munro felt the silence suddenly take on a different quality. The civilian in the blue suit moved forward. He had been introduced to no one, but he took over. His English was good, but his voice had an edge that grated on Munro.

"Why are you surprised to see a grave?" he asked Susan. Susan didn't see who was speaking at first. The man had come onto the terrace above them. "Did you expect no grave?"

God! thought Munro, why did I come here? There is going to be some incident. It's Cecil's fault. The girl is going to involve me in some bloody disaster. He closed his eyes for a second—faint as he had been on the sea-front at Eastbourne. Damn the girl! He was still holding her hand. She took it away, trying to take something from her handbag. If only it were a bomb—if she had a bomb and threw it. They might be able to race down the village and get across the bridge.

Munro pulled himself together. Susan was speaking, showing them a piece of paper.

"It is only a copy," she was saying, "and in your language, which I don't understand. But you will know if I have been misinformed."

"Why do you have this?" said the civilian sharply.

"Anyone can have copies of birth and death certificates in England," she said. She made it sound as though any other system would be suspect. "Besides, it is only a photocopy."

"But why do you concern yourself with it?" he insisted.

The girl was bland, totally untroubled. "For Peter," she said, "I knew he would want it. Stephan Aroso was his friend."

Rhodes came forward angrily. He felt the proceedings were being taken out of his hands. Perhaps it was his hearing: that was the only defect of his age. Sometimes he didn't hear too well. "What is it?" he asked, "what's all this about?"

Susan showed him the paper. "Do you understand Albanian?" she asked.

"Yes, yes, A little."

"Then you may understand this," she said. "It comes from Tiranë. I'm sure Major Pec will be able to tell us about it. It's a certificate for the cremation of Stephan Aroso, dated nearly two years ago. You see, that's what puzzled me. If he's cremated, why should they want to give him such a large grave?"

This girl! thought Munro. Does she know what she's doing? She's lit a time-bomb. She's pushed the button!

He looked at the photo-copy in her hand, an official certificate stamped, dated, headed like an Albanian Government document. And God knows, thought Munro, he had himself seen enough of those.

"May I see this, madam?" said the civilian.

Susan was still treating Pec as though he were in charge. Now she turned to him with an inquiring gesture. "Will that be all right, Major Pec?"

Pec was startled by this deference. The civilian frowned angrily. "Yes, of course," said Pec hurriedly. "This gentleman is Mr. Dejes. He is very important in this matter."

Munro took the paper from the girl and handed it up to Dejes.

"Here you are, Mr. Dejes," said Munro, rolling the name with pleasure. "Certificate of cremation as supplied by your government in Tiranë. Do you want to question it?" Dejes understood him, and looked as though he might kill him. Munro smiled back. It was nice to get even a small revenge.

Dejes ran his eye over the document. It was hard to tell, but it was probably authentic. Someone had made a bad blunder. To have let them expose themselves in this way— to have started two hares . . . which one was the truth? he asked himself. What story did Tiranë want propogated? What were they expected to do now? How could the crack be papered over? And this man Munro, grinning up at him—perhaps guessing the truth . . . They should have shot him when they had the chance. They must certainly do it this time.

Rhodes was to be contained no longer. The atmosphere of camaraderie had gone with the girl's damn interference,

105

its place taken by anger—and fear too. Yes, he had noticed that.

"What does this mean?" he demanded. "Is the man buried here or not?"

Rhodes brought everything into the open, blundering in where even Susan had stepped delicately. The Major cleared his throat. Dejes nodded for him to speak.

"There may be a mistake," he said, "of course we are not sure. This was where we supposed the body to lie. It is commonly believed to be here. If however the Central Authority had issued statements to indicate otherwise . . ." His voice drifted.

"We will investigate this," said Dejes sharply. He waved the certificate above his head. It was difficult to know how many onlookers understood what was said, but they seemed to have realized what was going on.

Rhodes made a brave challenge to resume control. "Very well. We will return. If this is the right place, so much the better. If not, then the cremation service will have a record."

Susan didn't let it be smoothed over that easily. "That is the cremation record," she said, pointing at the paper Dejes still held, "and I should like it back." Could she be deliberately pushing the man, Munro wondered. Did she guess how dangerous it was to cross him?

Dejes answered her. "We require this to check it. Then it will be returned."

He went up the slope and around the chapel out of sight. He left a shaken group of officials.

"It is best we return to the village," said Pec.

Rhodes struggled up the terraces, the buoyancy gone out of him, and Yanni helped him. He appeared to have shrunk a little. On the way back to the village he was an old man. It was downhill from the burial ground. The crowd melted away; a sense of gloom hung over the stone houses; no one looked out. Life had taken cover. They arrived back with only Pec in charge. The reception party had evaporated. There was another officer at the bridge, in a black uniform and a peaked cap. He had not been there on their arrival. As Rhodes began to cross the man stopped him. He put a hand up and called in Albanian.

Rhodes stared at him, then began to cross the bridge again. The man pulled a revolver from his belt. Rhodes couldn't believe it.

"He wants you to stop," said Pec. He was shamefaced about this.

"How dare he?" said Rhodes.

Pec and the man in the black uniform had a short conversation. Pec turned to the waiting group. "He says there is no record of your entrance. That must be made first, then you can leave."

"We are an official party," said Rhodes. "He must let us cross." Pec lifted his hands in helpless gesture.

"I demand it," said Rhodes. He began to cross again.

Munro called after him. "I wouldn't try it."

The man in black uniform was bringing his gun up. Rhodes watched him. He was trembling openly now—not with fear but with emotion. "I fought for these people," he said, "I have been their companion. We were together."

"Another war," called Munro, "history."

Rhodes came back, leaning against the bridge, suddenly tired.

Pec said something sharply to the man in black. The latter shrugged.

"What did he say?" Munro asked Vilaras. Vilaras had been lying low.

"He says he just obeys orders," he translated.

They sat on the wall, looking across to Greece. Munro felt he had lived through this before. This time he had quite a party to look after, like a sheep-dog with a flock . . . and he suspected the presence of wolves.

A man came out of the corner house. He spoke under his breath to Pec. Then Pec called over to them. "Will you please follow. They have prepared accommodation for you while the formalities of leaving are completed."

It was such a transparent device to hold them, that Munro almost laughed. But it was wiser not to.

8

They went into the house on the corner into a large room. Pinewood paneled the walls, and the windows overlooked the valley. A big wooden table was pulled against one wall, and wooden chairs stood against the opposite. It was like a village hall. From another room someone was shouting into a telephone, repeating the same phrases over and over again. Munro and the others sat and waited. After half an hour Dejes came in, flushed and tense. When Rhodes saw him he got up shakily. "I demand to leave with my party," he said.

Dejes waved him aside. "Later. Later," he said. He signaled to Pec, who followed him from the room. The party that Rhodes had brought that morning was left on its own. The man in the next room was still shouting into a telephone.

"Why are they so concerned?" asked Susan.

"They have lost face," Munro told her. "Everything was going right for them, until you brought out that certificate."

"Why did you have to do that?" grumbled Rhodes. He sat with his head on his hands, elbows on the table.

"But they seemed to be making a mistake," said Susan.

"Did it matter?" Rhodes was still angry.

Munro was about to say, "Damn it. He was her husband," when he checked himself.

"It landed us in trouble," Rhodes grumbled.

"That's not why we're here," said Munro. "Your friend Pec said it was an entrance formality. Don't you believe him?"

Rhodes glared across the room at Munro. "Why should he tell a lie?" he demanded.

"My point precisely," said Munro. He glanced at the door and went on clearly. "I'm sure Pec will soon tidy this matter up. These formalities must be carefully handled, or there will be questions at Central Office. Besides, we're here at the request of the British government, with the approval of the government here. If someone's made a mistake, it isn't Pec's fault. And it can't be Dejes. Some clerk in some orderly room—they're all the same. Just when we're trying to establish good relations—as you said yourself at the—er—grave—some clerk gets the certificate mixed, or something like that. The only thing that worries me, is I'd like to get back to contact London and let them know how well things went, before they take the matter to a higher level. We don't want our friends here getting into hot water with someone high up."

"Why the devil are you talking like that?" asked Rhodes. Munro had made the speech clear and distinct. It carried around the building.

"My throat's gone dry," Munro explained.

Shortly after a soldier brought in some wine. "As good as Greek," said Munro as he sampled it. The soldier smiled and went out. They drank a couple of bottles between the five of them very quickly, and things brightened up a little.

"They were very pleased to see us," said Rhodes wistfully.

"They will be again," Munro assured him. "I thought you said some very constructive things at the cemetery. It isn't time wasted." He didn't like to see the old man dejected.

The soldier reappeared. This time he had bread, cold sausage and cheeses. Munro was surprised to find how hungry he was. They sat at one end of the long table and had a meal together. It was later in the afternoon than they had supposed. The village was under hills, and at this time of year it lost the sun quickly. Shadows fell from the peaks to the south and west. It turned cold. Another soldier lit a wood fire in the big grate. It smoked away cheerlessly. Yanni looked out of the windows.

109

"It's late," he said. "How long do they keep us here?"

"Soon the border patrol will come and look for us on the Greek side," said Vilaras. He had said very little all day. Munro guessed things had not turned out as he had expected.

There was no light except from the fire. The wood panels gave off a sweet smell of pine. They stayed in the room all the time, except for a five-step visit down the corridor to where there was a primitive washroom. Now that Rhodes had stopped fretting, Munro thought they were all taking it very well.

There was something he wanted to ask Susan. He moved well away from the door. "Not too loud," he warned her, "There will be someone outside."

She looked at him expectantly. He went on. "You got the photocopy from Sir John?"

She nodded.

"Why didn't you tell me?" Munro guessed she was trying to hide her fears, but she wasn't entirely successful. Wide eyes betrayed her. "Why spring it on us at a moment like that? The Professor was right, you know. They're holding us here while they contact Tiranë and find out what do do. You put them on a spot."

"I'm sorry. I meant to tell you. I forgot. I didn't think it was going to be so important."

"It's important to them," said Munro.

She seemed to be trying to work out some puzzle. He persisted. "You've made the whole thing more important than it ought to be. Questions are flying back and forward now. That fellow in the next room hasn't been off the telephone all day. Bringing it up like that at the graveside—it dramatizes it."

She gave a wry shrug. "It wasn't the graveside, was it?" she said. Perhaps she was excusing herself, justifying what she had done. After all, buried or cremated—Stephan had been her husband. Perhaps she felt she had the right to seek out the truth, no matter how much that might disturb other people.

More wine arrived, then Turkish coffee.

"Reading the signs," Munro said, "they have got through

110

to Tiranë, and they've been told there's been a cock-up. My guess is that your certificate was correct, and the local people didn't bother to check. Stephan was shot here, so they thought he was buried here. Now they find out that Susan was right, they're going to swamp us with kindness—and bottles of wine."

"Anyone can make mistakes," said Rhodes. He was recovering. These simple folk were his friends. He couldn't let Munro be cynical about them.

But Munro proved to be right. Pec came in with Dejes, who forced himself to smile. "It is with the greatest regret we have to keep you today," said Dejes. The smile looked as if it hurt his face. "But there were difficulties."

He had a dusty old liquor bottle in his hand. "Let me pour you something special," he said. Pec handed around glasses. "It is so long since anyone used Karlovo as a frontier post, that they forgot how to do things. Exit permits were forgotten." The glasses were handed around with a bow from Pec. At least Pec smiled easily.

"To our eternal fraternity," said Dejes holding up his glass.

It was a very good liquor. Munro downed it gratefully. "And how about the other little problem?" he said. "Did they know in Tiranë what had happened to Stephan Aroso?"

Dejes was inspecting his glass thoughtfully. "Yes, Mr. Munro," he said, "the body of your compatriot had been cremated as detailed on the certificate." He hesitated. "I think, you of all people might have guessed the truth."

Munro was surprised. "Me? Why?"

"You were here, weren't you?" Dejes smiled gently towards him. "You must have been in this very room when they took the body past. You would have seen him from that window."

Munro remembered that he had been in this room before—after the shooting. He had been a prisoner here. And Dejes was right. They'd taken the body under the window.

Dejes moved across to look into the darkened street. "I understand it was a moonlight night," he said. "You saw the dead man on the stretcher?"

111

Munro could see it now. He nodded. His mouth had gone dry. Dejes poured another drink.

"He was shot to pieces," said Munro. "There was blood everywhere." It was all very vivid. "They left him on the stretcher just out there." He looked into the street.

"Exactly," said Dejes. "There was nothing anyone could do for him. He was in Karlovo for a couple of days. The local people assumed he had been buried here. In fact, the authorities were disturbed by the affair. They wanted an identification made. The body was taken to Tiranë. As you will have seen on the certificate, cremation was carried out there."

Munro was still seeing things, hearing things too. The whispering from the street outside; the soft sound of footsteps. The nightmare quality was coming back. He felt sick.

"Are we free to go?" asked Rhodes.

"Of course," said Dejes blandly. "You have always been free to go—apart from this matter of exit formality."

Pec was at the window. "I don't advise it, Professor," he said. "It is late and dark. Your safety is my responsibility. I would recommend you spend the night here and return to Greece first thing in the morning."

"It's not dark," protested Rhodes.

"It is very dark," contradicted Pec. "There is no moon, and the track is dangerous. You are my responsibility."

"I am my own responsibility," said Rhodes crossly.

"I think Major Pec is right," said Dejes. "And you have the young lady to think of. It is a long road for her after a trying day." He turned and called something to the soldiers outside the door. A couple of oil-lamps were brought in.

"As you know, we have electrification all over the country. This is one small area which is not yet connected," said Pec.

Another meal was being brought in. Piles of rice on large platters, and pieces of lamb and goat, smelling of charcoal. "Come," said Dejes, "make the best of a bad job and take our hospitality. Don't forget we are mountain people, and hospitality is a sacred thing. Eat and drink with us, and you are our friends."

"So it's all arranged?" asked Rhodes. "We go in the morning?"

Dejes nodded vigorously. "In the morning. When it is light, and there can be no misadventure. Please serve yourselves." Dejes turned to go then remembered something. "Ah, madam," he said, "I must return this. It was very fortunate you were able to give us the correct information." He handed the photo-copy of the certificate to Susan, and went out of the room, the smile still cracking his face. Pec followed him. It was some time before Munro felt like eating. He sat looking around the room, shocked that he could have forgotten it.

It was Susan who brought him to the table. She said, "Let's forget it."

When Pec came back they had finished the meal.

Rhodes was tired. "Are we supposed to sleep down here?" he asked.

"Certainly not," said Pec. "There are rooms for you. Do you wish to go to them?"

"I should like to," said Rhodes.

Later the others were shown to their rooms. Munro suggested they should have an early night, and they could make an early start next morning. He had a feeling that something else was due to happen, and if they hung around they would delay it. He couldn't put his finger on what gave him this feeling, but there was an air of expectancy. Munro believed in giving the opposition a lot of rope. "Time for bed," he said, "this air makes me sleepy."

They had rooms on the floor above. Munro noted carefully where they were. Rhodes had a room overlooking the ravine: they could hear him snoring as they went up. He had so much stamina for a man of his age, one was inclined to forget he was eighty-one.

Susan also had a room at the back of the house. Vilaras was given the room next to Susan's, while Yanni and Munro had smaller rooms overlooking the alley-way.

There were signs that the rooms had recently been occupied, with a soldier's great-coat still in a cupboard, and cigarette packets under a table. But the beds were made, and some effort had been made to tidy the place. "This is

113

charming," said Susan as she saw her room. Pec was delighted. Munro thought wryly about the childish and pleasant qualities of his enemies. They wished to be appreciated, flushed with pleasure at approval, but at the same time—what a pity—the rules of another game were observed, and men suffered or died for doctrines and dogma. Strange that economic theories turned into religions that few men understood, but many gave their lives for.

Munro sat by the window. People were moving about downstairs and the wooden floors creaked. He could hear voices and was surprised to recognize one of them. It was Vilaras's, but too faint to make out what was said.

Munro opened his door softly. Everything creaked in this house, and perhaps they had posted guards. But there was no sign of anyone. He tiptoed along the corridor to the top of the stairs. There was no one there, nor in the small hall below. The voices were much clearer now—Vilaras was talking to Dejes, and they were quite at ease with each other. They spoke in Greek. Munro knew more Greek than he pretended, but he wasn't able to follow. He heard his own name mentioned a couple of times. Vilaras was giving some kind of report. Dejes asked the questions. Occasionally Pec's voice chimed in. But it was mostly Vilaras.

Munro knew that this was what he wanted to hear. He went back down the corridor and opened the door next to his. Yanni started from his sleep.

"Keep it quiet," whispered Munro, "you're working."

"What do you want?" Yanni was wide-eyed in the dark.

"Just a little translation," said Munro.

He went to the top of the stairs, with Yanni trying to walk softly after him. "Listen," said Munro. The glow of an oil-lamp fringed the closed door. Vilaras was still speaking.

"What's the little bastard saying?" asked Munro.

Yanni stuck his head over the banisters. "He's talking about you," he said.

"You don't surprise me," said Munro.

"And the girl," said Yanni.

Munro frowned. "What's he saying?"

Yanni craned forward. He tried to listen and translate simultaneously. It wasn't easy and he couldn't hear every-

114

thing. "Dejes asks who she is . . . and Vilaras says she's your girl. Dejes is doubtful . . . you are married in their records . . . Pec says the English have no morals . . . Vilaras thinks your wife divorced you when you were in jail here . . . Dejes wishes they had shot you then." Yanni looked shocked at that.

"What else?" asked Munro. The voices had started up again, but they were muffled.

"Vilaras has a theory. He thinks the British Intelligence have used this girl to get you to Karlovo again."

"What for?" asked Munro.

"Sssh . . . He says the girl pretends to be interested in Rhodes and his poetry, but spends little time with him. He is a mere excuse for you to operate."

Pec seemed to be warning them to keep their voices down. There was a silence, then they heard Dejes. Yanni translated. "Dejes says there is nothing you can do. A spy cannot be effective if he is known to be a spy."

"He's dead right," whispered Munro.

"Vilaras disagrees. He says you have business here. And perhaps it has to do with the old business."

They could hear a confused but hushed outburst from Dejes. "Dejes says that's not possible. Vilaras says, 'Then why all this business with the grave? Why come back to Karlovo?' He is a bit excited about that."

"So I can hear," said Munro. He was in the dark himself. In the dark in every way, standing in his socks at the top of a creaking staircase listening to men who wished to kill him for no clear reason.

"Pec says, why don't you have an accident," said Yanni softly.

Munro swore. "I quite liked Pec," he said.

"Dejes is telling Pec not to be a fool," said Yanni. "They have instructions to find out what you are doing, and if you are dead no one can discover that."

"Good boy, Dejes," whispered Munro. "That's the advantage of a logical training."

Dejes started to talk again.

"He's telling Vilaras to send in a full report. There may be something in his theory."

"What theory?" asked Munro.

Yanni shrugged his shoulders. "I don't know," he said. "He is saying they must watch you. Only if anything fails, are you to be got rid of."

"Got rid of?" said Munro softly.

"That's what he said."

Munro had hoped they would help him to understand what he was involved in, but they seemed equally unsure. It was like holding two mirrors up to each other: they each reflected the other's emptiness.

Yanni held up a hand. "Dejes asks about your girl. Vilaras says you hold hands everywhere." Munro was glad they had done at least that much. The next thing Pec said horrified Yanni.

"They know all about me. Pec says—I am a running dog for the West and something should happen to me!"

"What does Dejes say?" asked Munro.

"Nothing," said Yanni uneasily, "no one disagrees!"

The door under the stairs opened. A light shone into the hall. A soldier came out. He went to the front door and turned a key in the lock. The light from his lamp made shadows dance on the wall. Munro pulled Yanni back. The man pushed home a couple of bolts. He was making a lot of noise. Munro signaled to Yanni to move. As he did so, the wooden boards cracked under his feet.

The man held up his lamp and looked up the stairs. He couldn't see anyone. Yanni was back at his door and Munro was out of sight along the corridor.

The man called up the stairs.

Yanni disappeared into his room. Munro had to pass across the top of the stairs to follow him. As he was about to move, he heard a door open below. Pec and Dejes spoke to the man. He answered, and a moment later there was a foot on the stairs. Pec called up. Munro backed gently down the corridor. He had no wish to be caught by that trio. He heard the click of a safety catch. Pec was the trigger-happy one, thought Munro. He hoped Dejes, if anyone came up the stairs.

Pec called again. It was too late to answer now. Pec sounded angry. Munro felt the handle of a door beside him.

116

Vilaras should have been in that room, but he wasn't. There were men on the stairs now. Several pairs of boots. They came up in a rush.

Munro was at the next door. He was grateful it wasn't locked. He turned the handle and slipped into the room. In the dark someone moved behind him.

"Who is it?" It was Susan. She was surprisingly calm. Munro got the door shut in the nick of time. The men had arrived at the top of the stairs. "Sorry about this," he whispered into the dark. "Nothing to worry about. Just a matter of waiting till the coast's clear."

The men in the corridor were talking together.

"I can't get back to my room," whispered Munro.

She seemed to take it all for granted. "Who's out there?" she asked.

"Pec and his men," he said. "Perhaps Dejes."

"Are they looking for you?"

"They don't know who they're looking for," Munro whispered. Someone was walking down the corridor. The floor-boards creaked at each step.

"I'm over here," said Susan. Munro could just make out the dark shape of the canopy above the bed. He remembered seeing it when they showed her the room—a large old-fashioned bed, a headboard carved with fruit and flowers. He moved further into the room, listening to the whispering outside.

"Are they going?" asked Susan.

It sounded as if they were. Then a door opened and shut, and Yanni gave a sleepy shout. Pec called an apology in Greek.

"Still looking," whispered Munro. "Always suspecting something, even when they don't know what." He realized that that could be a description of himself.

Another door opened softly. This time there was a shout. "They're in my room," said Munro grimly. He heard them talking excitedly along the corridor, his name used several times.

"Damn," he said, "they know I'm not there."

"What can they do?" she asked. She began to sound concerned.

117

"You never know," said Munro.

There was more noise in the corridor. Yanni could be heard again. He was asking what the matter was. Pec replied. Then another door opened and shut, then the door to the next room. Someone had gone in. Several people were next door.

"Quickly," she said. "Here."

He had become accustomed to the dark and saw her throw back the cover on the bed. His mind was still on the sounds in the next room. "Hurry up," she said, "pull your shirt off."

He heard them come out of the next room, urgent, nervous, still keeping their voices down to a terse whisper. He started pulling off his shirt automatically. She lost some of her calm. She said, "For God's sake, hurry," and he threw the shirt on the floor and got in beside her as someone touched the door handle.

She had one arm under his neck and was leaning over him, kissing him, as the door opened. Whoever stood there had a torch in his hand. In the sharp, white light, Munro realized she was naked. The beam hovered on them for a second. Then she took her lips away from his, and looked towards the door, as though dazed by the sudden brightness, or by passion. Munro also turned into the light as if he were coming back to reality. There were the shadows in the doorway. The light played on them for what seemed a long time. Then the torch went out and the door shut. No one had moved . . . no one had made a sound.

She still held him, listening to the steps moving away; the stairs creaked. Then there was silence. Munro lay back in the dark. His admiration for her was great, much more than gratitude. There was nothing he could say—but he had to say something. "I'm sorry. It was my only chance. I was on the stairs . . . they heard Yanni . . ." He guessed what he said didn't make sense. That didn't seem to concern her. "Who came to the door?" she asked.

Munro remembered the shapes. "Pec. Dejes just behind."

"Who had the torch?"

"Pec."

"He took long enough," she said.

"Well . . ." Munro gave her an admiring glance. "I think you took his breath away."

"What does that mean?"

"You were . . . well, a little spectacular."

She smiled. "Thank you."

Munro waited until the house settled back into silence. Then he left her, found his shirt, and went back to his room. The floor-boards sounded under his feet, but he guessed no one would investigate anything more that night.

Rhodes was awake early the next day. He sounded hearty as ever, noisily getting up, washing, and asking for a spare razor in a language the guards understood. Forgotten were any problems that had marred the day before.

Munro found the others ready when he went down. There was no sign of Pec nor of Dejes, but another officer escorted them to the bridge.

This time the short journey to Greece had no problems. Rhodes marched ahead, pointing out the magnificent views around them. He was rejuvenated; none of his illusions damaged, still believing in the brotherhood of man, the integrity of his fellows—peasant people especially.

Munro remembered to take Susan's hand, their fingers entwined with seeming affection. Vilaras would certainly notice. Yanni puffed up the slope. It was early and chill, but he still sweated, relieved to have to have escaped now that his identity was known.

The border patrol was down to one man again, and he was in his hut, with his feet over a fire. He pulled the barrier aside and watched them go. Munro looked down the closed road, and swore to himself. That was the last time anything would get him over that frontier!

They were all in a hurry to get away, and Yanni drove at speed. After twenty-four hours in another country, they felt Greece embraced and protected them. The car bounced over pot-holes, and slithered around corners, a horse that smelled home. They skirted the sharp drop in the valley. Loose rocks and scree edged the wayside. Stunted trees and shrubs clothed the hills.

Rhodes shouted "stop," and they came to a halt.

Munro wondered what had got into the old man. Rhodes was getting out of the car with delight. He called, "Come and look, Susan! You'll never see this again in your lifetime!" The others got out of the car. A little army was moving up the valley, men and animals, spilling through a narrow gorge between the rocks below. It was an army mostly of goats and sheep, but also a tribe of people, on horses, ponies, mules, some walking, moving slowly, delayed by the gorge and the uneven ground. From above, they looked like a tide seeping up the valley. A dark brown flow, moving over the land.

Rhodes looked down on the sight with reverence and love. "You know what that is, my dear?" he addressed himself to Susan. "They are the nomads of the mountains. They come and go with the seasons. Herdsmen, tribesmen, shepherds. They take their flocks and their dwellings with them—in spring up to the mountains which they believe are theirs by right. They move through the country like ghosts, using the old routes, seldom seen. And not just in Greece. Their empire goes further. Goes back to ancient times, ignores modern boundaries. You will find them in the hills of Albania, Bulgaria, Yugoslavia. You will find them as far as the Black Sea." The trickle of humanity moving in the valley had a significance for Rhodes that inspired him. "They are timeless," he said, "moving with the freedom of the human spirit. Independent, proud, primitive."

Yanni shrugged contemptuously. "They never wash."

Rhodes ignored him. "You see the men? In the black cloaks of goat's hair? No lowland shepherds—these are a hardy, tough race. They keep their customs and rituals. *They* have not been corrupted by Western civilization."

"Not by any civilization," added Yanni grimly. "Thieves and villains. More like wolves than men."

Rhodes looked at him in scorn. The nomads were symbolic and poetic.

"You know something," went on Yanni. "People are sorry for them. They think they are poor. Count the goats and the sheep, think what each is worth! Then multiply, and you will see they are rich men who pay no taxes. They have boxes of gold! They carry them with them, and bury them on the grazing land. And they pasture on other men's property."

Back in the car Rhodes had a fit of coughing. "It was that damn driver of yours," he told Munro, "he made me very angry."

9

The villa perched on the rocky outcrop was a welcome sight. The old woman who looked after Rhodes scolded him. They had been expected back the day before. The meals had been spoiled. Where had he been?

Rhodes sent her off to bring coffee. She came back to say that there had been messages all day from the postmaster in the village.

That surprised Rhodes.

"No," she explained, the messages were not for him, they were for Yanni. But Mr. Rhodes had taken him as his driver on that foolish expedition and . . .

She was cut short. Yanni was making his way up the path. He had a bundle of papers in his hand. They were cables. Yanni handed them to Munro when they were alone.

"Not one," said Yanni, "three."

Munro wanted nothing to do with them.

"They're addressed to you," said Munro.

"Of course," said Yanni, "but I understand no codes."

Munro was loath to touch them. He looked at the open cable. It had originated from London.

"There must be a mistake," said Munro. Vilaras came into the room. He saw the two men at the table together, excused himself and went out.

Munro hated getting involved like this. The cables were a series of letters and numbers. They could only be from Cecil, and Munro cursed him. He pushed them into his pocket. In the brief moment he had looked at them, he had recognized the Aroso code. He could afford to appear casual about that. It wouldn't matter who had picked up these messages, the Aroso code was safe, the outcome of work he and Stephan had done with Cecil. Munro was still proud of that job. He called it a "progressive code."

"They must be meant for you," said Yanni. Munro shrugged. "I'll have a look at them."

He couldn't think what the hell Cecil and Sir John were up to. Three cables in a day! He was angry with them. The village, and the district around, would know that there were cables from London. That would soon be common knowledge.

He examined the cables in his room. The Aroso code required two things. It was a code which developed from message to message. The previous code cable—or letter or message—was the basis of the code for the next message. In this way, the symbols never remained the same. There were other complications but that was the basis. Munro had come up with the original idea and Stephan had improved it. It was a private language, and Munro knew it better than he knew his own name.

The three cables were from Cecil. They asked for a report on the visit to Stephan's grave. The second cable must have been sent when there was no reply to the first. It expressed concern, and asked for acknowledgment. The third cable had been sent priority. Munro guessed it had been bounced off a satellite. The ciphers included Munro's old code-name. The message asked him to contact immediately: it had been received late the night before.

He went back to the big room where the others were finishing breakfast. He phoned a cable to Cecil. All he said was "Message received and understood." That should set their minds at rest in London. He was angry at the way he had been dragged further into their operation. This flurry of cables suggested their visit to Karlovo had some significance, whereas, in fact, all it had proved was that Stephan Aroso wasn't buried in these hills. His dust probably blew through the streets of Tiranë.

Rhodes coughed throughout the meal, and the old housekeeper came in from the kitchen to scold him again, telling him to go to bed. Rhodes ignored her. He went into his courtyard to say good-bye to Vilaras, and Munro had a feeling it was the end of term. He was surprised by a sense of anticlimax. The last few days had aroused instincts which Munro had thought long dead. Now he was going home, though it was hard to visualize life at Eastbourne. Besides, if he were honest with himself, he was going to miss Stephan's wife. That troubled Munro. Stephan had been closer to him than any other man—like a brother. Moments of near-death had formed a special bond between them. It was hard for Munro to think he wanted Stephan's wife.

Susan was with Rhodes taking notes about his poems.

"Won't keep her long," Rhodes called to Munro. He was still coughing. Munro wandered about the garden. He couldn't see the point of Susan keeping up this pretense. They would have to make up another story for Rhodes. Tell him they had to go back to London sooner than expected. The old boy would never guess the use they had made of him.

Later in the morning, Yanni had a message for Munro. "There is someone to see you in the village."

"Can't be," said Munro.

"Yes. They're asking for you," said Yanni.

"They?" Munro raised his eyebrows.

"Two men," said Yanni.

"I don't know anyone in the village."

"Not from the village," said Yanni, "they come from Athens."

Munro didn't like the sound of that.

"Who do I know in Athens—" he asked.

Yanni shrugged.

"Why don't they come up? They know where I am?"

"Oh yes," said Yanni, "but they want to give the impression they have come to see me."

"Oh, for God's sake," said Munro, "what for?"

"They don't want to come to you openly. They asked for me in the village. Then when I was alone with them, they said they had business with you."

"I have no business with anyone," said Munro.

"They know a lot about you," said Yanni.

"Are they the police?" asked Munro.

"I don't know. I think you should see them."

"Why?"

"They said they would come up if you didn't come down."

Munro thought about that. "What do they look like?"

"You know. Like men from Athens. One has a white jacket. They did not shave properly. One is balding. Both black hair . . ."

"All right," said Munro. He went into the villa and collected his gun, loaded it, and tucked it under his arm. He didn't understand how two strangers arrived in this isolated village to look for him, and he didn't intend to take chances.

"You're sure they are Greeks?" It occurred to him they might have some connection with Karlovo.

"Of course," said Yanni.

That didn't put Munro's mind at rest. Vilaras was also a Greek, and he was an enemy.

They went down the track into the village street.

"Where are they?"

"They don't want anyone to see you with them, so they are outside the village."

Munro gave Yanni a quick look. He had a sudden wave of distrust that included the fat man. What did he know about Yanni anyhow?

A closed car was parked on a piece of waste land, under trees. Two men waited in the shadows. They greeted Yanni, who indicated Munro with a shrug. The two men looked at Munro. They spoke Greek to him.

"What do they say?" he asked Yanni.

"They need you to go with them."

"Just like that?" mocked Munro.

Yanni shrugged. "They say they have orders to take you."

"Whose orders?" asked Munro.

There was another burst of question and answer between the three men. The strangers looked at Munro.

"They cannot say, but you have to go," said Yanni.

"Have to?" Munro didn't like that.

Yanni tried to explain. "It's something to do with your business here."

Munro looked at the two men. What could these two

unprepossessing characters have to do with him? And what could they know of his business? Come to that, Munro thought, what was his business?

"Where are we going?" asked Munro. He was wary, but he wanted to find out all he could.

"They don't say," said Yanni.

Munro laughed. "They don't want much! What identification have they got?"

Yanni translated that, and the strangers grew angry. One man started shouting. He pointed to the car and pointed to Munro.

"Tell him . . ." began Munro.

"Please, Mr. Munro," said Yanni, "I think you had better get away. Perhaps they have guns."

Munro calculated the odds. If they were both armed, someone was going to get hurt.

"Hold it," he said to Yanni. "Tell them I'll go if they bring me back."

Yanni told them. The shouting died down. "Yes," said Yanni, "they say they will do that."

There was still a good chance to run for it, but Munro was intrigued, concerned to find out why he was summoned and by whom. "You coming?" he called to Yanni.

"Not me," said Yanni. He stood at the side of the road and watched them go. They turned off from the village—away from the Albanian frontier, Munro was happy to note. He was surprised that they had let him sit in the seat behind them. They weren't as alert as they ought to be.

He waited until the car was on an open stretch of road, then he put his arm under the chin of the passenger, and he let him see the gun he had against his head. "Now take it easy," he said to the driver. "No trouble or your buddy gets his head blown off. You get number two before you take your hands off the wheel."

They didn't understand a word he said, but they knew exactly what was intended.

"Just keep going nice and smooth, my friend, while I see the hardware situation." He was going over the man in front. He went over him twice, still watching the driver. The passenger didn't have a weapon of any sort.

126

"Okay," said Munro to the driver, "stop the car."

The man understood that. Both of them were very taken aback to find Munro had a gun. The car stopped, and Munro went with practiced skill over the driver.

"No gun," said the driver. He was shaking.

"So you speak English?" said Munro. He glimpsed himself in the driving-mirror. He was smiling the meaningless smile he sometimes had when under strain. He didn't like that aspect of himself, but he had to put up with it.

"No gun," said the driver. It seemed about the limit of his vocabulary.

"You don't have to tell me," said Munro. "No guns. Either of you. What sort of a hijack is this? Suppose I had said I wasn't coming. You didn't come prepared for trouble, did you? Why not? What made you think I'd like the idea of a trip with you grubby bastards? Suppose I take the car and leave you to walk home?"

They looked at him blankly.

"All right," said Munro. "Relax. See . . . no gun."

He put his own gun away. The two men were clearly relieved. "Just one thing," said Munro, "where are we going?" They didn't understand that, so he raised his voice. "Where are we going?"

They went blank again.

Munro saw a map by the driver's seat. He tapped it. They understood then. "Kotsi," they told him.

It meant nothing to Munro. "Kotsi?"

The driver opened the map. He pointed to a bare space of Greece that looked as though it must be open mountain to Munro. But it wasn't far.

Munro slowly nodded agreement. "Kotsi," he said.

The two men were more than anxious to be friendly. "Kotsi, Kotsi," they said grinning and nodding. Munro had stopped smiling. He could feel his little gun tucked under his arm. He was glad he had brought it. A few days ago he thought he would not have had the stomach to use it. Now he knew he would.

The road started to climb, heading south, Munro guessed, going over a spur of the Pindus mountains. The view was spectacular, but he kept his eye on the men in front, leaning forward so they were constantly aware of him. But he noted the road; he liked to know where he was going, so he could come back. They began going down into a valley. The snows had gone except from the distant mountains, and cattle fed on the plains below. The country grew more gentle, with an air of well-being—meadows, poplars. Munro remembered that the world was not all bare rock, and latent enmity. It could also be tender, even civilized.

They turned on to a rough track and the passenger called "Kotsi." It was a village on the edge of a forest. The track branched again. The surface got worse; they skidded on loose pebbles when they came to a stop.

The men smiled encouragingly and the driver opened the car door. Munro lifted a hand, and they waited. He looked around. The forest spread out ahead of them. On one side a slope led up to the wall of a farmhouse. The wall was topped with flowers, but the big wooden gate was spiked.

Munro indicated the farmhouse. "That it?"

They understood and nodded.

"Who is it?" asked Munro. That was too difficult for them. They shrugged. The driver began to get out. This time Munro didn't stop him.

As they shut the car doors a man called. The driver called back. They walked to the gate and Munro could hear someone coming. The gate was unlocked. A young man beckoned them in. "Come, come," he said.

Munro could see the house beyond, framed in the archway of the gate, at the end of a path through a trelliswork of creepers. There was no one else around. They went in and the young man closed the gate. "Come," he said, and hurried towards the house.

A verandah ran along the front of the house and someone had been having a meal there. A table was set with dirty dishes and an empty packet of cigarettes. Munro recognized the make. His brain photographed and translated as one function, and he knew who was there before he went in.

Cecil was on the phone in the front room. He covered the mouthpiece and turned to Munro hurriedly as he came in. "I'm through to London, old boy," he said. "Won't keep you a moment. Just had to tell Sir John we'd found you." He turned back to the phone and called into it, "Yes, sir, just this very minute. Looks as right as rain. No, we haven't had time to compare notes. Will call you back, sir. This was just to let you know he's safe."

Cecil put the phone down and looked at Munro with a wide smile. "By golly. That's a great weight off his mind. We thought we'd done for you. He couldn't forgive himself."

"What the hell are you talking about?" said Munro. He thought that Cecil had deliberately had that phone conversation as he came in so that he should hear it. And at the same time, he couldn't fit Cecil into the picture. He was in his city clothes, his dark gray suit, white shirt and sober tie, looking like a caricature of an Englishman.

"Sir John," explained Cecil. "We didn't get any answers from you. He was nearly out of his mind. Said we were mad to have sent you. Said they'd kept you in Albania, thrown you back into jug like before. You look splendid. This part of the world always did agree with you. By the way, what the devil happened? Why didn't you acknowledge or something?"

"I did," said Munro, "when we got home."

"Ah! We were right. They *did* hold you."

"There was a brief delay at the frontier." Munro was being guarded. Whatever Cecil wanted to know, he would have to come out into the open and ask.

"Delay?"

"Nothing serious. One of those things that can happen anywhere. Exit formalities. They soon ironed it out."

"Ah. I see." Cecil was thinking fast. Munro knew the signs. "But everything went off all right? No incidents?"

"Like what?" said Munro.

"How long did they keep you?"

"They let us go this morning." That seemed a long time ago.

"All of you?" asked Cecil. He was still trying to get his bearings.

"They kept us all," nodded Munro.

"And let you all go this morning?"

Munro nodded gravely. "That's right. No one got shot."

Cecil laughed. "Good Lord, old boy. No one expected that."

"Then why the panic?" asked Munro. He detested Cecil—detested the game of chess he played with living pieces.

"What panic?" Cecil looked innocent.

"What takes you so far from Whitehall?" Munro didn't disguise the sneer.

"We . . . well, Sir John that is . . . got a little alarmed. We expected you back yesterday. Anything could have happened."

Munro nodded. "I hadn't seen it that way. Last time in Karlovo, Stephan got killed; this time it could be me."

"Exactly," said Cecil. "The old boy began blaming himself for sending you. I said you'd be all right. He doesn't know you like I do."

"That's true," said Munro. "Your staff are driving me back. Mind if I go now?"

That upset Cecil where all else had failed. "For God's sake, Munro! Don't be such an unpleasant bastard. I have to do my job the same as you."

"The difference is," Munro was quick on to this, "you know what your job is."

Cecil had a split second of indecision, and Munro knew his suspicions were just. "What are you using me for, Cecil?" He was relaxed, pleased with himself. It wasn't often anyone got under Cecil's skin.

Cecil hesitated. If you knew the man well you could tell when the real question was going to be asked. It was just coming. "Well, your last trip was sensational. You and Stephan got very close to the exit. Then neither of you got across."

Munro tried not to show he was hanging on every word. Cecil went on. "One of you gets shot and one gets jailed. In fact you were nearly shot as well. So let's suppose that on that trip something happened . . . I mean . . . and this is all supposition . . . suppose you, or Stephan, had been involved in something unofficial. Suppose you or Stephan had some sort of unfinished business in these parts—or you had some sort of loot hidden away—and someone else knew about it, but didn't know where it was. But they hoped you would be trying to pick up this unfinished business or collect this hidden loot—then, don't you see, my dear chap, all these things would begin to make sense."

"What do you mean?" said Munro. "All what things?"

Cecil had a briefcase on a chair. He picked it up. "Something I thought you might like to see," he said. He pulled out a newspaper. "You read German."

Munro knew that this was a trump card coming up, and he couldn't for the life of him guess what it was.

"German?"

"Berlin newspaper. East German publication. But there are stories like this all over the so-called Iron Curtain countries." He handed the paper to Munro. It was open at an inside page and an item was ringed in pencil.

Munro read German well enough to translate. The headline said "The Criminal Returned To The Scene Of The Crime" and then it went on to say how the infamous English spy, Munro, had gone to Karlovo on the borders of Greece and Albania. Munro could hardly believe it. He looked at the date.

"It's this morning's paper," he said. He was trying to work out the time between the event and the deadline for the paper. "We were there only yesterday."

"Someone thinks you're important," said Cecil.

Munro wondered who that could be. "This man Vilaras," he said, "is he Greek?"

"Oh yes." Cecil started looking through his briefcase. He found some papers. "He is a very good Greek in his own lights. That means he is opposed to the present Greek government. He has a long history of agitation—communist, anarchist and Maoist."

"How does Rhodes know him?"

"Does Rhodes really know anyone nowadays? Don't you think he stopped knowing people years ago?"

"Why did you use the Aroso code?" asked Munro abruptly.

"For the cables?" Cecil was giving himself that extra

split second, editing his answer. Munro nodded. "Because it's your code, of course," said Cecil. "No one except you and Stephan could ever use it."

"You didn't need code for those cables," said Munro. "There was nothing in them of a confidential nature."

"Sir John thought you would prefer to keep your movements secret."

"The Aroso code will alert the whole bloody Balkans," said Munro.

"But no one will know what was said."

"So they think the worst," said Munro. "They think I'm here on a mission that warrants the Aroso code."

Cecil seemed to get the point. "I see what you mean."

"That sort of thing's been happening all the time," said Munro. He pushed back his chair, and walked to the window. The flowers had started to bloom. Spring was further on in this south-facing valley than on the other side of the hills. It was typical of Cecil to find such a place for himself.

"Why all the cloak-and-dagger stuff?" asked Munro. "Why didn't you just phone me at the villa, and ask me to come over?"

"Friends of ours in Athens arranged the meeting," said Cecil. "When I left last night from Heathrow we didn't know if you were alive or dead."

Cecil was moving around the room. He was nibbling at a green fig. They were like two animals, each trying to outflank the other. Munro saw that, and promptly sat down.

"There *is* one thing that perhaps you should know," said Cecil. He didn't look at Munro as he spoke.

"Oh yes?" said Munro.

"You're unhappy about some of the aspects of our collaboration, and you have a right to be."

Munro distrusted the liberal prologue more than most.

"Obviously you sense our caution in this matter, you feel we haven't been frank with you. You're quite right. But we felt obliged to be careful."

"Careful about me?" repeated Munro.

Cecil pursed his lips. He still didn't look at Munro. "Yes," he said, "we have to take several things into account, especially after we realized what this incident with the so-called Group-Captain in London might be."

"What might it be?" asked Munro.

"It was a way of contacting you, was it not?"

Munro nodded. "You could say that."

"Perhaps we should start a little further back," Cecil went on. "That will show you some of our thinking."

Munro restrained himself. Did Cecil think he was giving a bloody lecture?

"Let me take the occasion of your exchange."

"Exchange?" That surprised Munro. Why was he bringing that up?

"You were exchanged with the help of Yugoslav officials for an Albanian," Cecil indicated the German newspaper, "just like the paper said. And just like they say, that Albanian was nothing."

"What do you mean, he was nothing?"

"He was a businessman."

"I was a businessman myself," said Munro.

"True," Cecil gave him a friendly smile, "but you turned into a first-rate agent—and by the time they picked you up, you and Stephan were the best we had."

"Thank you very much," said Munro grimly.

"The point is," said Cecil, "they jumped at the chance to let you go. *Jumped* at it. We put up this simple shopkeeper as the other half of the swap, and they said, "Yes." Now, doesn't that seem odd to you?"

"I don't think I'm with you," said Munro softly.

"Look at it another way," said Cecil. He was back nibbling the green figs and looking out of the window, so Munro couldn't see his face. "Put it like this. You had the bad luck to fall into their hands for just over a year."

"Eighteen months," said Munro.

"Eighteen months," Cecil nodded slowly. "Now that's a long time. We don't know exactly what they did in that time, but we have a good idea. We know the technique. Solitary confinement; de-personalization; psychological abuse; the disintegration of the personality. It's a hard assault to withstand. Far harder than physical assault."

"I know," said Munro.

Cecil nodded again. Perhaps he thought he was being objective, but Munro resented being treated as less than a man.

"Different people can stand the treatment longer than others. Everyone has a limit. A deeply religious man can keep whole, keep sane you might say, longer than others."

Munro looked up at the ceiling. "I did it by reciting extracts from Professor Bressle's *Pornography of Our Time* and *Mrs. Beeton's Cookbook*."

"Oh yes," said Cecil, "we think you held out quite a time."

"Quite a time?" breathed Munro. He stared at Cecil.

"As I say, no one holds out forever; then, unwittingly, he is vulnerable, and begins to relearn what they want him to relearn, and to absorb material they want him to absorb."

"They?" Munro had his fists clenched. He thought about his gun. He would shoot Cecil if the man went on.

"The opposition," explained Cecil. "It just depends which team you're playing for. It's a technique everyone uses."

"I don't," said Munro. "If I wanted to degrade a man—no matter what fashionable words you might dress that up in—I'd use the tried and true historic methods. I'd bind him, chop off his ears, castrate him. You know. Great princes became great kings that way."

"You're uncouth, Munro," said Cecil. "The disintegration processes are used to learn from the victim, or to recreate him along the lines required."

"God help us," said Munro, and meant it.

"They never laid a hand on you, did they?"

"Not a hand," said Munro.

"But the other pressures were all there."

"Too true."

"So you see how we did our sums? Eighteen months under reconstruction, as you might say. Then this extraordinary exchange for a nonentity, indicating how keen they were to get you back on our side of the fence . . ."

"What the hell are you saying?" Munro didn't believe he could have understood.

"Then this chance to come back to this happy hunting-ground turns up, and you have a remarkable meeting with someone with alien interests . . . which you don't fully report."

"I don't work for you," said Munro, but he was still dazed by the implications of what the man had said—what he was still saying.

"Then this bit in the East German papers. It's like a signal flashed out to all it may concern. "To all who want to contact Peter Munro: his exact position is eight kilometers south of Karlovo." So you can see, with all these bits and pieces fitting into place, Sir John and I had second thoughts, and began to speculate how much you have changed—for believe me, dear boy, you have changed considerably since you and Stephan used to set out with such gay abandon to penetrate the intricate defenses of the other side."

Munro looked blankly at Cecil. He could no longer see him clearly. It was as if he had gone under water. He was walled in by the dark and narrow space of a cell. He knew this was an illusion, but at the same time it was real. And Cecil let the words flow on and on, with the arrogance and composure of one who had never suffered; of one who had designed the plots, pulled the strings, and never been assailed by the nightmares. And what he had said was right. Humiliation overtook Munro, degradation swept back into his being. Once again an old terror shook him. Terror of being less than a man, being a thing, sitting in the dark in a tiny cell. No one had mocked him then. They had done more—or less. For he had been treated as though he were not there; as if he didn't exist; as if he had never existed. And he had held on to the core of his being by an effort of will; a daily, nightly, summoning of strength. And Cecil! who had been having his meals in his London clubs, and having his women in various beds around Knightsbridge . . .

He knew he had his hands on Cecil's throat, and he knew he was shaking him so that his head swayed and his eyes popped. And at the same time it seemed to Munro that part of him was looking down on this spectacle of violence in a detached, observant fashion. Munro could hear his voice, though he didn't recognize it. "You're right, Cecil," he was saying, "I did change. From second to second, and I couldn't stop it. You know what the change was?" Cecil was trying to speak. He was choking. "You know what the change was, don't you, Cecil? I was dying, Cecil." Cecil's face was gray, blue. Munro couldn't decide. "I was dying by little pieces. In the dark little by little."

Munro became aware of the other two men who had burst into the room. One of them was breaking his grip on Cecil's neck, the other was pulling his head back. He let go of Cecil as though he was giving up a lifeline in a heavy sea. The fury went out of him and he slumped against the wall. He looked at Cecil with dawning realization. For a long time no one spoke, while Cecil drew breath, wheezing and gasping. His face had changed color again. Now it was white. Cecil, to give him his due, didn't collapse. He stared balefully at Munro as life crept back. He tried to speak once, and his voice cracked. He tried again and said, "You are a madman."

"If I am," said Munro, "it was some of your doing."

"You tried to kill me," said Cecil.

Munro shook his head. "If I had wanted to do that, I'd have used a gun."

He was suddenly a little sick. Cecil was no more in control of his life than was Munro himself. And Cecil's white shirt had been rumpled, his image put out of shape. What a pity, thought Munro. It was like watching the actors take off their grease paint. Imperfections appeared below. He just wanted to get away.

"I'm using your car," said Munro. "I don't need both of your men. I'll take the driver."

It was the driver who had helped drag him off Cecil. He signaled to the man and went out. He went down the path regretting what he had done, but knowing he had not been responsible. A part of his life had been recalled—as from the dead—by Cecil. And Cecil had exorcized it. So how could Munro regret it? He had said aloud what he had kept in his heart for a long time. He had felt again an unbearable pain. If Cecil had taken some of the load on to his shoulders, it was no more than his due.

They drove without a word from Munro. The driver watched him warily, accelerating as soon as he hit the main track, uneasy about being alone with this passenger.

10

It was late afternoon when they re-crossed the mountain range. Munro felt like a man convalescing, a new feeling revived him. Colors were clearer; the air fresher; images sharper. His wits were more alive. He was treading on an imaginary foot-brake as they rounded a band, and came squealing to a stop. Ahead was a collection of black capes, and some hundrd sheep and goats.

It was a moment of alarm. Black capes were suddenly still, caught in the afternoon sunshine crossing a road. This shattered their defences. Usually they moved in valleys away from the roads, and if they went through villages, they did so at night. Munro saw the indecision in their faces. Primitives at the mercy of an urban civilization. The driver was angry and anxious to get moving. He righted the car that had swerved to a standstill.

The black capes watched with concern. Sheep and goats bunched across the road. They knew the man in the car would drive through.

"Switch off," said Munro. He turned off the ignition himself. He got out of the car and waved to the herdsmen. He smiled. They understood the smile and waved back. There was a hurried chasing of animals across the road. At times the black capes would salute Munro gratefully. He returned the salute, waiting until the last of the herd had crossed before he gave the driver the sign to move on. For Munro had a special attitude to the black cape men. He had owed them much in his time. An old man, wiry, dignified, came to the car. He ignored the driver, and spoke to Munro. Munro replied, "And the best of luck to you, Dad."

They didn't understand each other, but they parted

friends. "Okay," said Munro, and the driver threw the car along the road in an effort to make up time.

It was nearly dark before they saw the stone houses of the village. At this time of day it was usually deserted, but now there was a crowd in the street, and Munro had a sudden dryness in his throat. They were directly below the villa. He didn't know why he should think something had happened to Susan. An ambulance was parked at the side of the road, a man in uniform standing by. Everyone looked up towards the villa.

Some men were leaning over the wall in the garden above, playing out a rope. At the end hung a bundle in netting, swinging backwards and forwards as it was lowered. From above came shouts, and from below the man in uniform shouted directions. Munro watched the bundle ease slowly downwards.

It was getting dark. Twilight was short; light one minute, and night the next. The man in uniform turned on the headlights of the truck. They lit up the swinging bundle. One more shout from above, and the rope jerked to a stop. In the netting Munro could see a figure. "Who is it?" The man by the ambulance was startled to be addressed in English. "He is ill," he said, "the English poet."

"What's the matter?"

The man said something in Greek. The netting was on the ground, and the crowd hurried to pick it up. They carried it to the waiting truck. Munro caught sight of dozens of faces in the lights. Rhodes might be a forgotten figure in the literary world of England, but in this small corner he was loved.

The truck started. Only then did Munro see Yanni sitting beside the driver.

He shouted to him. But Yanni was more concerned with Rhodes.

"You are back. Good," called Yanni. "He will be all right." He indicated Rhodes. "They will tell you in the villa." The truck backed out and drove away.

Munro went up to the villa. Susan was talking on the telephone when he went in. She put the receiver down as she saw him. "That was the hospital," she told him.

"What hospital?"

"I don't know. They took hours getting here."

"What's wrong with him?"

"He passed out. All that coughing. And he had a temperature. I think it's pneumonia or something."

"Poor old boy," said Munro. He thought the girl looked a little nervous. She must have had a difficult time. "Sorry I wasn't here."

"Where were you?"

"Dropped in to see an old friend of your's."

She looked blank. He went on. "Cecil is around."

"What!"

"Flew in this morning apparently. They were alarmed when they got no reply to those cables. Sir John thought they'd done a foolish thing sending us here."

"Where is Mr. Cecil?" she asked.

"At a village called Kotsi. Didn't Yanni let you know?"

"No."

"He should have told you," Munro frowned. "Where did you think I was all day?"

"I didn't know. But we had so much to do looking after the Professor, I had no time to worry."

"How long will he be away?"

"It could be some time." She looked uneasy. The villa was suddenly very empty. They were perched up in the night sky—electric lights shining forth as usual—like a beacon at an airfield, the village huddled below them, the mountains dimly rolling away. It was doubly quiet, for the coming and going of visitors had made this a noisy time when Rhodes was at home. Without the old man, the villa was a shell.

"It's lucky in a way," said Munro, "now we don't have to make up stories to cover our tracks. We can just go."

She nodded. "Yes. There is nothing we can do for him."

Munro realized she was still thinking about Rhodes. "I told Cecil," he said. "I said we'd be ready to go in a couple of days." Munro had thought they were the only people in the villa, but the housekeeper came in. She wore a shawl and was on the point of leaving. She had a note in her hand which she gave to Munro. She was distressed, and said something. Munro understood she was telling him about Rhodes. He tried to find out from her who else was in the house, but she waved him aside and hurried out.

Munro looked at the paper. It was from Rhodes, written in a scrawl. He read it aloud to the girl "Phone calls. Ask Susan." He looked at her. "Does that make any sense to you?"

She hesitated before she nodded. "There were some phone calls," she said.

"To whom?"

She shrugged her shoulders. "To you. To me. It didn't seem to matter."

"I don't get this," said Munro. He was beginning to understand why she might be nervous. "Who from?"

"They didn't say," she said.

"They?"

"Perhaps it was the same man."

"How often did he phone?"

"Twice."

"Look," he said, "what's all this about? Any trouble and I want to know."

"I'm sorry," she said. "All these things seem to fall on your shoulders, and they come through me."

"Through you?"

"You wouldn't be here if it hadn't been for me."

"Okay," said Munro, "now just tell me what happened."

"This man wanted to know why you were here."

"You told him?"

"I said you had brought me to meet Professor Rhodes—and I said it was none of his business."

"Good."

"But he phoned again. He said he knew why you were here. You had abused Greek hospitality in the past and you were doing so again. You had escaped with your life once, but you would not always be so lucky." She pretended not to be concerned, but he could see she was nervous.

"Look, my love," said Munro cheerfully, "we'll be out of this place the day after tomorrow. After that, they can hang themselves. Perhaps we should go down to the village to eat."

"I can cook a meal," she said.

As she went around the kitchen opening drawers and cupboards, he followed her. He wasn't so much talking to her, as using her as a means of clarifying his thoughts.

"I nearly strangled our mutual friend," he said.

"Cecil?" She didn't take him literally.

"Yes. I blamed him for Stephan's death."

"That wasn't very sensible."

"I wasn't very sensible. You go a little insane in solitary. Today I went a little insane."

She was mixing something in a bowl. "Do you like salad?"

"Love it," said Munro. He was happy with whatever she did. "Another interesting thing," he said, "Cecil was picking on me. Accused me of doing some job. He suggested I'd been given back to the Travelers in exchange for rubbish. You know why?"

"No," she said. She was looking in a larder. "You like chicken?" she asked.

"Yes," said Munro. "He said I had been given the treatment. Brainwashed. I was back in England working for someone else . . . And now I was in Greece to make contacts."

Susan was cleaning a chicken. Munro thought over what he had just said. "When you think about Cecil, he just isn't consistent."

"No?"

"Cecil was deliberately provoking me. I see it now. Attacking me. Why should he do that? All the way from London to make accusations. Why?"

"You're very clever," said Susan. "How do you light these stoves?"

He showed her. He still talked. "You know why?" he asked.

"No."

"Because attack is the best method of defense. He was frightened . . . or Sir John was frightened, or both of them . . . So he flew from London and told me they suspected me."

"Garlic?" said Susan.

"Great," said Munro. He knew he was on to something. "But what are they afraid of?" There was wine on the shelves. He poured two glasses. He couldn't see any reason why the Travelers should feel threatened by him. "I think I've got all the questions," he told Susan, "but I don't see the answers."

"That will take about an hour." She shut the oven door.

They went through to the big livingroom—huge now they had it to themselves. It was strangely domestic to be alone together. Munro found it restful. He was surprised to realize how much he had accepted the girl. He liked the way she listened to him.

"Cecil is concerned in case I've found out something. He accuses me to confuse the issue." Munro frowned. "But I haven't found out anything to accuse them of . . . or have I?" He looked up at the ceiling. "What could they have used me for?"

"You haven't done anything, have you? I mean, nothing for them?" Susan sounded thoughtful.

"You know all I've done," he said. "We went down to the bridge . . . we went to the grave . . . we came back."

"Then I don't see . . ." she began.

"There is one thing," interrupted Munro, "whatever we did, there was always some sort of fuss about it. I don't know how—but we certainly got publicity."

"Where?"

"Cecil had a German newspaper. I suppose there were others."

"That wasn't your fault," she said.

"What good would it be to me anyhow?" said Munro. "If he thinks I'm sending out smoke signals, to whom am I signaling?"

She was looking at the lights shining out into the garden, attracting the moths. "Where can we turn off some of these?"

Munro found the switches in the hall. He cut the beacon down by half. "That's better," she said, "I feel exposed."

Later they had supper. "I hope the Professor won't mind," she said.

"He'll be delighted. He loves to play host. I'll tell him we enjoyed ourselves in spite of his absence."

They sat at the window looking at the great sweep of the night, the moon low over the mountains, very yellow and heavy. Munro lifted his glass to the moon. "It's twice as bright, twice as big. Macedonian moon, I call it," he said. "We used to pick a full moon to move over these hills. It seems a hundred years ago." He hadn't spoken like this for a long time; he hadn't thought about it. "I was like another person in those days," he said. "I didn't think what we were doing. Never the politics. Just the fun of the thing with Stephan . . ."

She might resent him talking like that about her husband.

"Tell me about Stephan," she said.

"Tell you about him?"

"Yes. You knew him better than I did."

He thought about that. "I suppose I did."

Munro was not a man who shared confidences easily. Perhaps that was part of the attraction of the work Cecil had offered. Secrecy appealed to him. Life had depended on it at times. He was good at keeping things to himself— even his wife never knew what he was doing. For the years he had spent as an agent, Munro's wife had thought he was still buying and selling porcelain in East Germany.

"You know Stephan and I were contacts?"

"Yes, I knew that."

"We worked together as a team . . . if such a thing is possible in that game."

"Sir John told me." She was very frank, unaware of the implications of talking freely.

"Stephan was born in this part of the world. His father was an engineer with the oil companies. He was killed during some civil trouble." Munro stopped for a moment and looked into the dark. "Funny to think of armies in these hills. It doesn't seem real."

"Go on," said Susan.

"Stephan was a little boy. Rhodes wasn't the only one to fight with the partisans. Kids of twelve and thirteen have been soldiers out here."

"But Stephan wasn't in Greece all the time," she said.

"That's true. He was in Yugoslavia, Bulgaria, Albania. He spoke all the languages, and most of the dialects."

She nodded proudly. "I heard him sing in these languages." The memory made her smile.

"The thing about Stephan was his charm," said Munro. "He used to get out of trouble by some magnetism. People liked him. I admired that. I think I was jealous."

She gave him a quick look of wonder. "Why?"

"I didn't have that quality. People didn't like me."

"That's nonsense." She almost laughed.

Munro warmed towards her. "Anyway," he said, "Stephan was a charmer. He ran rings around the men they put on to us."

"Did you know they suspected you?"

"We guessed. The last few weeks were tricky. I was all right. I had documents, letters from Trade Commissions in the countries where we operated. I'd extended my so-called business, buying antiques. Giving good money for them."

"That was how you started, wasn't it?" she asked.

"Yes." There was a time when life had been lived at a simpler level. "I saw this opportunity to have my own business," he said. "I built it up. I had regular trips to Dresden and one or two other towns in the East. I was investigated a couple of times, but I was above board in those days. Besides I was bringing some cash into the country— dollars. Later I got this note from some obscure office in Whitehall. It was from Cecil. I didn't know what he was up to, I was so innocent I thought the Board of Trade was trying to put business in my way. I'd done a couple of simple jobs for them before I realized the implications."

"When did you meet Stephan?"

"About six years ago. They used me to bring out information that Stephan had put together. He seldom went back to England. I think that was why they took so long to catch up with him. If he hadn't gone back that last time, they would never have got him."

"And we should never have met," said Susan.

Munro made no comment. He didn't like to think about

his involvement with the Travelers. "They conned me into it," he told her, "but I was ready to be conned."

"Was Stephan like you?"

Munro drank slowly. He saw Stephan in the dark, heard him laugh. "No. He was as clever as they were. He didn't feel they manipulated him."

"Why not?" She was very quick with that question—very interested. Munro tried to think why. Sometimes he thought, you could sense people's reasons. But he couldn't sense anything from her.

"No one could manipulate Stephan," he said. "He was one step ahead. He knew what they were up to. He would laugh at Cecil and his mob. Stephan could cope with them."

"But Stephan was the one to get shot."

"That was just bad luck," said Munro.

The moon was moving slowly over the hills, picking out peaks in jet-black shadows. "I think I'm telling you this because you're Stephan's wife. It's like talking to Stephan."

"You loved Stephan, didn't you?"

"That's a strange thing to say."

"I think you were closer to him than to anyone else."

"That's not saying much," said Munro. "I'm not a person that takes easily to his fellow men."

"What about his fellow women?"

Munro wasn't sure if she was laughing at him.

"In my time I have been close to five or six. At least it felt close. But I don't share easy."

"Why not?" she said.

"It's Stephan we're talking about," he reminded her.

It was very easy to sit and talk with her. "You're like Stephan in one way," he told her.

"What's that?"

"I knew I could trust him. We were living a double life most of the time, both of us. Fooling the opposition, and some of the time we were fooling our own HQ. But we were never fooling each other."

"You think I'm like that?"

"Yes. You seem like Stephan to me."

"Coming from you, that's a very nice thing."

146

"God. He wasn't perfect. Too damn conceited. Thought he could do anything. Wouldn't learn."

Munro got up and opened another bottle of wine. The villa echoed with the pop of the cork.

"Why did Yanni go?" asked Munro.

"He wanted to see the Professor safely to the hospital."

"I don't know how much I trust Yanni," said Munro.

"You don't trust many people," she said.

"I have reasons," said Munro.

"He seems a nice man," she said.

"What does that prove?" asked Munro. "Cecil employed him."

"Cecil employed you," she said. "I don't mistrust you for that."

"Cecil employed me?" Munro savored the thought as he did his wine. "I suppose he did."

"You should forgive people," she said.

"What for?"

"You can't forgive Cecil for what happened to you when you were a prisoner."

He saw the connection, and the truth of it.

"Can you talk about it?" she asked.

"Do I have to?"

"Not if you don't want to."

"Perhaps one thing concerns you," he said. "I didn't react very well. I lost touch with reality. That isn't easy for me to say."

"I know."

"But as Stephan's wife . . ."

"Go on," she interrupted.

"I was shocked by his death. The game ended. That cell was like a grave."

There was a silence. They didn't feel the need to speak. And then she said, "I read your reports."

"They were secret."

"Sir John gave them to me. What happened before you got to the village?"

"What a strange thing to ask." He couldn't follow the pattern of her thought.

"Have you forgotten?"

147

"Of course not."

"You two were not on your own?"

"Does that matter?"

"In the report you said you stayed the night before with nomads."

"That's right." He smiled at a memory. "The women were very taken by Stephan, but their men told them we were living together. Stephan understood their dialect."

"Did you pay these nomads anything?"

"What are you getting at?"

"If you didn't give them money, perhaps they betrayed you?"

"They have this thing about hospitality. They wouldn't take money."

"So they might have given you away."

"Nonsense," said Munro, "they didn't even know we were hiding. They wouldn't know one side of the frontier from the other. They aren't part of that game."

He had a strange mixture of feelings about her. At one moment she seemed concerned for him, and at another she was like an interrogator.

"Don't you think I put everything in that report?" he asked her.

Before she had time to reply he realized what had happened. "I get it," he said, "Cecil has been talking to you. You think I've got something else going."

"No. I think you may not remember everything, that's all."

He felt himself getting angry. "You don't know anything about this."

"Why do you think they took us to that churchyard?" she asked. Some of her questions had no background.

"What the hell does that have to do with it?"

"They agreed to let us visit Stephan's grave, and then they take us there."

She had lost him. "This has nothing to do with my report," he said. "I told Cecil everything that happened."

"Everything?"

Now she was getting him angry.

"I know you're concerned about Stephan . . ."

148

"That was a long time ago," she said quickly.

He couldn't believe she had said that.

"I told you. You knew him better than I did. I loved him like a stranger, for a week or two. Then he'd gone."

"Then why are you here? I mean, if you didn't want to see where he died . . ."

"They took us to the wrong place, didn't they?" she asked.

"What does that matter? They thought he was buried there."

"Did they?"

"Why not? Anyone can make a mistake. I'll tell you what happened. Their officials get a request from London to show us the grave. The officials want us to know they can do things as correctly as the West. So they show us a grave. Any grave. Just to keep us quiet and send us home happy."

"So that's what happened?"

"It must have been."

"I knew about your exchange as well." She seemed totally inconsequential.

"What about it?"

"Before we left London they told me that you had been given back in exchange for someone of no importance."

"They said that before we left?" Cecil had told him they got suspicious afterwards. Why were they lying? Who was lying? They were spreading a net around him.

"Why did those people want you back in England?"

He felt his hand shaking. This *was* a form of interrogation. The girl was echoing what Cecil had said. Just echoing Cecil! He determined not to lose his temper. "Maybe you have some theory," he said.

"Do you know why they exchanged you?"

"No."

"Do you know why people are interested to see you back in Greece?"

"No." A wave of sadness swept over him. She was the only person he had met since Stephan's death for whom he had felt any warmth. She had seemed to respond. Why had she been friendly? He had never trusted Cecil, so Cecil

149

could do him no harm. But he *had* trusted her. He had felt protective. "What are you trying to say? What do you think I've done? I wasn't coming back. It was only through you . . . you asked me to take you . . . *you* wanted to see the bridge. . ."

She tried to walk past him. He caught her. "You're accusing me of something. What is it?"

"Leave me."

"You can't just walk away."

"You are hurting."

"Susan. What did you mean?"

"Nothing. Let me go. . ."

She tried to pull away. She too was very angry, trembling.

"I'm sorry," he said. "We'll be out of this place tomorrow. You said something, and I just couldn't take anymore."

Her anger seemed to evaporate. She gave a gesture of resignation—as if she too were sad.

His heart went out to her. They had been so close. Only a moment ago. What had she said that had disturbed him? He could think of nothing.

He said "Susan" but he didn't know what else to say. "Susan," and then he did the only thing he could to comfort her, taking her in his arms and being sorry for her, forgetting he had lost his desire for women, and kissing her. She was frozen for a second, not moving away nor responding, then her arms went around him and she was kissing him lovingly. It seemed to Munro, that they had both been waiting for this—unaware that they had been waiting.

She drew back. "Did you do that because you were sorry for me?"

"No," he said, "because I wanted you." He hadn't known it until then, but he was sure.

She smiled and kissed him again, slowly, deliberately, happily.

11

When Yanni came up in the morning they were still in bed. He walked into the villa, calling for Munro. Munro heard him, and thought he was dreaming. Even as he woke and remembered what had happened, it still had the quality of a dream. The girl moved beside him, turning to him, opening her eyes. For a second she was startled to see him; then she looked so happy, touching him, a possessive pleasure that made it difficult for Munro to speak. He had so much he wanted to say; many important things, but no words. The great weight of sadness had been taken from him.

She put out her arms, pulling him to her, with conscious pleasure, sleep still in her eyes. She was very pretty, lying back lazily on the pillow, a blonde tumble of curls. Her assurance delighted Munro.

He whispered, "It's Yanni."

She looked blank, listening.

"He's gone to my room," said Munro.

She didn't seem to care. She said "Peter . . . Peter . . ." and ran her fingers over his face, his neck, his arm, his chest, admiring, loving.

"Mr. Munro," called Yanni.

They heard the door bang. Yanni was looking through the villa.

"Mr. Munro."

Munro got out of bed and pulled on a dressing-gown. The door opened. Yanni looked in anxiously. He saw them and he was surprised.

"I'm sorry," he said, "I have something to show . . . I will be out here." He shut the door as he backed out.

"What is it?" called Munro.

"It's all right," Yanni called back, "just some newspapers. I shall be here."

"Newspapers?" Munro frowned. He began to dress quickly. "I'm sorry he came in."

She laughed at him. "He is a nice man. He can be helpful."

She watched him with a lazy delight.

Munro joined Yanni in the big living room.

"I am sorry." Yanni was apologetic. "I saw your room was empty. I was alarmed for you."

"Forget it," said Munro.

"I thought, what could have happened to Mr. Munro?" He carried a bundle of newspapers.

"Those papers?" asked Munro.

Yanni gave them to Munro. "On this page," he said. "Do you need me to translate?"

Munro glanced at the papers. He could read Greek. He looked for his own name but didn't see it.

"It is an Athens paper," said Yanni. "Bad politics, but many people read it."

"What do you want to show me?" Munro had a feeling Yanni was softening the blow.

"I say that to let you know they are not important," said Yanni. "And they do not mention any names. It might not be you."

"What?" said Munro. He could not be angry with Yanni. He could not be angry with anyone, with the sweet taste of love still on his tongue.

"They have a page by the staff," explained Yanni. "Here it is. They say—to summarize—that we should not allow our soil to be exploited by foreigners who carry out their own vendettas. They say Greece is a proud and free country and neither our allies nor our enemies must be allowed to abuse our hospitality."

"Sounds nebulous," said Munro.

"They say no names," repeated Yanni. "But here they say that there is evidence to suggest that foreign security services are using Greece as a base for activities of their own."

"Happens all the time." Munro gave a shrug.

Yanni went on translating.

"They say one of the western governments is using a known agent to return to Greece—to the north of Greece they say—in order to complete a mission that he failed to complete two years ago."

"Let me see that," said Munro.

Yanni showed it to him. Laboriously Munro translated.

"Can't be me," said Munro.

Yanni continued. "It is known that nomadic tribes in the north had assisted this agent, and an agent now dead. Why is this agent back? Whom does he wish to contact?"

"Well, well," said Munro softly.

Susan came into the room.

Yanni was apologetic. She stopped him. "Don't be silly, Yanni," she said. "What are these papers?"

"I brought them from the hospital this morning," said Yanni. He didn't want to tell her about them.

Munro showed her. "Some bloody journalist thinks I'm here to find the people who helped Stephan and me on the way to Karlovo."

"Why should you?" she asked.

"They don't say."

She smiled and put her arm through his. "It doesn't matter, Peter," she said, "tomorrow we'll be gone, and they can say what they like."

"You're going?" Yanni sounded dismayed.

"We've finished," said Munro.

Yanni looked doubtful. "Finished?"

"We had a look at Karlovo," said Munro. "That's why we came."

Yanni gave an involuntary glance at the papers. He shrugged. "As they say," he said, "I thought you came to find some people."

Munro stared at him. "What in God's name put that in your head?"

"I always had that impression," said Yanni.

"Who from?" asked Munro. "Cecil? Sir John?"

"Nothing that was said," said Yanni quickly. "Nothing written. I asked myself why should you come to this place?"

"And?" said Munro.

"I thought it must be to do with the shooting."

"Stephan's shooting?"

"Of course. If you wanted to find out something—like who betrayed you that night, how did they know you were going to use that escape route—then you would have to make inquiries from someone who was also there."

"I don't know who else was there," said Munro.

Susan pressed his arm, reassuring him. They were together. Everything else had happened a long time ago.

"It doesn't matter," she whispered.

"It does," said Munro. The thought of the girl filled much of his being, but not all of it. He was concerned with what Yanni thought, with his logic. Perhaps the same logic was used by a shadowy enemy watching him journey through Greece—waiting to test theories, no doubt. Yanni wanted to drop the subject. He looked to Susan for help. "I have disturbed you this morning."

"Come on, Yanni," said Munro sharply, "who the hell could I be looking for?"

Yanni was annoyed that Munro persisted. "There were these people," he said sharply, "the Sarakatsans—or the Koutzovlachs. I don't know which of these nomads you were with."

"Who are they?" asked Susan.

"They are shepherds," said Yanni. He sounded deprecating. He didn't like nomads. He felt they gave Greece a bad name. It wasn't civilized to wander about like Arabs. "They are the people Mr. Rhodes stopped to show you. Some have villages they go back to. Some have no villages and always move with their animals."

"Like gypsies," said Susan.

"Am I supposed to be looking for gypsies?" mocked Munro. "Who in their senses could have started this rumor?"

Yanni nodded. "It would be difficult, but not impossible. These people go back to the same mountains at the same time of the seasons, year after year. They are like birds migrating—always to the same places."

Munro shook his head. "Forget it, Yanni," he said. "This little jaunt is over. We're going home."

Yanni had coffee with them. "I regret you are going," he told them. "It is always a pleasure to work with British Security."

"You haven't been working with British Security," Munro told him. "This is a private visit. You knew Susan and I were engaged?"

"I heard that," he said.

"What do you think?" said Munro. It amused him that the cover story should turn out to be prophetic.

Yanni was puzzled. "I wasn't sure," he said.

"Yanni," said Susan, "you are a friend. I can say in front of you how much I love Peter."

"Yes. Now I know," said Yanni.

He went off down the rocky path still puzzled. "I will see to the arrangements for tomorrow," he told them. "I'll check the car."

They spent the morning wandering through the empty villa, and in the tiny garden, leaning on the stone parapet, looking over the mountains. Village noises floated up.

"Half-way to heaven," she said, watching to see if he thought that sentimental.

All he said was, "What are we going to do when we get out of here?"

"Let's wait and see," she said.

He had not made love since a warm night in Athens, just before he had gone into Albania after Stephan. That was many months ago. Desire had deserted him during interrogations and the months of solitude. Now he wanted her overwhelmingly.

"Didn't you want to make love to me in Athens?" she asked.

"No," he said truthfully.

"I'm surprised."

"Why?"

"I wanted you," she told him.

It was a warm spring day. The sun bathed everything in a clear, hard light. "Is that Albania?" She pointed into the distance. Rocks glittered. Munro nodded. "Men draw lines on a map. One side of the valley is alien. But the birds don't know; they sing on both sides. The wolves don't know; come winter time they'll kill Greek sheep, Albanian sheep. Doesn't matter to them. Did you know they had wolves?"

She wasn't listening to him, but peering down to the village. "Yanni is coming back," she said.

"Already!" Munro frowned.

Yanni came puffing up the steps.

"What is it?" Munro called.

Yanni shielded his eyes against the sun. "I have a message from Mr. Cecil. He wanted you to phone him."

"Phone him?"

"I have a number for you."

"Let's go now," said Susan. Her smile had gone. She was suddenly urgent.

He was startled. "Why?"

"Let's go back to London. Don't phone him."

He put an arm around her. "It's all right," he said. "Better hear what he has to say."

She recovered herself.

Yanni puffed across to them. "He was trying to call you all morning. Couldn't get through." Munro nodded. They had taken the receiver off. "Let's get it over then." He went to phone.

Yanni followed him.

"What's all the panic about?" asked Munro.

"I don't know," said Yanni.

Munro wasn't sure if he believed him.

"Let me get the number," said Yanni. A moment later he handed the receiver to Munro. "He's on the line."

He heard Cecil. "Is that you, Munro? I've been trying . . ."

Munro interrupted. "Look, Cecil. We don't have any more business with each other. The job's over."

"I know, old fellow." Cecil sounded cheerful as ever, as though Munro had never had his hands around his throat. "The point is, I have to see you."

"What for?"

"It's urgent."

156

"I'm listening," said Munro.

"Dear fellow," said Cecil, "you know these telephones. Where's your security?"

"I don't need any," said Munro, "I don't work for British Intelligence."

"You should read the papers," said Cecil.

"If that's all you have to say . . ." began Munro.

"I'm not far away," said Cecil, "Yanni knows. He'll bring you. Everything aboveboard. But it *is* serious. Affects both of you."

"Who?" asked Munro sharply.

"You and Susan," said Cecil. "I'll give you the details. Just pop down. It won't take twenty minutes." He put the phone down. Munro was about to get the number again.

"I know where to see him," said Yanni.

"You know more than I do," said Munro grimly. He would be careful what he said in front of the plump, friendly Greek.

Susan watched him from the door. "I'll let him know this is where he gets off," he told her. "You and I can make our own way home without help from the Travelers."

"Look after yourself," she said. She seemed unduly concerned. He grinned at her. "Don't worry. Cecil's smarter than I am back in London, but not out here."

She didn't say anything, but she kissed him and watched from the wall as they went down.

"I'm sick of you, Yanni," said Munro. "Don't come up to the villa again."

"Mr. Munro," Yanni was apologetic, "I am doing what I can to help."

They walked along the village street. "Where is the stupid bastard?" asked Munro.

"I will run you in the car."

"He said he was near here." Munro was suspicious.

"Just outside the village," agreed Yanni.

"What's the cloak-and-dagger for," snarled Munro. "Will he never learn?"

"So no one connects you with him," said Yanni. "He does it for your sake."

"He never did a thing for my sake," said Munro coldly.

Yanni had his car outside the café.

They drove from the village and turned off on a narrow track.

"I'll shoot you, Yanni, if this is another of your games," said Munro unpleasantly.

Yanni shrugged. He was much misunderstood, but there was no point protesting.

The track dropped below the road. On a slightly wider section a car was pulled up. Cecil and the driver waited.

"The whole set-up bores me," said Munro as Cecil joined him cheerfully.

"I don't blame you, old fellow," said Cecil, "it's got out of hand." He took out his wallet. "We have a reservation for you on the night flight tomorrow. Yanni will drive you back to Athens first thing in the morning. These are the details." He handed Munro a few papers. "How are you for money? You'd better take this anyhow."

He was offering Munro a bundle of notes.

"What's the idea, Cecil?" Munro touched everything, papers, money, as though it were explosive.

"Remember that little gun of yours?"

"Yes."

"Still got it?"

"Yes."

"Oh good." Cecil smiled encouragingly.

"Someone you want shot?" asked Munro.

"Nothing like that," Cecil laughed. "You know that, Munro. The Travelers never work that way."

"What's the problem?" asked Munro.

"No problems," said Cecil. "We'd just like you out of the country in one piece."

"Is that supposed to mean something?" asked Munro.

Cecil looked thoughtful. "You did a nice job for us, Munro. It would be ingratitude to let you be the victim of someone's silly mistakes."

"Are you telling me something?"

"Just that some people are getting the wrong idea why you are here. They think you might be dangerous. We don't know how far they might go, but Sir John doesn't like it. He wants you out immediately."

"I wouldn't trust you if you were pulling me from a blazing house," said Munro. He looked at the money and tickets. "What's so special about this flight? Someone sabotaged the engines?"

Cecil grinned. "Could be, old fellow," he said. "Just be on it."

Yanni interrupted. "You didn't tell Mr. Munro about the radio."

"No need," said Cecil, waving him aside.

"What's that?" asked Munro.

"We monitor radio," said Cecil.

"I know that," said Munro. He was angry. Something was being kept from him.

"We've been picking up items about you."

Munro blinked at him. "About me?"

Cecil nodded. "You were mentioned."

"My name?" Munro didn't believe it.

"Yes. Peter Munro. You are here for a special job. The Greek officials should take action. You are a threat to their neighbors."

"Who says this?"

"Lots of people. Not that we take it seriously . . ."

"Who the hell says this?"

"My dear fellow. They said it on Radio Tiranë. Then it was given air-space in Bulgaria, and points north as far as Poland and East Germany. Nothing much. Just a tiny mention here and there. News items. You know, they point a moral. Insidious British. Trouble-makers; people of bad faith. What did they say? Something like, 'Peter Munro comes back for more punishment. Has he not learned that to meddle with the free republics is a dangerous game?' "

Munro shook his head. "What are they excited about?"

"Beats me," said Cecil. "Still, you never know, with that sort of talk they may try something funny. They have agents in Greece as well. Must have, if you come to think about it. Otherwise, how would they know you were here?"

Munro didn't have to think hard. "They must have read reports about those visits to the bridge."

Cecil looked unconvinced. "I doubt that."

"And our famous trip to the grave," said Munro.

"H'm," said Cecil.

Munro remembered the crowd at the Professor's villa—Vilaras among them.

"Call it a day," said Cecil. "We know they're wrong, but let's play for safety. Off with Yanni when the sun comes up, and back to dear old Blighty."

Everything that Cecil did or said smelt wrong to Munro. Even his "old fellow" jargon was out of date; his humor forced.

"All right," said Munro, "we'll be on the plane tomorrow."

He went back to the car with Yanni. Cecil watched them drive off with a cheerful wave. He gave Munro the feeling of a man winning all the tricks.

They drove back to the village. Munro left Yanni and went up to the villa.

He looked for Susan. There was no sign of her. That puzzled him, but he told himself she had probably gone into the village. He wanted to tell her what Cecil had said. He was glad to be going in the morning, and he felt she would be, as well.

He supposed she might have left a note, and looked through the villa, but there was nothing.

Munro tried to settle in the garden under the olive tree with a book. It was a volume of poems by Rhodes. The old boy had written well in his time, but Munro couldn't keep his mind on them. It was strange for Susan to go out like this.

The telephone rang and he guessed it was her. But there was only a slight noise at the other end, and no one spoke.

"Who's that?" asked Munro. There was no answer. He could hear a faint breathing.

"Don't be bloody funny," said Munro. "Who is it?" Then he thought it might be the hospital with news about Rhodes, but the phone went dead.

Munro went back to his seat under the tree, but he couldn't read. He got up and wandered about. If Susan had gone to the village, she was probably shopping; perhaps buying the lace they made in this district. But Munro didn't believe his comforting thoughts. He looked around the rooms again. In her bedroom a chair was pushed against the bed. Some books beside it were on the floor. Munro picked them up thoughtfully. Perhaps Susan hadn't noticed them. A rug in the corridor was in a heap, as if someone had kicked it aside. Who would do that? A number of solutions jumped to his mind. He didn't like any of them.

He went back to the garden and looked down into the village. He could see the main street, almost deserted. He began hurrying down the steps from the villa. He had to find out where the girl had gone.

Yanni was staying in a room over the café. It was just possible Susan had gone to see him. Munro spent half an hour looking for him. It was incredible that you could lose anyone in such a small place. As if Yanni had tried to hide, and Susan too! He found Yanni drinking with a couple of men on the edge of the village. There was no sign of Susan.

Yanni was pleased to see him.

"Join us. These gentlemen would be honored. One was a seaman when he was young . . ."

Munro ignored them. "I'm looking for Susan," he said. "Have you seen her?"

Yanni was surprised. "Not at the villa?"

"If she were, I wouldn't be looking for her." Munro was on edge.

Yanni shrugged. "She goes home tomorrow. Perhaps there are places she wants to see."

"Like what?" said Munro.

"There is beautiful country," Yanni gesticulated.

"She hasn't a car," said Munro. "She knew I'd be away only a short time. Where would she go?"

"I don't know." Yanni didn't appear disturbed. He thought it no problem that the girl should go off by herself. Perhaps Munro was making something out of nothing.

"She will turn up." Yanni was cheerful. "Best to have a drink."

"No thanks," said Munro.

He went back to the villa, promising himself she would be there. But she wasn't. All was silent. He noticed the mat again lying in the corridor, rumpled as though kicked aside. He cursed the girl for bringing him this anxiety.

He felt like a man overstating something, an actor giving too big a performance; but he had no way of restraining himself. The noises of the village drifted up to him—an occasional shout, the sound of sheep bells, faint conversation as people passed below. Munro sensed something was going to happen. And when it did happen, he was not surprised. He heard a car coming into the village. It stopped below. Doors banged. Someone was coming up to the villa. When he looked down and saw Vilaras, it was as if he had expected him. Another man walked behind him, and a third stood by the car. Vilaras saw him, hesitated, then came on. It was all perfectly clear to Munro. Vilaras was responsible for Susan's disappearance.

Munro waited as the two men came into the garden. Vilaras smiled tenuously, but the smile quickly died.

The man with him took in the villa and the garden in one swift flicker of an eyelid. A professional, thought Munro. He had met the type before. He looked for the bulge in his jacket pocket, and, sure enough, it was there. Munro congratulated himself on the fact his own gun was never seen, but was easy to get at. The man wore a blue suit with an open shirt. He appeared uninterested in Munro; but this, of course, was part of the routine. He had dark, curly hair. Munro photographed him in his mind . . . "Age—late twenties; professional killer." Munro also knew that whatever file there was on the man, it would list his assignments and his success. How did they phrase his current assignment? Munro wondered.

"The Professor's in hospital," said Munro. He felt he was making a first bid in a poker game. And it was a bid none of them took very seriously.

"I know," said Vilaras, "it was a pity."

"What can you expect," said Munro chattily, "gadding about at his time of life?"

"Gadding?" Vilaras didn't understand the word. He was being very polite. The other man was still keeping an eye on the villa.

"That jaunt to the bonny hills of Albania," said Munro. He made it sound flippant, suggesting that nothing troubled him, least of all this visit. "That's Rhodes. Always game for

162

a bit of excitement. The old breed. Fast dying out. When Rhodes goes, the sun sinks on the British Empire. But you know the old boy, don't you . . . now that's a point. You don't know him all that well, do you?" He was smiling blandly at Vilaras.

The other man said something in Greek.

"What does Curly say?" asked Munro.

Vilaras shrugged. "He wants to know who else is in the villa."

"Now?" asked Munro.

"I suppose so," said Vilaras. He looked at Munro with some surprise.

Munro pretended to give the matter thought. He marked off his fingers as he spoke. "Now let's see . . . the old man has gone to hospital . . . the housekeeper nipped off smartly soon after . . . the other members of the staff have vanished like the winter's snow . . ." He looked at Vilaras inquiringly.

"But you have stayed?" said Vilaras.

"Love the place," said Munro. "Just can't tear myself away."

Vilaras was still uneasy. "I understood that Miss Marsh came here to discuss poetry with Professor Rhodes."

"That's correct," said Munro. He didn't know why, but he sensed how important the question was.

Vilaras went on. "Now that he is ill, this is very bad luck for her."

"Very," Munro nodded amiably. It was impossible to guess what Vilaras had on his mind, and Munro was usually good at identifying the other man's thoughts.

"There will be little chance of her doing any more work with the Professor now," said Vilaras.

He was marking time, thought Munro. Not sure what to say.

The man with the dark curly hair was listening intently, but not to Munro nor to Vilaras. It was as if he were trying to catch a sound from the villa. Munro was baffled. What the hell did these two want? If they had taken Susan, why had they come back? They must have something to tell him. Why didn't Vilaras get to the point?

"What's the matter with your friend?" asked Munro. The dark man had moved towards the villa door.

"I think he has heard something," said Vilaras.

"Impossible," said Munro, "there's nobody there."

Vilaras looked at him doubtfully.

"But take a look by all means," added Munro. He waved Vilaras towards the door. He had suddenly made up his mind to go into action. There were two against one, and at least one of them was armed, but Munro felt he could handle them. They were so concerned with something else, he could take them off guard.

Vilaras called to the second man. The latter hesitated.

"Go ahead, Curly," said Munro encouragingly.

The two men went into the villa. Munro followed, keeping up a casual chatter.

He displayed the empty living room like a conjuror revealing a rabbit. "You see. Nothing in the villa. Take a look. Open any door. Don't bother to knock. Make free. Please," and as the dark man pushed open the door to the next room Munro put his gun in the small of his back.

"Just keep your hands against the door," said Munro cheerfully. "No one wants to get hurt."

The man looked swiftly at the gun in Munro's hand, and he kept very still.

"What are you doing?" Vilaras was alarmed.

"Just clarifying the situation," said Munro. He took the gun from the man's jacket pocket, and quickly went over him for another weapon. There was nothing else.

Vilaras and the man said something in Greek. "Don't try anything." Munro looked at Vilaras with a wide but mirthless smile.

"I have no gun," said Vilaras.

Munro believed him, but he checked. "Now what are you here for?" asked Munro.

The other Greek was very angry now that Munro had moved away. He shouted at Vilaras.

"Tell him to keep calm," said Munro.

"Mr. Munro," Vilaras spread out his arms deprecatingly. "We have come to help you, and he does not expect to be treated like this."

"Does he always carry a gun when he comes to help people?" asked Munro dryly. "And why do you think I need help?"

"I have a message for you," said Vilaras.

"Who from?"

Vilaras waved the question aside. "Do you know the village of Mesara?" he asked.

"No," said Munro.

"It is to the north near Florina."

"Oh yes?" said Munro. He showed no interest.

"It is a small place in the hills. Indeed it is little more than a place for summer pasture."

Munro watched Vilaras. He had a good idea what he was being told, but he would make the other man spell it out.

"I don't know that part of the country," said Munro.

"Perhaps you do," said Vilaras. "You used the route in the past. This is a village which you and Stephan Aroso had as a base."

"Now how would you know that?" said Munro.

Vilaras didn't bother to make excuses. "I know some things about you, Mr. Munro. Many people do."

"But not that," said Munro.

"So you remember the place?" asked Vilaras.

"It has the advantage of being on three frontiers," said Munro, "the Greek, Albanian and Yugoslav."

"That is the place," said Vilaras.

"My dear fellow," said Munro, "there's no secret about who I am. But who are you?"

"I think there is no secret about me also. I work against the present authority in Greece," admitted Vilaras.

"But why are you telling me about Mesara?"

"You are to go there," said Vilaras simply.

"I'm not sure how to take that," said Munro softly. "Is it a threat?"

"Advice," said Vilaras.

"Why should I go?" asked Munro. He tried to remain casual.

"Mr. Munro," Vilaras was guarded, "we think we know why you are here—and why you stay."

"Yes?"

"It is not for me to make decisions," said Vilaras. "I am told to give you this message. Some people might think there were easier ways of dealing with you."

"Meaning?"

"If a man is a danger, it is as if he were an enemy in war. He threatens us, we threaten him. These are simple facts, Mr. Munro. You know all about them."

There was only one thing clear to Munro. They—whoever "they" were—wanted him to go to this tiny village. He remembered the place. It was a wild stretch that ranged into three countries and was impossible to police. He and Stephan had stayed there once. He remembered living on sour milk and olives.

"So you had to make sure I would go," said Munro thoughtfully.

"We were not sure," said Vilaras. "And this man came because we know your reputation." Vilaras was almost apologetic as he indicated his companion.

Nothing sounded quite right to Munro. They had a trump card, but they seemed loath to play it. They had not told him what would happen if he didn't go. Perhaps that was too obvious to need stating.

"If I don't make this trip?" asked Munro.

"No one can make you go," said Vilaras. "It was thought you would be prepared to take this chance. After all, you have found out nothing since you arrived here."

"What should I want to know, Mr. Vilaras?" asked Munro.

Vilaras smiled as though sharing a secret with Munro. "It must be something important, before you come back to this area and take part in such an involved disguise."

"I'm in disguise?" mocked Munro. What the hell was the man talking about!

"A married man who pretends to be engaged, to bring someone to see the Professor!" Vilaras smiled again. "You and your employers must think we are stupid. And did Mr. Cecil think we would not learn he had come himself to see you?"

"He's a fish out of water as soon as he leaves London," said Munro confidentially.

"So with all these things, we guess what you wish to learn."

"Well, well," said Munro. His mind was a blank. "And if I go to Mesara, I'll find out?"

"I am of no importance," said Vilaras with a shrug, "I know nothing. Like you, I guess. But my guess is you will learn something."

Munro knew they had him over a barrel. If he didn't go, there was a good chance Susan would be found at the foot of some ravine.

"If anything has happened to her," he said, "I will come back and kill you, Vilaras."

Vilaras looked at him in amazement. His jaw dropped, and he seemed unable to say anything. If Munro had not always expected to find wheels within wheels, and disguises masking disguises, then perhaps at that moment he might have asked himself what so bewildered the little man.

He tossed the gun back to the other Greek.

"Do you intend to go?" asked Vilaras.

"I'll think about it," said Munro.

"There is a question of time," said Vilaras, "tomorrow would be too late."

Vilaras and the other man went down the steps towards the village. Munro could hear the second man's angry protests. Vilaras replied quietly. It seemed to Munro that he was as puzzled as Munro himself. It occurred to Munro that perhaps a third party was pulling the strings of this marionette show. But he couldn't think who that might be.

He waited until later that afternoon. There was still no sign of Susan. He tried to control his fears, but the equation now seemed clear to him. Susan had been kidnapped to bring pressure on him. They had taken her to make sure he'd have to go. He decided to drive himself. He wasn't sure what to take with him, nor how long he would be away. A small voice said "Forever", but he ignored it. He took nothing but maps, ammunition and his pistol. He knew he was going to kill someone, and he knew he might die himself. But he didn't know who—nor why.

This time Munro found Yanni in his room above the café.

"I'm taking the car," he told Yanni.

"Where are you going?"

"This is private," said Munro.

"Have you found Susan?"

"I expect to," said Munro.

Yanni looked anxious. "You are going to look for her now?"

"That's right."

"But where?"

Munro hesitated. "Mesara."

"I don't know it," said Yanni.

"Beyond Florina," said Munro, "just a bit off the track."

Yanni frowned. "That is going over the frontier."

"Not quite."

"There must be some reason, if she is there," said Yanni.

"I think someone took her," said Munro.

"Mr. Munro. It's better I come with you."

"I can handle it," said Munro. He took the car keys from Yanni. Yanni came out with him. He was still protesting as Munro drove off. Yanni stood watching as the dust rose behind it. He could see it thread through the streets and start climbing the mountain road. He watched until it was out of sight, going north. Yanni had a great sense of having betrayed Munro. He should have told him all he suspected, even though in doing so he might have betrayed the men who paid him.

One of the larger houses a little way out of the village had been taken for a few days by a family from Athens. No one yet had seen the visitors. But they were understood to have moved in.

Visitors were indeed there, but they were not from Athens. Cecil stood at the window on the top floor watching the car speed past. He saw Munro at the wheel without the aid of the binoculars he held.

"There he goes," he said in triumph. "Running true to type." He saw the car again between two outcrops of rock, going at speed. "The thing about Munro," he went on, "is that he is such a predictable mixture of cynicism and romanticism. He knows exactly what makes everyone else tick, but he doesn't realize how he ticks himself. Lucky, in a way. Gives one a chance to make use of his finer qualities."

He turned to the girl who watched from behind. She was pale, and her eyes bitter. "He hates you," said Susan.

"Does he?" said Cecil with a smile. "I take that as a compliment."

She had been waiting in the room for hours, standing by the window looking up at the villa. The strain showed in her face.

"You've done an excellent job," said Cecil. "Of course, the essential factor was the timing. There was no point you disappearing until we were sure they were about to make a move. That was the crisis. Did this visit by Vilaras mean anything? A tricky moment. I think we judged it to a nicety."

"He hasn't forgiven you for the last time," she said.

"Yes, he blames me for that," nodded Cecil. "Not Stephan, you notice. Me. And I wasn't even there."

Cecil was rubbing his hands. He could not disguise his satisfaction. "This has been one of the most tricky operations to regulate," he said. He was talking more to himself than to her. "In fact, I'd say, the trickiest. Sir John thought we hadn't a chance. He said we'd never get him there. I had doubts, oh yes, I had doubts. You were absolutely masterly, my dear. I realize what happened. I've had reports. And Yanni, you know, I heard from Yanni, how things were going, and all that."

"Does Yanni know the overall plan?"

"Good gracious, no," said Cecil.

"I'm glad to hear that," she said. "I didn't think he would have been such a bastard."

Cecil ignored her. "Yanni took things at face value. You're the only person, other than Sir John and I, who knows the facts."

"Do you know where he's going?" she asked.

"No. But that's not important. This rendezvous won't be the destination. They aren't *that* simple. But the interesting thing is that he has been sent for. I think that proves something."

"What?"

"Well, my dear, at least they are very concerned. Someone wants to know what he's doing and how much he guesses. Someone wants to know very much."

Susan put her knuckles to her mouth. "Have you any idea what'll happen to him?"

"That depends on whether we're right or wrong. I mean, if we're wrong, then probably they'll just want to find out what he's up to, and Peter Munro can look after himself."

"And if we're right?" asked Susan.

"I don't see a clear answer to that," said Cecil thoughtfully.

"If he runs into danger? If he gets killed?"

"My dear, of course he will run into danger. He has been in danger here already. We all have. And why should he get killed?"

"I don't know," she said. "I'm just frightened he'll get killed."

Cecil glanced at her. "Yes," he said, "I heard you had to go a little further than your brief to make sure he would be concerned about you. I hope that hasn't complicated things."

She flushed angrily. "I didn't go to bed with him on your behalf, Mr. Cecil."

"No?"

"That was something I did for myself." She went out of the room.

It was hard for her to stay in the same house. The sound of Cecil moving above reminded her of her complicity. It disgusted her to think what she had done, the part she had played, although she realized that it was something she would not have thought twice about on other occasions.

Cecil saw her later that evening. "You must be exhausted after all you've done," he said. "I was most unsympathetic. It's been nerve racking. We'll get you back to old England just as soon as possible. Tomorrow probably."

"I don't want to go back yet," she said.

"I'm afraid you must," said Cecil. "Don't forget you're still working for Sir John."

She walked in the garden that evening. Cecil told her to

170

be careful not to be seen. "News travels fast," he said. "It would be upsetting if Munro goes chasing over the mountains after you, then a little bird tells him you're here."

Susan kept out of sight, although she was certain that it was too late for Peter to learn that she had not been abducted, that she did not need protection from unknown enemies, but that he most certainly did.

12

It was a bright night with a big moon, which soon disappeared however. Munro was stopped twice by the border patrol, and explained he was heading for Florina. They examined his passport but didn't recognize him. Before he began the long slope down to the valley, he branched off on a side road. The track led to a village which he could see from a long way off. He had been there before. It was Mesara.

Tall sentry boxes on the top of wooden stilts acted as lookout posts. But none was manned. The border patrol preferred to keep warm in some cottage kitchen with a bit of a fire and a glass of ouzo. If anyone was smart enough to try to get out of the countries to the north, then good luck to him. Munro put his headlights out, and drove until he ran out of track. It reminded him of the road to Karlovo. Munro left his car close to the steep rocks, giving it some cover.

He stood looking up at the huddled buildings that formed the village, like a ragged castle in the night sky, growing out of rock. Who would be there at this season, Munro wondered. It had been a hide-out for outlaws in the past. Well, he thought, in a sense he was an outlaw, for those in his profession put themselves beyond the law of many countries; and they certainly put themselves beyond its help.

As he started towards Mesara, a shadow rose from the ground—at one moment part of the track, the next a black shape at the side of the path. Munro's hand moved for his gun.

But there was no need. The figure waited, motionless,

and Munro saw a young man in a black cape, one of the
nomads now moving through these hills. Munro was going
to give him a greeting and go on his way, but the young
man held up a hand. He was smiling, showing he was
friendly. "Out late for a lad of your age," said Munro non-
sensically. The young man held something, offering it to
Munro. Munro took it, puzzled. It was an ordinary
playing-card. Someone had written on it with a piece of
charred wood. Munro read his own name "Peter Munro."
The young man smiled and nodded. He moved down the
track, waving to Munro to follow. Everything was clear to
Munro. He had been expected to pass this way, and the
playing-card was the only sign he required.

The young man beckoned to Munro and they started
down, zigzagging between rocks. The descent was steep,
but the man ahead kept going with the ease of a goat. He
halted to let Munro catch up, then on he went again.
Munro looked at the stars to get his bearings. Clearly they
were not going to Mesara. They had turned off the track
and were heading away from the main road, closer to the
frontier. They could, in fact, be over it now by Munro's
reckoning. Munro knew the little gun under his left arm
was no more than a token defense, but it gave him some
assurance.

The valley curved under steep cliffs, opening to form a
small basin. The ground under their feet had more soil in
it. Munro noted that they were still going north. A kilo-
meter one way or the other in this area could be signifi-
cant; they might be one side of the political world, or the
other. Not that Munro gave a damn for their politics, but
he cared for his own safety. Suddenly the darkness ahead
was lit by a score of fires, with an army of figures, coming
and going, shadows leaping and shrinking on the rocks.
The night was full of the bleating of animals, the sound of
cattle bells. Munro followed the man to one of the fires.
The figures around it rose. Munro had seen these black-
caped nomads often before, but in this place they were
transformed. This was their home, a setting that had not
changed in a thousand years.

A powerful old man with a huge moustache greeted

173

them. He took the playing-card from the man who had brought Munro. This seemed to be valuable to him. He looked at Munro, and pointed at the writing on the card. He spoke in a dialect that even a Greek would have found difficult to understand, but Munro knew what he meant.

Munro nodded and pointed to himself. "That's me," he said. "Now where's the girl?"

They had no idea what he was talking about.

The old man bowed and pointed to a place at the fire. Munro spoke in Greek, "Look," he said, "let's get on with it. Who wants me here? Where's the girl? The English girl?"

They looked at him blankly. The old man spoke to his companions. One of them hurried away. Bowls of food were being carried towards them from a beehive-shaped hut on the fringe of the firelight. He could make no sense of this. He was a guest at this camp-fire! He shrugged his shoulders and sat. The old man sat beside him, then the other men took their places. The food was handed around. Munro hadn't thought he was hungry, but he ate. He drank also from the big jars of wine, and the flames leapt up and warmed him. They had roasted goat—it was a special occasion. It occurred to him that he was the occasion. They had known he was coming. They had prepared this in his honor. It also occurred to him that killing a goat was a sacrificial gesture. It wasn't too late, he could still get up and walk away. None of these clansmen would have stopped him.

He was still eating when the young man appeared at the fire. There was a hurried conference. They looked towards Munro. The feast was over, but they waited for him to finish.

The old man stood up and indicated to Munro he was to follow; then he went off through the camp with Munro close behind. It seemed especially dark when they left the firelight. The old man moved at a more sedate pace than his young kinsman, and Munro kept with him. They crossed the valley covered with thornbush. In the light of the moon, coming and going behind clouds, Munro could see an expanse of plateau, undulating into the night.

They went over rough terrain for about an hour, and Munro knew he was out of Greece. "Well out," he thought grimly.

At one time he could see, away to the east, a sheet of water, and he remembered the big lakes that lay between Greece, Albania, and Yugoslavia. Which country he was in he couldn't fathom, and he was beginning not to care. They dipped down into a grassy valley about midnight, and for the first time saw signs of people—a sprinkle of buildings on the hillside, and a village ahead.

They struck a track on the other side of the village, where the going was easier. Munro was beginning to think of taking a rest when he saw lights on the road. The old man pulled him to the side, and they kept out of sight while the truck lumbered past. Munro watched grimly. The driver was in uniform; a couple of men were singing, and the language wasn't Greek.

The old man started off again. Munro stopped him. "Where are we?" he asked in Greek. The old man pretended not to understand, and Munro cursed him in English. About a half mile further on, they stopped again. They were outside a big farm, a mud and stone wall surrounding the buildings. The old man went up to double iron gates and pushed them. They were locked, and a bell started to ring. Munro heard men shouting, and a couple of soldiers came hurrying out, pulling on jackets, carrying rifles. It took all his willpower not to turn and run. He knew these uniforms well.

He realized he was shaking. He stood against the wall to recover. It was the old nightmare all over again. It couldn't be real! No one but a lunatic would court such disaster twice in a lifetime. Yet he was here, and the soldiers were shouting as they unlocked the gate. The old man motioned to Munro, and he went in. He had an odd feeling of watching himself from above. He was not quite orientated within his own body. The gate was locked behind them. God! It was the sound of a cell door closing. Munro couldn't think why he didn't scream.

The soldiers hurried ahead. They showed no signs of sur-

175

prise. It was as if this charade had been rehearsed, expected, Munro playing a part.

The place had indeed been a farmhouse, but now a flag hung over the door. A man in a white jacket waited, standing aside for Munro and the old man. Once inside Munro was ushered one way, and the old man another.

The man in the white jacket, self-important, unsmiling, said "Please" in English. They went down a wide corridor. Munro sniffed the air. There was a smell of disinfectant about the place. They passed a couple of doors. It reminded Munro of a hospital. A nurse came out of a room—it *was* a hospital! Munro was swept with panic. Was Susan here? He was appalled. He followed the man blindly. A door opened ahead into a small room. There were four beds against the walls, but three were empty. The fourth was partly obscured by a screen. A figure lay under the sheet. Munro's heart pounded!

Two men stood at the foot of the bed, looking at the figure behind the screen. Both turned as he came in. One said, "Mr. Munro?" inquiringly. Munro didn't answer. He was too terrified to speak. What in God's name had happened? He pushed past to the foot of the bed. The figure was partly obscured by plaster casts. Arms, shoulders, neck. But he had no difficulty in recognizing the face. Unreality shook Munro: he couldn't speak. The face above the plaster smiled. An old, familiar smile. The same charm, same wry amusement. "Hullo, Munro," said Stephan Aroso. He lifted an arm, partly covered in plaster. Munro didn't know what he was doing as he took it. Stephan's grip, though faint, was real . . .

13

Susan had insisted on going back to the villa. Cecil objected. "You can't possibly stay the night there by yourself."

"I prefer it," she told him.

He walked up the steep path with her.

"Someone may see you," she said bitterly.

Cecil was his cheerful self again. "It doesn't really matter," he said, "Munro will be there by now."

"Would it mean anything to you if he got shot?" she asked him. The thought of Munro getting killed haunted her.

"Of course it would," he said indignantly. "An excellent fellow. Got the courage of a lion, and thinks fast."

"That won't help him," she said grimly.

"My dear young lady, this is a totally different operation. I can't see anyone taking a crack at Munro. They have contacted him for one of two reasons. In neither case is he in danger."

She knew he was lying.

Cecil looked around the empty villa. "Are you sure you want to be here alone?"

"What have I to be afraid of now?" she asked him.

"Very well. Let me help you to pack."

"What for?"

"You know about the arrangement for tomorrow?"

"I have to stay until we know about Peter."

"My dear, your assignment is over. There's no reason for you to stay."

"I'm staying," she said.

Cecil said coldly, "You go in the morning as scheduled."

She walked to the bedroom and locked the door. A few moments later he could be heard walking down the path.

She looked at herself in the mirror with bitterness. She began to write to Sir John, a letter of resignation. But she couldn't sit still—getting up, walking about. Then she tried to pack her bag, and cried as she did so. She was still crying when she heard someone outside.

"Who is it?"

"Me." It was Yanni's voice. She opened the door. It was a relief to see him. He asked her, "Why has Mr. Munro gone to Mesara?"

She didn't know how to tell him. "You have worked for the Travelers before," she said. "You know they don't take anyone into their confidence."

"Of course I know," said Yanni. "They tell no more than they need. That is the best thing, then if a man is caught he can reveal only very little."

"Or nothing at all," said Susan.

"Nothing?"

"Nothing. If what he believes is the assignment is *not* the assignment, then the agent would know nothing."

Yanni frowned. He wasn't sure he understood. "What I had to do," he said, "was simple. To look after you and Mr. Munro."

"And be a little clumsy about it," she said.

"Clumsy?" He was startled that she knew that.

"To leak a little information about him. To indicate he was here for a special reason, that I was an excuse for him to be back."

Yanni looked at her, and flushed slightly. "I did not know Mr. Munro when I took those instructions," he said. "When I knew him, I did not like to carry them out."

"But you did?"

"I had orders."

"To suggest that Peter was here for what reason?"

"I didn't know. Just some other possibility. I am sorry, Miss Marsh."

"That's not my name," said Susan. Yanni goggled at her. "I am not engaged to Peter."

Yanni couldn't believe that.

178

"I told you," said Susan, "they don't tell you the whole story, and what they do tell you is a lie."

"What is the truth?" asked Yanni.

She hesitated.

Yanni saw she had been packing. "You are going?"

She nodded.

"Didn't you care for him?"

"I loved him," she said.

"Why has he gone to Mesara?"

She sat on the edge of the bed and told him. His big eyes gazed at her. "What do you think will happen?" she asked.

Yanni had no doubts. "They will kill him."

Munro sat at the foot of Stephan's bed and drank whiskey. An explosion had gone off in his head. He had stopped thinking.

"That's my medicine," said Stephan. Awkward in plaster, he poured Munro another glass, spilling a little.

Munro found it hard to focus. The room swam; the lights were too bright. "You were shot to pieces," he said. He had a vision of the bridge, Stephan clinging to it. He stared at the figure in bed.

"You don't think it's me," said Stephan.

"You *have* to be dead," said Munro.

The two other men left the room. "Doctors," said Stephan. "They did a good job—nearly two years ago, now. But this is my first long journey, so they came."

"What sort of state are you in?" asked Munro.

"As good as new," Stephan grinned.

"What's this place?" Munro looked around the room.

"Some sort of nursing-home. For special cases. Or very important people."

"Which are you?"

"Both."

"Can you walk?"

"Why?"

"Got to get you out of here."

He could see Stephan's eyes light up. "You don't change much. In fact, you don't change at all."

"Oh yes," Munro nodded soberly, "I've changed . . . How far can you walk?"

And then the full force of what had happened swept over Munro. Stephan Aroso was alive! The one man for whom he had respect and affection, who had been fused with him in times of danger. Together they had suffered and sweated, shared alarms, fears—and triumphs, with alarms over and enemies outwitted. Then they had celebrated, got drunk, found women. Like men after a battle. He had identified with Stephan—like a younger brother, or part of himself. When Stephan died, that part of Munro had died.

Now the old intoxication flooded back. They were throwing down gauntlets left and right, to East and West. Cavaliers who could take on the world! The explosion in his head still echoed. The whiskey melted into the warmth of his feelings. "I might have known you wouldn't die that easy," said Munro.

They poured more drinks, knocking them back, not a word said. But they were giving a toast . . . to their own immortality, invulnerability, the illusions of the young that death is not for them. In more sober mood, Munro would have seen the folly of this, for he was no longer as young as he had been two years before. In that short time, the rings around his heart, like those around the trunk of a tree, had etched in an unconscionable number of winters.

But at this moment nothing seemed real; nothing serious. Life was like a comic strip. They could get killed—as Stephan had been killed—and, as he had done, come alive again. What more proof did one need of their indestructibility? The feeling engendered a recklessness in Munro. "Let's make a run for it," he said.

"This place is bugged," said Stephan.

"You're sure?"

"Bound to be."

"Right. Here we go."

Munro stamped his feet on the floor as though he were running. Then he stopped and listened. The place was silent. Nothing moved. Stephan lay on the bed, smiling. Munro's was a joke from a time long past.

"I don't understand what you're doing or why you're here, Munro, but it's great to see you."

Munro was looking around the room for bugging devices. "Light bracket; water pipes." He knew the patterns of old. "Probably the ventilator." Somewhere someone was sitting with a tape-recorder, noting all they said. How painstaking and foolish, thought Munro. He turned to Stephan. "I just came over the frontier."

"From Greece?"

"Of course!"

"When?"

"Last night." Then Munro glanced at his watch. "This morning." He looked at Stephan. "How about you?"

"They brought me here two days ago."

"Where from?"

"Germany."

That puzzled Munro. "East Germany?"

"Of course. That's where they did this job." Stephan indicated the casing around him.

Munro was still working out the puzzle. "They brought you here?"

"Yes."

"Why?"

"Search me," said Stephan.

"Did you know I was in Greece?"

"How could I?"

"They might have told you." Munro gestured to include the villa.

"How would they know?"

"It was in the papers."

Stephan started laughing softly. "Don't make me laugh. It hurts my ribs."

"It was in the German papers."

That stopped Stephan laughing. "Why was it?"

"Someone thinks it's important," said Munro.

Gradually the outside world was oozing back into his consciousness. They would have to come to terms with reality; this splendid moment of reunion couldn't be indefinitely prolonged. There was a cold morning to face in the Albanian hills.

"Where are we exactly?" asked Stephan. "How close to our old escape route?"

"Too bloody close," said Munro.

Stephan put down his glass. "Well, what are you doing here?" he asked. Munro was on the point of telling him, but he stopped—suddenly sobered. What could he say? That he was with Stephan's wife in Greece? Making love to her? Loving her? Planning to keep things that way? What did you tell an old friend when you wanted his wife? "It's a long story," said Munro.

There was a chill in the room, but perhaps it was the first taste of dawn. A breath of wind from the snows to the north-east. Munro sensed that some magic was vanishing. There was some hard accounting to be done. All puzzles had an answer. The bits and pieces of a jig-saw picture were accumulating in his hand—perhaps he and Stephan could put them together. But he was sad about one thing. He could no longer be totally honest with Stephan. He would be unable to tell him about Susan. For the first time he would have to be wary of what he said—to edit his thoughts. Some of the bubble evaporated at that moment.

Something else was making Munro uneasy. He couldn't quite pinpoint it.

"Keep it till the morning," said Stephan.

"What?"

"The long story."

Munro lay down on one of the beds, and expected to sleep; but he couldn't rid himself of one vivid picture—the bridge! His old nightmare. The men at the far end, Stephan staggering to the parapet, clinging to it, covered with blood. Suddenly Munro realized that was the vision that so disturbed him! Stephan *had* to be dead!

A nurse put a tray on Stephan's bed as Munro woke. She looked startled, Stephan reassured her, and she hurried out.

"She's bringing your breakfast," said Stephan. "Nobody told her we had guests."

The nurse came back with a pot of coffee. Munro drank some quickly.

He felt edgy in the light of day. He had slept with his

jacket on, needing to feel the gun against him. Moments of panic shook him.

"The whiskey's finished," said Stephan. "Things look different in the morning." He could read thoughts, Munro told himself. Better not think about his wife.

"You were going to tell me," said Stephan, "why you are here?"

Munro took his jacket off and washed at a sink. He wondered why he kept his gun hidden from Stephan. He didn't seem to trust anyone now. Perhaps he was paranoiac.

He drank the rest of the coffee after he dressed. Anything to delay examining reality too closely.

"I came here looking for someone," he said.

Stephan said nothing, motionless under the plaster cast.

"For a girl," said Munro, "she disappeared from the place we were staying." He sensed Stephan's eyes on him. Munro got the feeling he didn't believe him.

"What girl?" asked Stephan.

"I'm engaged to," said Munro. He stirred his coffee: the spoon seemed to make a loud noise.

"Engaged? What do you mean? You're married."

"You know how it is," said Munro, "my wife got tired of waiting."

"I see," Stephan sounded as though he were working it out. "You got divorced. This is some other girl?"

"That's how it goes."

"And this girl disappeared?" Stephan looked across at Munro.

"Yes. She vanished. There were a couple of men watching me. They've been around since I arrived in these parts."

"That doesn't surprise me," said Stephan. "What did you come back for?"

"This girl wanted to . . ." Munro broke off. He couldn't tell Stephan that the girl wanted to see the place he had died. What could he say? "She wanted to meet Rhodes. She's doing a thesis on poetry. They had sessions together."

Stephan grinned at him. "Munro! Don't give me that! The girl was a cover to get you back. Who did you think you were fooling?"

"I wasn't fooling anyone."

"I'm surprised to find you working for Cecil again."

"That's the last thing I'd do," said Munro.

"Peter . . ." Stephan seldom called him that, except in mockery, "my dear Peter. Are you concerned about the unseen listeners?" He indicated hidden microphones.

"I don't work for the Travelers. I sit by the seaside at Eastbourne. I watch the tide go out, and I watch the tide come in."

Stephan laughed. "I told you. No laughs! My bones are sore."

Munro remembered winter by the English Channel. The picture he gave of himself seemed ludicrous now. Stephan was right to disbelieve it.

"What are you going to tell them?" asked Stephan.

"Tell who?"

"These people," said Stephan, "they're going to ask questions."

Munro had been thinking about that.

"You can't just say you strayed over the border," said Stephan.

"No?"

"Anyone but you," Stephan grinned. The danger of the situation was obvious.

Munro repeated. "I came to look for this girl."

"They don't hold with romance in this part of the world," Stephan reminded him. "A woman is a commodity. It isn't so long since they stopped wearing the veil."

"This man Vilaras . . . the man who's been watching me . . . he gave me the route to follow. I was picked up by nomads. One of them brought me here."

"As simple as that?" Stephan looked amused.

"So they must know where Susan is."

"Susan?"

The name had slipped out. There was no going back on it. But he didn't get the question from Stephan he expected. "This girl vanished? Then you got instructions that brought you here?"

"That's it."

"They kidnapped the girl to get you?"

184

"That's all I can think of," said Munro.

"What for?" asked Stephan. He was waiting for the answer. It seemed important to him. Why? thought Munro.

"I've no bloody idea," he said.

Stephan nodded towards the ventilator and winked. He didn't believe Munro and he knew no one else would.

One of the doctors came in. He greeted Stephan, then signaled to Munro. An orderly stood in the doorway. "Please go with him," said the doctor.

"Good luck," Stephan called.

They went down the corridor, around a corner, and stopped at a door; the orderly knocked. Someone called. The orderly showed Munro in.

He recognized the man behind the desk. It was Dejes, the official who had been at Karlovo.

"You are causing us a lot of trouble, Mr. Munro," said Dejes.

"How's Major Pec nowadays," said Munro.

Dejes lifted a hand to dismiss anything frivolous.

"Why do you come back into our country?"

"I'm regretting every minute of it," said Munro cheerfully.

"It is a violation," said Dejes. He was marking time. No accusations.

"I was looking for someone," admitted Munro.

This didn't surprise Dejes. "Mr. Munro. We would have expected you to look for your fiancée. But your fiancée is not missing. She is perfectly safe with your employer."

That shook Munro. "With whom?"

Dejes didn't want to play games. "We are old hands as you, Mr. Munro. Let's waste no time. She is with Mr. Cecil."

"Is this true?" asked Munro. He didn't know whether to be relieved or angry.

"Yes. We have reports from Vilaras. You know about him?"

Munro nodded. "He told me how to get here. I thought you had Susan."

"No," said Dejes. "But you still come as Vilaras tells you. This was not necessary. We have no power, nothing to make you come. But you still come . . . Why, Mr. Munro?"

Munro couldn't work that one out. "She had disappeared," he said.

"She is still in the village, Mr. Munro. At the villa."

Munro was aware they were both looking at each other blankly. Dejes went on. "Who is taking the tricks in this game, Mr. Munro?"

"I wish I knew," said Munro. He was thinking very fast.

"You have come into Albania unlawfully," Dejes reminded him. "You are a known spy."

"How's that for an understatement!" said Munro. His smile had no mirth in it. "I am the most known spy in the world."

"A very good basis on which to function," said Dejes. "Everyone will dismiss you as harmless. A good cover?"

"That would be smart," admitted Munro. He began to wonder how close to the truth Dejes might be. Had he been working for Cecil? And if he had, what had he been doing? The possibility fascinated him.

Dejes went on. "We want to know why you came to Greece. Why you came back to Karlovo. Why Cecil found the matter so important as to come and see you. What did you expect to learn?"

"I'm retired," said Munro. "I came out here as a courier. I was with this girl-friend of mine. She wanted to meet . . ."

Dejes held up his hand again. He was weary of this story. "Mr. Munro. You could be back on trial, I can only deal if you cooperate. Otherwise everything goes to higher authorities."

Munro did not like the sound of that.

Dejes went on. "Nobody wants you back in our country. You embarrass us."

"Fair enough," said Munro, "I could go out the way I came."

Dejes seemed to plead with him. "All I ask is a little honesty, Mr. Munro. Please do not suppose you can bluff yourself out of this. I am glad to help you—to close the incident—but only if you tell us what you are doing."

186

Munro was going to speak. Dejes stopped him. "No stories, that will only delay things. One fact. Why are you here?"

Yanni insisted on talking to Cecil. He didn't care what time it was. If Cecil wouldn't see him, then Yanni would telephone the Athens newspapers. His eyes had lost their sleepy depths. "I will make it so hot for you . . ." he said.

"Don't go on," said Cecil, "you're seeing me now." He walked up and down in his dressing-gown, angry with Yanni, angry with the girl who must have told Yanni something he didn't need to know. "You did not tell me what would happen to Mr. Munro," he said. His loyalty had been abused. Cecil's calm did not comfort nor reassure him.

"I'll tell you the worst," said Cecil. "If we are totally wrong in our calculations, then Munro will land up in Albania with the locals amazed to see him. We'll suggest another exchange, and they'll send him back again."

Yanni was about to protest again.

Cecil interrupted. "Mr. Yanni, you have done what was required of you. You are now free to return to Athens. In fact, I insist on it."

"You don't think what happens to him," said Yanni. "You will find what you want to know—and that is sufficient for you. Mr. Munro is no use to you and Sir John. You have him like a goat tied to a tree."

"A goat?" That puzzled Cecil, impatient as he was to hurry the man away.

"A goat," said Yanni, "to catch tigers! Or you make him a pawn to sacrifice, so you are in a good position." He felt murderous towards Cecil. He knew he had helped to trap Munro.

Cecil knew that Yanni would make trouble for him if he let him go without putting his conscience at rest. Below his breath he cursed the Greek. He would never again employ him. But he had to give the man his due, he had been ideal for this job.

"For your information, Yanni," he told him, "Vilaras and that friend of his intended to kidnap Miss Marsh."

"I know," Yanni shrugged. That was not important. He could have handled those two.

"They intended to use her to induce Munro over the frontier. And that is exactly what's happened." He spread his hands and smiled.

"They did not find her," persisted Yanni.

"Exactly." Cecil seemed to be agreeing with him. "We knew what was planned. So we saved Miss Marsh an unpleasant experience."

"That made no difference. Mr. Munro thought they had taken her, so he did as they said."

"That wasn't our doing, Yanni. You can't be blamed for that."

Yanni was angry. "Of course it's my fault. All the fuss we make, the things you do! That made it seem he was back for his old spying."

"If people want to draw that conclusion . . ."

"It's as you intended."

Enough was enough, Cecil decided. He did not usually spend time on his subordinates. Normally he had no connection with agents. "You will have to go now," he said sharply. "Munro has every chance. The only danger I see for him is if anyone is foolish enough to intrude, or do anything to alarm the opposition."

Yanni looked at him blankly. Frustration welled up inside him. There was nothing he could do to help Munro, and by his reckoning Munro was going to need a lot of help.

It was the very blank look in the eyes of the man opposite that decided Munro. Dejes wasn't playing a part, he was genuinely at a loss. Munro worked on instinct, and instinct told him that they would both have to trust each other a little.

"We stand to lose a lot," said Munro. "You could lose face; I could lose my life."

Dejes protested. "It would not be so bad."

"I could be in a cell for another year or two," said Munro.

Dejes shrugged, but said nothing.

"So let's get this straight," Munro was thinking aloud, careful what he said. "You meant to kidnap Miss Marsh and use her to get me here."

Dejes didn't deny it. "We know you are living together. You must care for her."

Munro nodded. "I care for her."

"But the girl vanished. It is almost as though she knew what we intended. Then she appears at the villa again." Dejes was frowning. "One must ask where she was? With Mr. Cecil? Did he arrange it? Is she part of his organization?"

"Cecil wouldn't need her help," said Munro coldly.

Dejes went on. "You thought she had been kidnapped; so you take advice from Vilaras and come here." He looked thoughtfully at Munro. "That is very odd."

"Why?"

"No one stopped you. Cecil didn't warn you. They let you come back over the frontier where it could be dangerous. Do you think Cecil is betraying you?"

"I always think that," said Munro.

"This time?"

Munro couldn't say anything. He didn't know.

"Why didn't the girl stop you?" asked Dejes.

Munro felt his skin prickle. He couldn't follow the reasoning, but he had a sudden sense of a vast betrayal—more than he could stomach. "Now look here . . ."

"Don't be angry. This is a puzzle we can solve only if we are honest with each other."

It sounded like a conspiracy between the two of them. Susan was under suspicion—as were all people and things, familiar, safe and sure.

"I know there are things you won't tell me, Mr. Munro, as there are things I won't tell you. But if we look at what you have done since you came to Athens you will see the problem."

"Let's start a little earlier," said Munro sharply. "Let's start with the phoney Group-Captain and that Intelligence set-up."

Dejes nodded. "Yes. That was ours."

"But why?"

"We wanted to know the truth of a rumor."

Munro could hardly believe it. "You knew I was coming back here?"

"We thought so."

"That isn't possible! I hadn't made up my mind. No one could have known."

"I think your friends were confident. We had to be sure."

"Then you got the wrong answer," said Munro.

"Yes." Dejes made no pretense about it.

"I'm seeing a new side of you, Mr. Dejes," said Munro drily. "You and I are playing fair. Too fair. One of us must be preparing the big cheat."

Dejes spread his hands. "If I knew how to cheat I would."

Munro thought fast. What could have alerted Dejes and his friends while Munro was still in London? While he was still in Eastbourne, for that matter.

Dejes was ahead of him. "Somewhere there was bad security. Or . . ." The little man hesitated. "Or perhaps someone was drawing attention to you."

"Who would bother?"

"That's just what we're finding out," said Dejes. He began to make notes. "In Athens there is no real security. Yanni is a known agent."

Munro took up his reasoning. "Oh yes, Munro's back in town, pretending to be engaged to a pretty girl."

"Pretending?"

Munro realized he'd have to be careful. "A lot of people know I'm still married."

"Then who is she?" said Dejes.

"You said it yourself," Munro told him, "she's a girl I care about."

Dejes didn't look convinced, but he went on. "Then you came north to Professor Rhodes. You can imagine this intrigued us."

"I can imagine," said Munro.

"But that is not all. You go to the bridge, to the edge of our country. The mind reels at what you are doing."

The thought made Munro's own mind reel. The memory of an insane journey!

"She wanted to see where it happened."

"What?"

"The shooting." He had to phrase it carefully. "Where I could have been killed."

"Miss Marsh?"

"Yes."

"Is she always so morbid?"

Munro didn't answer. Sooner or later he knew he would have to say who she was, and face Stephan.

"So," went on Dejes, making notes, "you measure things, you examine the bridge. You bring the girl into the village."

"That's not how I remember it." Munro had a clear vision of that moment.

"No?"

"She crossed; I followed."

Dejes didn't think that important. "You both come over."

Munro wiped his hands. The vision had made him tremble.

"Why?" asked Dejes.

"I must have been mad."

"You take many risks to find out something, Mr. Munro."

"Wrong deduction," said Munro grimly.

The phone rang on the desk. Dejes picked it up. He listened for a moment. When he put the phone down he asked Munro, "How long have you known Miss Marsh?"

Munro wasn't ready for that one. "Not very long."

"A week? A year?"

"Three or four months."

"You have formed a very close relationship in a short time," said Dejes.

"Things happen that way," said Munro.

"Where did you first meet?"

"I saw her in Eastbourne." That was true enough.

"What do you know of her background?"

"Where's this getting us?" asked Munro.

"You don't know her very well?" suggested Dejes.

Munro wondered how well he knew her.

The phone rang again. Dejes replied, then he looked up at Munro.

"Thank you, Mr. Munro." The interview was abruptly over. Dejes called and the orderly opened the door. Munro went with him to the ward. He felt excited—as though he were on the verge of understanding everything. The solution was almost in his grasp. It just needed an insight. But insight was like inspiration, or love, or magic. It might present itself at any time, but not to order.

There was no one in the ward, but a few minutes later a nurse pushed in an invalid chair.

"Hi!" called out Stephan. "What's the verdict?"

Munro had a great longing to blurt out the truth about Susan. It weighed on him. God knows how Stephan would take it. But it had to be done. "They want to know about the girl," he said, "how long I've known her. All that stuff."

"Routine," said Stephan. The nurse had wheeled him to the window. It was all so relaxed that Munro had to remind himself where they were.

"They had someone else on the end of a microphone, listening."

"Well, of course," said Stephan.

The nurse poured two glasses of colorless liquid, and went out of the room. Stephan handed one to Munro.

"Isn't it too early in the morning?" asked Munro.

"Never too early." Stephan drank. Munro followed suit. It seemed easier to talk after that.

"I told them the cover story about the girl."

"So she *was* a cover?"

"No. I was the cover."

Stephan looked puzzled. Munro noticed that some of the bandage had been removed. He didn't appear marked or scarred.

Munro went on. "She wanted to visit this area. I thought you'd be on to it immediately."

Stephan still looked blank.

"You know her name?"

"Susan?"

"Dejes knows her last name, the one she's been using. They haven't told you?"

Something told Munro that there was more wrong than he suspected. He went on. "The name on her passport is Marsh. Susan Marsh."

There wasn't a flicker of response from Stephan.

"Doesn't that mean anything to you?"

Stephan shook his head. "Should it?"

"She's your wife," said Munro.

The whole building took a moment to recover from that one. Stephan put his glass down, his eyes on Munro, incredulous. Unseen listeners froze over recording-tapes.

"Peter," said Stephan gently, "I'm not married."

Munro had guessed what was to come, a split second earlier. The insight he had asked for had been granted, and he wished it hadn't. Stephan went on. "I never heard of anyone called Susan Marsh. You would have known. You knew about me . . ." Perhaps he sensed the shock Munro suffered; he was being more than gentle.

Munro said nothing. The implications were bitter. Stephan passed the bottle to him. "Have another. You've been taken for a ride."

During the time they had worked together, they had dovetailed as a team. As one had flagged, the other had supplied the drive, operating in a self-adjusting fashion, sensing what was required in times of crisis. It was like that at this moment. Stephan sat at the table, quietly. Munro stood, faculties ticking over slowly, doggedly working things out. The equation was coming down to a manageable size. He was beginning to guess what X would equal. There was a dry taste in his mouth, he felt sick. It was impossible to believe the truth.

"Why did Cecil need to saddle me with a wife?" Stephan asked him.

"To bring her here," said Munro. "She wanted to see where you died, and I was the only person who could show her."

"You agreed?"

"I came around to it."

"You didn't smell a rat?"

"Many rats. But I fell for the girl."

"My wife?" Stephan grinned.

"You were dead," said Munro.

"I was forgetting."

They had another drink, and the bad taste began to go.

"They knew I wouldn't lift a finger to help them, so they set up the one drama that might get under my skin. I had to do your widow a good turn." He was seeing things clearly, objectively, no trace of bitterness. That could come later. For the time being he had to re-create Cecil's plan. Or was it Sir John's plan? It was more intricate than Cecil's usual operation.

Stephan sat motionless, absorbed.

"When we left, she told me our cover was that she and I were engaged."

"Why?"

"To avoid unpleasant publicity. 'Mrs. Stephan Aroso goes back to see where her husband the spy died.' "

"A bit thin," said Stephan.

"It is, when you think about it. But I went along with it at the time. Perhaps I wanted to be with her more than I knew."

"They went to a lot of bother to get you out here, didn't they?"

"More than I thought." Munro was amazed to uncover the machinations that had gone into the plan. What could be the prize that Cecil and Sir John hoped for? Why all this careful preparation, this elaborate and artful design? Nothing that Munro had ever had to handle for the Travelers was worth this endeavor.

"What's it all about?" asked Stephan.

"I'm still working it out," said Munro. "From the moment I got here, they made sure it leaked. No doubt about it, everyone knew about it. I was back picking up the pieces of an old job."

"Which one in particular?"

"Just like Dejes says, I was back measuring the bridge—going to the graveyard; cables passing back and forward, all in code. The Aroso code, Stephan. Your code. Oh yes, they put it together nicely. I was working on our last operation."

"But what?"

"God knows. Something must have come to light."

"What could that be?"

"I've been out of touch," Munro said. "In jail in Tiranë then solitude in Eastbourne."

"Why rake over old ashes?" mused Stephan.

"No idea," said Munro. He glanced out of the window. Uniformed guards patrolled the stretch of land between the buildings and the surrounding wall. Somewhere in a corner of his mind nagging suspicions began to come to life.

But Stephan persisted. "And nothing's happened while you've been here? You still don't know what they were after?"

"Nothing's happened," said Munro.

Stephan hesitated, then he said, "One thing's happened. We're back in partnership."

Munro absorbed that. "They wouldn't know about that."

"Why not?"

"They don't know about you."

"Let's just suppose," said Stephan, "suppose that Cecil wanted to contact me."

"He thinks you're dead."

"On what evidence?"

Munro frowned. "On mine."

"Suppose he didn't believe you?"

"Why shouldn't he?"

"He could have reasons."

Munro shook his head. "I told them I saw you cut to pieces."

"You told them that?"

Munro nodded. "After the exchange I made a report. I was so sure you were dead they had to believe me."

"All right," Stephan gave way. "Suppose later on Cecil began to wonder if I *was* really dead."

"Why should he?"

"We're just supposing. A hypothesis. To see if anything takes shape. Suppose they guessed I might be alive—and they wanted to be sure . . . what could they do?"

195

"Send an agent to look for you."

"But where? I could be anywhere."

"A needle in a haystack," admitted Munro.

"But if they were clever," said Stephan, "they could get Stephan Aroso to reveal himself. They send Peter Munro—and Stephan Aroso is so intrigued to learn that his old partner is gallivanting all over their ancient stamping-ground that he can't resist the temptation, the excitement, of taking the bait, rising to the surface . . . Cecil is fishing with an irresistible fly!"

Munro had the impression he was being hypnotized. Every word Stephan said held him motionless.

"Bait?" said Munro softly.

"It's just supposing," said Stephan.

But Munro knew at that moment that, give or take five percent, making allowances for errors and omissions, all Stephan said was true. Amongst all the other emotions that crowded in on him, there was one of admiration. The very intricacy of Cecil's logic. "He guessed you might be alive?" Munro reasoned it out carefully. "If you *were*, then his best chance of confirmation was to have me back in the district. Making it look as though I were picking up old threads?"

"Something like that." Stephan was watching him.

"Then everyone begins to wonder what I'm doing. It might be something important. Intelligence over here needs to know. Dejes and his friends try to frighten me off."

"Did they?"

"Yes. They got nervous. Perhaps they supposed the Travelers—me, Cecil—knew something about them. Now Dejes is alarmed: something big is at stake. So they decide to get me here for questioning?"

It was all a speculation, but growing, putting flesh on its bones, becoming more credible.

"The trouble is, you don't know very much. You don't know how you're being used. Cecil hasn't taken you into his confidence—only the girl, Miss Marsh, seems to know the facts. She's been the means whereby they got you here. She helped Cecil to find out what he wanted to know."

"Spell it out," said Munro.

"They want to know for certain if I'm alive." Munro

196

didn't follow. Stephan seemed to see it very clearly. "It's so important to them, they create this elaborate charade. You had to be tricked, a complicated trick, with everyone playing at least two parts. Did she appear to care for you?"

Munro couldn't bring himself to answer that one. At that moment he hated the girl.

"Are you going to help them?"

Munro was quite pale. He shook his head.

There was a telephone in the ward. It began ringing. Stephan picked it up, listened, then handed it to Munro.

"It's for you."

The timing was just a little too fast for Munro to keep pace. Nothing that happened was entirely real.

"Munro here," he said into the phone.

"Peter . . . Peter . . . thank God you're all right."

He didn't believe it was her at first.

"Who is it?"

"Susan. Where are you, darling?"

He didn't answer. It was so moving to hear her.

"Peter . . . Can you hear me?"

"Why did you do it, Susan—" he asked.

She sounded as if she were crying.

"I'm sorry, Peter. I didn't know you when I started. I didn't want to go on. They said you'd be safe . . . Are you still there?"

He said, "Goodbye, Susan."

"Peter, Peter! I'm sorry." She sounded in despair, but by now he had good reason to know she was an excellent actress. He could hear another voice in the background. Then Cecil came on the phone. "Hello, Munro." It was incredible he should sound so cheerful. "We've been kept hanging on for this call of yours for ages. Anything wrong that end?"

"What's the program, Cecil?"

"Don't worry old boy. We'll get you out . . . everything all right?" Cecil was urging him to give some indication.

"Just get me out," said Munro.

He was putting the phone down as Cecil called, "Any news?" Just before the receiver went down, the phone went dead. Someone else had cut the line.

"Well, they didn't learn much," said Stephan.

They sent for Munro a few minutes later. Dejes went through the phone-call as a formality. The case seemed to be closed for him. Munro wondered about that vaguely, but he was too disturbed to give Dejes much thought. He couldn't hate the girl, no matter what she had done. He scarcely heard the questions Dejes put. He wondered if she *had* been crying. In a way he felt like tears himself. Life had been growing warm in her company—now that warmth had gone out of it.

"Now you know what you have been doing here?" suggested Dejes.

"Flushing out Stephan," said Munro.

"You know why this was important to them?"

Munro hadn't given it any thought.

"No," he said.

14

Susan had been crying at the sound of Munro's voice. Now she was white-faced, but with no tears. Cecil played back the telephone conversation on a tape-recorder. It came to a finish and he sat back uneasily. "I can't make anything out of that," he said. He ran it again. This time he repeated the last few seconds. "They were listening of course."

"Taping us taping them." Susan sounded very distant.

"Yes," agreed Cecil, "cutting us off I think. The line went dead as soon as I asked for news."

They were in the big room in Rhodes's villa. The old man had arrived back from hospital, and was in bed along the corridor.

"The thing is . . ." Cecil got up and moved about restlessly. "The thing is he had plenty of time to say something. He could have reacted. He might have been bitter."

"He was bitter," said Susan.

"He was bitter about us," Cecil nodded. "But he would have been bitter in a different way if he had found out about Stephan."

"If your theory's right," she said.

"Must be right," said Cecil. He stood at the window looking over the village to the hills, tapping his teeth. He went on. "They wouldn't go to the trouble of trapping him, if they didn't have Stephan."

"Wouldn't they do that anyway? Just to find out what he was up to? She was drawn willy-nilly into his calculations. She had to know what might happen to Munro.

Cecil cleared his own mind. "They must suppose he knows what he's been doing. That means Munro suspects Stephan's alive. It all points to that—in their eyes. So they'll test their theory just as soon as they can. Face to face."

It was the first time she had seen Cecil without his self-assurance. In spite of what he said, some of his omnipotence had evaporated.

"There's been time for a meeting," she said, "and he says nothing. Surely that means Stephan isn't there. Perhaps he's been dead all the time. Perhaps they really killed him on the bridge."

"I don't think so," said Cecil.

"You should be sure one way or the other by now," she said sharply.

"Why?"

"You don't suppose they are going to telephone us again!" She no longer hid her anger. "Your plan ended with Peter going. Well, he's gone. What have you learned?" Her voice rose.

They heard the old man faintly along the corridor. "You all right, girl?"

Susan went and sat by his bed. Rhodes was thinner, grayer, gaunt, a minor God hacked out of stone. He was soon asleep again.

Left by himself, Cecil poured a drink. He thought about contacting Sir John. But what could he say? That the plan had failed, Munro had been sacrificed, they were still in the dark? And what should he do about Munro? Leak the story that he had wandered back over the frontier accidentally? Very suspect. He had another quick drink. The girl was right, they ought to have solved the problem by now. Munro should have given something away—if only by inflection. But not a thing. It had been as if the man had blotted out everything except the girl's betrayal. Cecil was shaken. But he grasped at straws—perhaps Munro was holding back, consciously and deliberately giving nothing away. In that case, the information he was withholding must be the information Cecil was testing. Was Munro holding back? Was Stephan with him, just a few miles away?

"Heads will roll," said Cecil softly to his reflection. He was thinking of himself primarily, but also Sir John.

Ioannis Soüstäs, code-named Yanni, was a man much moved by his emotions. An affectionate man, never happier than when he was at one with his fellows, never happier than with his stout frame wedged into a taverna surrounded by people eating, drinking, shouting about crops, politics, or sport. Sometimes it was hard to be an agent, to play one part and long to play another.

Yanni's job was over. Cecil had paid him off, and added a small bonus. He had told Yanni to take his car, which was expected back in Athens next day.

Yanni knew a woman in the capital with whom he could get drunk and happy, and forget Munro. After all, the ethics of the business was not his concern. But when he drove out of the village, he took the mountain road that Munro had taken and headed north.

He calculated the odds as he drove into the hills. He had one possible advantage, for although he spoke slightingly about the Sarakatsans, the men in the black capes, he had known them as a boy. They pastured near his village on their travels. He could understand their dialect, and spoke it a little.

When Munro got back to the ward a nurse was making notes. Munro hadn't seen her before. She wore a badge on her uniform, and an air of importance. She peered over spectacles at him. "He has gone to the doctors," she said in English.

"Is he all right?"

"Of course. he had the best attention. Now they take some bandage."

"Take some bandage?"

"He is improving."

She left the room. Outside in the corridor Munro caught sight of a guard. They were being watched all the time, but discreetly.

The door opened and Stephan walked in. He leaned on a stick, grinning. Behind him were a couple of orderlies.

"Don't touch me." Stephan waved them away. "I can do it." He came slowly into the room.

The nurse had said he was going to lose bandages, but

Munro wasn't ready for this. He was quit of the casing around arms and shoulders.

Munro felt he was seeing a ghost, a phœnix risen from gunfire. His uneasiness grew. The sick taste was back in his mouth. There was no reason, but he was shaky with apprehension.

Stephan was triumphant. "How about that? As good as new."

Munro breathed softly, "Worth a guinea a box."

Later on, they took a stroll in the garden. No one stopped them as they went a few steps along the road.

"A little more time," said Stephan, "and we'll be down that track for the frontier."

"What about Cecil," Munro reminded him. "If he sees you he's going to start thinking."

"Like what?"

"Like he was right. You're alive."

Stephan grinned. "By that time he's too late." Munro didn't ask what he meant, and Stephan didn't explain. But Munro guessed there was another play being enacted. He wasn't quite sure what it implied, but he would find out. One thing impressed him; the ease with which Stephan walked—as if no longer concerned to keep the appearance of a man coming back from death. Careless in the performance. It no longer mattered to him.

Why? wondered Munro. What had happened? Distrust, suspicion, awareness, aspects that had served Munro so well in the past and which had been lulled of late, all whispered warnings, analyzed, detected. One insight made sense. He had spoken on the phone to Cecil, and he had not mentioned Stephan. He had left an impression that nothing as startling as Stephan's existence could have come to his attention—so no one knew. That was all that had happened. Perhaps it was enough.

It was later in the day that they saw the first of the nomads going past. Munro and Stephan watched them.

Dejes joined them. He said, "They use the mountain pass to go to the spring pasture land. It is hard to legislate for them."

"I understand your government confiscated herds of

202

more than four hundred." Munro had his attention very much on the disappearing black capes.

Dejes did not rise to Munro's bait. "All mountains are wild, Mr. Munro, you know that. These people have traditions. They are in families. Old things are important to them. As much as possible, the authorities let them be. They are disappearing anyway. Gradually they join our farms." The black capes disappeared.

"They are not important," said Dejes, "they come and go." He went back into the house.

"Thinking of making a run for it?" Stephan asked.

"You're not ready for it," said Munro.

"On your own?" said Stephan.

"What's the matter with you, Stephan?" Munro protested. "We're a team."

Stephan's smile sparkled, but like glass.

Before nightfall another small herd went past, the men calling to their animals. They took the same track as their fellows. It might as well have been signposted. Munro had recognized one of the men in the first group—he now saw him going past again. He wondered how often Yanni was going to make the trip, and how he was going to get in touch with him, in front of Dejes and the guards. Most of all in the presence of Stephan.

They had a meal together that evening, served in the ward; in silence, Stephan preoccupied; the bonhomie, effervescence, the shock of reunion, gone. It was as though they had passed some watershed in the last twenty-four hours.

"You have problems?" asked Munro. It wasn't yet the time to drop all pretense, to make accusations, or even to begin to clarify the grim suspicions. There was nothing to gain in forcing hands. Besides Munro needed time to recover, to reorientate himself. He was an animal in a trap, having lost his last defense. He knew that now. But he had to conceal what he guessed, and to talk to Stephan as though he were his friend, not his jailer.

Stephan looked at him wryly, as if to say he knew all Munro knew. But he had grace enough to keep up the pretense too. He still wore some plaster around his chest—Munro wondered why.

He seemed to go off at a tangent, but Munro understood him. "You know I was born in these parts," said Stephan.

Munro could answer equally inconsequentially, and Stephan understood. "My dear Stephan, you never did anything for a sentimental reason any more than for a mercenary one. Your motives are sensational."

"Is that the right word?" asked Stephan.

Munro nodded. "You do things for excitement, for feelings of being alive, in danger, hiding, a fox hunted. Take away those, and you sicken. The moment you get bored, you move away. Or stir it up . . . or drop a bomb."

"What do you do, Munro?"

"I'm the man who just wanted to make a living, remember? I'm the buyer and seller."

"Are you going to marry my wife?" asked Stephan.

"Do I get back alive?" asked Munro.

Stephan sat quietly over his drink. They were sharing wine as they had done often before.

"You must understand one or two things," he said gently.

"I do," said Munro.

"Once Cecil knows for certain I'm alive, then my usefulness here has gone." He indicated with a wave the world outside.

"What about . . .?" Munro did a mime of people listening to their conversation. Stephan shook his head. "You don't know my authority. I turned everything off."

"Any reason?"

Stephan gave a gesture of resignation. "There are things to be said."

Munro nodded. "Of course. Reality is never for the record."

That made Stephan smile. "That's why I have always been fond of you. Never totally predictable."

"But fairly true to type," said Munro, "or Cecil couldn't have used me. Nor anybody else."

Stephan nodded. "Cecil is in this business because he believes in it. Thinks these silly games are important. Thinks it's for the good of England, so for humanity." Stephan hesitated. "I do it for fun."

"How do you think he got on to you?" asked Munro.

204

"The Aroso code," said Stephan.

Suddenly Munro saw it. "That makes sense," he said. "He was sending messages in Aroso code about me on this trip."

"I know. I was getting them."

"Puzzle you?"

"Yes."

"So it worked?"

"What did?"

"That's why he sent them—for you. So you should know what I was up to. Or rather, what he wanted you to think I was up to."

"Oh yes. I know that now," said Stephan. "I might have guessed. All the bad security about your trip, what you did! It got more incredible. I had reports that you made measurements on the bridge."

"Where were you?"

"Further north." Stephan was still cautious. "We thought . . . my superiors thought . . . you must have been sent to check something."

"Like?"

"Like how was I killed and you weren't."

"That came up," admitted Munro.

"Were there bullet-holes on the wall? My superiors thought we might have forgotten such a detail. Did you really report me dead after they exchanged you? Was I still free to operate? Was Cecil using the Aroso code or was I interpreting material that he was just feeding me?"

"Worked it out?" asked Munro.

"Most of it."

It was in this oblique fashion that confessions were made, confessions for which Munro guessed no guilt was felt. It was sufficient for Stephan that he satisfied himself, gained his own ends. It wasn't likely he worked out the consequences to others. The consequences were going to be tough, Munro realized.

"One question," said Munro, "do you need any of that plaster?"

Stephan shook his head. "No. But you had to believe in me at that moment, or we could never have let you phone

205

Cecil. You had to be on my side because of *their* betrayal."

"I see. And not on their side because of *your* betrayal?"

That hurt Stephan. "How did I betray you?"

"Eighteen months in jail."

"They would have caught you anyway."

"Through you?"

"Besides, I arranged for your exchange."

"So that I could report your death?"

"My dear Peter, you can't have it both ways! I *did* get you home. It was Cecil and that girl of yours who brought you back."

There was no answer to that.

"What happens to me now?"

"I don't want anything to happen to you. As you said— we're a team. All the authorities here want is for you to lie low. Cecil has no proof I'm alive. It will take time to phase out Aroso code. Besides there is a backlog of information for us to work through."

"Us?"

"You could help me."

"Not my cup of tea," said Munro.

Stephan shrugged. "They're surprisingly civilized. You won't be shot in the back or anything. Cecil will be told you're rearrested. Perhaps in a year we could fix you up with another exchange." Stephan grinned. "Nothing to hurry back for, have you?"

"I'm paying rent at Shaw's Hotel," said Munro.

"What?" Stephan didn't follow.

"Eastbourne," said Munro.

They finished the wine.

"The guards would like your gun," said Stephan.

Munro wondered how far he'd get if he started shooting. He took the tiny pistol from under his arm and handed it to Stephan.

"I'm very fond of that," he said.

"I know. I'll see you get it back."

The guard tapped on the door.

"You have a room of your own," said Stephan.

Munro was glad about that. The more he thought of the way Stephan had exploited him, the more a cold anger grew. His enemies were to left and to right. Where he had given something of himself, to Stephan or the girl, they had used it as a chink in his armor. Both had abused him. He lay in the dark, telling himself that what he wanted was not revenge, but a sort of bloody justice.

15

At first light he had the nomads on their trek. Herdsmen shouted, dogs barked, he could hear goats and sheep. He also heard Yanni. Three times, to be exact. He timed the intervals. Yanni was going along the track at hourly intervals with each small group that passed. This was his one hope. Munro searched his brain how to use it. Munro was a man of some ingenuity, and his mind was much concentrated by the danger he was in, but the sun was well up before he thought of anything that gave him the ghost of a chance. Then he searched in the wastepaper-basket in his room, and in the drawers and bathroom, as there were a few things he needed. One of the nurses brought him coffee. It was the girl who spoke English, and he knew she wasn't a nurse.

"Okay if I take a walk?" he asked.

She shrugged. It didn't seem to matter. Obviously he wasn't going to get far if he tried to make a run for it.

Munro waited until he could hear the distant cries of the herdsmen. He didn't wait to identify Yanni. He knew the fat man would be there. He sauntered down the corridor, and stood at the door in the cold sunlight. The sounds of sheep were close. He was still holding his coffee-cup, sipping his drink. Everything was calculated to give the appearance of a relaxed man. He moved to the gate as though interested in the strangers driving their flock.

He knew one of the guards was suddenly interested in him, keeping him in sight, becoming alert.

Munro stepped out on to the track. Fifty or sixty yards away three men were driving a collection of sheep and goats. Munro was aware of movement in the house behind him, but he didn't look around. He knew what he had to do regardless of the risk, for Yanni was the middle man of the three, trailing a step or so behind the others. He had seen Munro, but gave no sign.

Munro waited until they were almost alongside, then he suddenly stopped drinking his coffee. He put the cup down on the ground, and shouted to the three men. "Hi! Hold on there!"

He was going to hurry across to them, when he heard Dejes call, "What is it?"

"That's the man who brought me here," said Munro. He was already moving towards the three men. They came to a stop.

"What's that, Mr. Munro?" Dejes was nervous.

"Won't be a moment," said Munro. He was walking quickly. The three men stood and watched him.

"Mr. Munro!" Dejes was giving a warning, but Munro chose not to hear. The guard came after Munro. He heard the catch come off his gun. He ignored it and began fishing in his pocket.

The guard shouted: Munro waved to him to wait, but the man broke into a run. Munro was with the nomads before the guard caught him up. One of the men was elderly, a little like the man who had guided Munro, but not the one. Munro played it very coolly. He offered the man a Greek note. "Sorry," said Munro, "that's all the currency I have—unless you want English pounds, and I don't recommend that." The man didn't follow. He took the note a little doubtfully. Munro saw he looked quickly to Yanni who nodded.

The guard was now angry. He shouted and took the note.

"Oh, come on!" protested Munro. "Give the old boy his cash. I owe it to him." He spoke louder as if to make it clear to the guard. "I owe it to him. He did me a favor."

Munro's calm unsettled the guard. Dejes called from behind. The guard called back.

"Look," shouted Munro, "I have to give him something." He took the note out of the guard's hand as if he had authority, and handed it back to the old man. Then he turned to the guard. "Any cigarettes?" he asked.

The guard was ready to be angry again, but this puzzled him.

"Cigarettes," shouted Munro at him tolerantly. "Any cigarettes? Give me a couple of cigarettes." He indicated the other two men. Yanni was looking at him from under his black cape in wonder.

The guard glared at him. He glanced towards Dejes. Dejes was now walking towards them. He called something. The guard pulled a packet from his pocket with bad grace.

Munro took two from the packet. He held them up to show the guard.

"You see. Two. Only two. These poor devils have to smoke goat dung. Albanian cigarettes very good." He pulled a packet from his own pocket. It was empty. "You see, I've run out." He pushed the cigarettes in the empty packet and tossed it to the other man. All the time he avoided contact with Yanni. The second man caught it. He handed the guard back his packet. The fellow was watching all he did like a hawk. He didn't see any sense in it. Munro was aware of Dejes at his side.

"Thank your man for the cigarettes. Tell him I'll pay him back. He didn't take too kindly to my gracious gesture. Doesn't he like the itinerant travelers?"

He failed to distract Dejes. The little man took the note and glanced at it. "This is Greek. He can't spend this here." Dejes took some money from his pocket and handed it to the old man. "The local currency," he said drily to Munro.

"And at a very favorable rate of exchange," said Munro appreciatively.

Dejes gave Yanni and the other man a brief glance.

In the distance another party of nomads was coming over the hill. Dejes waved to the three men. They stood for a moment, uncertain, then turned to shout to the animals, and moved on.

"What's all that about?" said Munro. "They can't do much harm."

"One hopes not, Mr. Munro," said Dejes.

They walked back to the house together. Stephan waited for them in the doorway. "Anything wrong?"

"I've been giving my money away," said Munro, "all of a pound."

Dejes gave Stephan a reassuring nod. "I have the note." He showed it to Stephan.

"That all?" Stephan was puzzled.

"And cigarettes," said Dejes. Stephan frowned. "You don't smoke." He looked at Munro.

"I borrowed them from the guard. The ungenerous bastard wasn't going to cough up."

He went into the house and the others followed. He knew that Stephan was still mulling it over. He didn't want to give him time to think.

He went back to his room to finish his coffee. Stephan poked his head around the door. "Mind if I join you?"

"Have some cold coffee," invited Munro.

Stephan was uneasy. He took his time pouring his coffee. He guessed Munro had been up to something, but he couldn't think what.

"Better not dash about like that," he said. "You're not a prisoner, of course. But those guards aren't too bright. They might let off a shot."

"Won't do it again. Promise you." Munro couldn't keep the smile off his face. That troubled Stephan. He knew Munro of old. He never underrated him. It was just that in the past Munro had never had reason to keep secrets from him. Now his ingenuity would no longer be to Stephan's advantage.

"Dejes is naturally suspicious."

"Of course."

"He thought you might be sending a message on that banknote."

"Who to?" grinned Munro. "Those poor peasants? You mean like, 'leave two pints of goats' milk in the morning'?"

Stephan smiled; but he guessed he was being outmaneuvred and he didn't like that.

"Who were they?" he asked.

"You know, the Sarakatsani. You remember. You can

211

sing their song, do their dance. Why's Dejes worried about them?"

"It's you that worries him," said Stephan. "He has a high regard for you as an agent."

"Get that in writing and I'll put in for Cecil's job." Then Munro remembered something. "Where can I get a few cigarettes? I'll have to pay back that guard. Can't afford to make enemies."

Stephan kept close to Munro all morning. Munro got the feeling that he was trying to sense what was going on in his brain. Stephan was good at that. Munro actively kept his mind on other things. He chatted non-stop. He didn't know how long it would take Yanni to get back across the frontier, but he wanted to give him plenty of time. By noon Munro decided the fat man would have made it.

"How did you operate the Aroso code set-up?" he asked.

Stephan gave him a quick look. He didn't see any connection. "Cecil used to use it all the time," he said.

"Used to?"

"Not so much now. But he did for over a year."

"When he thought you were dead?"

"Yes."

"And I was in jail. And no one but his agents could decode it?"

"That's right."

"So for all that time, top-level material was being picked up by you, decoded, and passed on?"

"That's how it worked."

"Very smart," said Munro. "Why do you think Cecil got suspicious."

"You can't pull a trick like that forever," said Stephan. "After a bit the opposition . . ."

"Opposition?"

"Cecil . . . and his friends—they must have begun to wonder what was going wrong with their schemes. How did we know what they were planning, who their agents were, and where they were?"

"Did you?"

"Some of them."

"So you think Cecil began to analyze the situation, and

212

realized that there was only one answer. The opposition . . . you in this case . . . were able to understand the Aroso code."

"That's how I see it," said Stephan.

"But Cecil had a theory the code was unbreakable. He said you were the man to outwit computers."

"Nice of him."

"So if the code couldn't be broken, and yet the opposition were reading it, there could only be one answer. You hadn't died, as I reported. You must be alive and well in Albania, translating your own code with the ease of an expert."

"Good thinking . . . if a little late in the day."

"Don't forget, I gave a graphic description of your death . . . as I saw it."

"That must have confused poor Cecil," Stephan grinned.

Munro continued. Once started, he liked to lay it all on the line. "But Cecil had to prove his theory, he had to find out if you *were* really alive. So he recalled me, although I didn't know it, sent me back on what looked like a mission, and waited to see if there was any reaction from this side of the fence."

"Very clever," said Stephan thoughtfully. "But he still isn't sure. Not after he spoke to you on the phone."

Munro nodded. "You took a risk. I might have blurted, 'Stephan's here.' "

"Not after the way they treated you."

Munro marveled at the accuracy of their timing. The following day he would have been more balanced—he would have seen the cracks in the walls. He might then have told Cecil all he needed to know.

"You cut it a little fine," he said.

Stephan nodded, "That's the fun of it. You know that, Munro."

"Of course it is," said Munro. He was thinking of his trial and the judge telling him he ought to be shot. "Just so long as no one gets serious."

Stephan looked at him sharply, so he gave a grin. He had something else to talk about. "There's one sure-fire way of knowing if we've fooled Cecil," he said.

"How's that?"

"Well, if the Travelers go on using the Aroso code that shows they don't think it's been broken. That means they've dropped any idea you aren't dead."

"That could be." Stephan thought about that. He still couldn't make out what Munro was leading to, but he sensed his confidence.

"So we could always find out."

"How?"

"Check. See if he is using the code." Munro made it sound irritatingly simple.

"What do you mean?"

"Look, if Cecil is sending messages in Aroso code, then you're in the clear. Your plan will still work. You can stay on forever, picking up information from Cecil and Sir John."

"I can see that." Stephan was letting Munro get under his skin. His voice rose sharply. He hated an explanation to be labored as though he was a child. He had always been one step ahead of Munro.

"Only trying to help," said Munro.

"I'm sorry. What did you mean . . . we could check?"

Munro indicated the building. "Got any equipment here? I mean, can you pick up stuff transmitted now?"

"Why should Cecil be transmitting now?" Stephan felt uneasy.

"*If*," said Munro. "Can you tune in and see if he's using the Aroso code?"

"They have a watch on his channel all the time in Tiranë," said Stephan.

"Naturally." Munro nodded. "That means *they* get any message, but will you?"

"I get them later to check on their decode."

"So they have someone decoding already?"

"Yes. I have a staff. But everything comes to me for approval."

"Everything?"

"Yes."

"How do you know?"

214

"Why shouldn't they show me everything?" Stephan was getting rattled again. It was Munro's air of confidence.

Munro shrugged. "I wouldn't know. I just wondered what would happen if they wanted to do without you."

"Why should they?" Munro amazed him.

"Well, could they?" Munro's smile was bland, almost as though he were concerned for Stephan's sake.

"You know this code as well as I do," said Stephan. "They could go on using it for a time. But it's a progressive code. The basis for it changes. I haven't told them how to calculate the dynamics of the basic yet."

"Very wise," said Munro with approval, "that keeps someone like you as essential."

"Someone like me?" Stephan repeated.

"Well, someone like me," said Munro. He knew he'd sown many and varied seeds of doubt in Stephan's mind.

"Now don't get any ideas about taking over . . ."

Munro interrupted him. "You know me," he said, "you know that's not my style. I'm loyal old slowcoach. I wouldn't work for the enemy for ideals, love or money . . . not even for fun, Stephan. I'm just suggesting you check transmissions yourself, in case stuff is being picked up in Aroso code by some ambitious second-in-command who would like your place. Someone who might hurry to his boss with a promising signal in pink ribbons—something special. Then this second-in-command might say, 'Look what a good boy I am. I should be running the show.' "

Stephan was sure Munro was talking at two levels. One, the concern he pretended to show. Two, another level. Manipulative, devious, getting him to do something, take a step, a false step at that. The trouble was that Stephan couldn't think what the hell Munro was on about.

"You think I should check transmissions?"

"Not a bad idea." Munro seemed to imply it was Stephan's suggestion.

"No harm in that," said Stephan. He was being cautious.

"No harm at all." Munro nodded cheerfully.

"I'll put someone on it," said Stephan.

Munro seemed to have lost interest. "Trouble is, one gets

215

bored in a place like this. Sun's over the yard arm. Time for a drink?"

Stephan put a couple of operators on the receiver they had in the room Dejes used. He tuned the channel himself. Munro looked on encouragingly.

"That's the ticket," he said. "Never trust your associates. That's something you've still to learn, Stephan."

They walked up and down outside after they had eaten. Stephan was silent. Munro chatted for a bit, then he too fell silent. He knew that whatever happened, a test, one way or another, was coming.

They went back into the building. Stephan left him for a couple of minutes. When he came back, Munro called cheerfully, "How's it going?" Stephan said nothing. "I mean," went on Munro, "how's the Aroso code trick?"

"What do you expect?" asked Stephan.

"I expect they'll use it," said Munro thoughtfully. "My guess is you've fooled them."

"I don't see why you should expect anything from Cecil."

"Bound to contact Sir John."

"He won't use the code for that."

"Why not? He used it last week about me."

"Yes. We picked that up."

"So," Munro went on breezily, "anything on the air?"

"No," said Stephan. He was getting angry with Munro.

"Care for a stroll?" said Munro.

"No," said Stephan.

"Just something I wanted to chat about." Munro indicated the hidden microphones.

"I don't need to talk in secret," said Stephan loudly.

"All right, all right." Munro lifted a hand, a calming gesture. A few minutes later they went through the garden on to the road.

"What is it?" asked Stephan coldly.

"Do you have to have Dejes around all the time?" asked Munro.

"What do you mean?"

"Surely you have authority. You don't need him here. You have all these people, these guards."

"Why shouldn't he be here?"

"I just thought."

"What?"

"It might be better for you without him?"

"Better for me?" He began to wonder if Munro was perfectly sane.

"Yes. He's a political officer, isn't he?"

"Yes."

"If he goes, I suppose you're in charge. You give the orders. No one's going to question you?"

"I don't know what you're talking about." When Stephan lost his sense of humor, he was indeed disturbed.

"I thought . . . in a crisis . . . you'd be better without competition. You know—you just say to the guards, 'I'm going for a walk with Mr. Munro. Don't worry. Everyone stay indoors and give him back his little pistol with enough rounds of ammo to get him safely home.' You know, then if Commissar Dejes isn't around, no one is going to say you nay."

Stephan stopped and stared at him. "What's the matter with you, Munro?"

Munro sighed. "I've had a bad time these last two years. Jail, and all that. Eastbourne, and all that. I think my brain's gone addled."

Stephan went back to the house without saying anything. Munro followed. Stephan shouted to the guard. The man looked coolly at Munro, and nodded.

"Let's check on the radio operator," suggested Munro.

"Look," said Stephan, "you can walk up and down here by yourself. I told the guard."

"You said, 'Shoot him if he runs'," said Munro.

"I've just told you," said Stephan, "you can walk."

He went into the house. Munro waited outside. He had to keep on the alert. He had to do something to keep himself on this knife-edge of activity he had engendered within himself. At any moment he was going to have to make new decisions. The excitement must be kept alive. He began to walk up and down at a snail's pace, close to the guard.

The man was getting uneasy. He shouted at Munro, but Munro pretended not to understand.

Stephan appeared at the door. "What is it?"

"Anything on Aroso code?" called Munro.

Stephan went back in angrily.

Munro decided not to tempt fate. He sat on a pile of chippings not far from the guard. He began to wonder if his scheme—fragile, imaginative—had failed to work. Perhaps Yanni had not understood.

Stephan came out of the house. He shouted, "Munro!"

Munro knew by his voice that the scheme had worked. He said "Thank God" to the cold sky.

"What do you know about this?" Stephan was holding a message sheet. He was cold with fury; at the same time he was shaken.

"Aroso code?" asked Munro hopefully.

"What do you know about it?" Stephan's voice rose.

"Hold on," said Munro amiably. "If it's Aroso code, then they think you're dead. Remember? We worked it out. You're in the clear." He had the satisfaction of seeing Stephan look at him blankly.

"Is it?" asked Munro.

Stephan nodded.

"Worked through it?" asked Munro.

"Not yet," said Stephan, "but I've seen enough. We'd better go inside." He was suddenly subdued. The hunter had turned hunted. He sensed the trap, but wasn't quite sure if he was in it. Munro could see his mind ticking at speed. To have thrown Stephan on to the defensive was a feat, and Munro was pleased with himself. As they went back he said softly to Stephan, "Think you can get rid of Dejes?"

Stephan looked at him, eyes wide with incredulity. Munro was calling the tune. Surely he, Stephan, should be in command. He went on ahead. He guessed Munro was right; he'd have to think of a way to get Dejes out of the place. They went into the ward. The beds had been cleared away, and desk and tables took their place. It was clearly Stephan's office.

"So they have a copy of this in the Tiranë office," said Munro. "We'd better get to work on it quickly. Never know what that up-and-coming second-in-command might do."

"Don't you know what it says?"

"Not in detail," said Munro. "I didn't compose it, you know. Cecil's so much better at that sort of thing."

They sat down together and went through the message. It was indeed from Cecil to Sir John. It listed information that could only have come from Stephan. It implied a great deal more. Anyone reading the transcription could only have assumed that Stephan Aroso had been supplying information to his old employers for some time . . . for a year or two perhaps. There was an indication that more was to follow, that Stephan and Munro were back in harness together, that in fact they had never been out of harness. Without overstating it, the message was clear. Stephan was double-crossing Dejes and those who worked with him.

They sketched in a translation between them. Munro saw the sweat on the other man's brow.

"Nasty jam to be in," sympathized Munro. "Cecil does this sort of thing very well. He has that type of warped mind. He's been doing it to me for the past few months. Of course, one doesn't appreciate it at the receiving end, but when you see it like this, you really have to hand it to the man. That's why the Travelers has stayed in business for so long. It's really Cecil's baby."

He chatted on, as he clarified a sentence or two. Stephan was dumb. Munro let concern creep into his voice. "What will they do? Shoot you?"

Stephan pushed back the paper. He understood clearly what it meant. "How did they know all this?"

"Guesswork basically," said Munro, "inspired guesswork." He smiled gently at Stephan. "You told me some of it; Dejes indicated bits. You could fill in the gaps if you were in my place."

"How did they get it?"

"Transmitted this morning, first thing. Remember? The lads with the sheep and goats."

Stephan didn't take his eyes off Munro. The execution of the game was an end in itself for him. He was fascinated to learn how he had been outwitted.

"But how?"

"Well, I wrote the gist, plus instructions, to Cecil, on the inside of an old cigarette pack. Then I put a couple of cigs from the guard on it—chucked it like bread upon the waters . . . and hey presto! What have we? A genie from the bottle. Let's have a drink."

Stephan was shaking a little, "Suppose I go to Dejes. Suppose I explain."

"Oh come on, lad!" exclaimed Munro. "Do you think I would have told you if I hadn't worked it out? What! Go to the big boys here? Say that Munro put a message in a packet of cigarettes and somehow or other it flew to Cecil? Waken up, Stephan! That's not like you. What would that imply? That a friendly Sarakatsan happened to be passing by with nothing better to do than dash off to British Intelligence with messages from me? Who would that be? Little Bo-Black cape who'd lost his sheep?" Munro made it sound ludicrous. But Stephan thought it might still be a way out.

"It's up to you," said Munro doubtfully. "You know these chaps better than I do. If they had good reason to suspect us of working some trick against them, I think they might come down a little heavy. They aren't notorious for sympathetic measures."

Stephan knew that. It would be a risk.

"How do you plan the rest of it?" he asked Munro.

"How about an understanding with Cecil," suggested Munro. "After all, you must have quite a fund of information that could be useful to him. You two speak the same language. Betrayal, double-cross, that sort of thing." He didn't sound bitter, but there was a cold hard look in Munro's eyes.

"He couldn't keep me out of jail," said Stephan.

"Why not?" Munro was encouraging. "If Cecil thinks you're worth it, he could fix you up in some neutral spot—Beirut, South Africa. A pleasant climate, a small, but steady income. That should do the trick."

Stephan was silent. Munro felt he needed another nudge in the right direction. "The thing is," he said softly, "what's the alternative? What will they do to you here?"

220

The door opened and Dejes came in. Now, thought Munro, the decision is upon us.

"We have a matter to discuss," Dejes reminded Stephan.

"Of course. I'll join you," said Stephan.

Dejes saw the paper on the desk. "Am I interrupting something?"

Munro marvelled at the little man's sharpness.

Munro held up the message sheet. "Working out the old codes," said Munro buoyantly. "Keeping our hand in. Dreaming up a twist to the Aroso code. You know, wheels within wheels—simple once you get the hang of it. Like working out, not just the shape of a black cat on a dark night, but where exactly is that black cat's shadow."

Dejes watched him steadily, small eyes magnified behind his glasses. Munro guessed he wasn't satisfied. He was going to ask another question, but Stephan got up.

"I'll come now," he said, and went out with Dejes. Munro was left at the desk with the message sheet in front of him. He tore it into tiny pieces. Then he sat and waited for Stephan. He waited for about twenty minutes, and it seemed a very long time. Stephan came back on his own. "Where's the message?" he asked.

"Gone," said Munro. "What did you tell him?"

Stephan hesitated. Then he said, "Nothing," and Munro guessed he was speaking the truth.

"And it's been picked up in Tiranë?" queried Munro.

Stephan nodded. He was under pressure, trying to see a way out. "Will it be decoded yet?" Munro sounded merely interested.

"They are very slow," said Stephan.

"That's good." Munro sounded relieved. "Gives us a bit of time."

"What for?" asked Stephan.

"To decide what to do." Munro was still not pushing him. He guessed Stephan would see the answer for himself. Much better that way.

"Why do you think I'll go your way?" he asked Munro.

"Why didn't you tell Dejes?" countered Munro. He looked swiftly around the room. "Not bugged, are we?"

221

Stephan shook his head. "I do the bugging," he said.

"All right," said Munro briskly, "let's make assumptions. If they're working on the message now, how long before the bubble bursts?"

"They'll be here by morning."

Munro nodded. "I thought so. That gives us tonight." He tapped the desk. "Got a map anywhere?"

"I haven't made up my mind," said Stephan.

"I know. Just covering all possibilities," said Munro.

Stephan threw him a map from one of the drawers. Munro was hesitant about opening it. "Where's Dejes? Would be much easier if he wasn't around."

"Well, he *is* around," said Stephan sharply.

Munro was still cheerful. "I know," he said, "if he bursts in again, I'll tell him we're playing another game. It's called 'Escaping across the Greek frontier.' "

Stephan couldn't restrain a wan grin. They pored over the map. Their location was marked; they were well into the mountains, not far from the boundaries. "The trouble is," said Stephan, "most of it is ravine."

Munro agreed. "Perpendicular at that."

There seemed to be two alternatives. "The way I came?" suggested Munro.

"That could be patrolled now," said Stephan. He didn't say why, but Munro understood.

"Well, further west there are a couple of bridges over the ravine. It gets narrower at one or two points."

"We get into the villages that way." Stephan was uncertain.

"Who's going to pay any attention to us?" asked Munro. "All these nomads went through."

"They don't try to cross bridges," said Stephan.

Munro knew he was right, but he felt they would have to take that chance.

"We still have to get rid of Dejes," said Munro.

Stephan sat staring at the map. Munro said nothing, but he could hear his own heart thumping. This was the moment someone had to shout heads or tails.

"You can leave that to me," said Stephan.

222

16

Later in the afternoon Stephan went to see Dejes. The chill sun was already going down over the hills, and the earth was hard and near-frozen in the garden under Munro's feet. He found the guard who had given him the cigarettes and presented him with a packet. The man didn't know what to make of that. Then Munro saw a car draw up. A uniformed driver waited. He was still waiting when Munro went back into the building.

He looked for Stephan in the ward, but there was no one there. He went to his own room and sat on his bed. Soon after, the car drove off. Munro guessed what had happened.

Stephan came in. He was grinning, a changed man.

"I saw a car," said Munro.

Stephan nodded. "Dejes has gone to Tiranë."

"How did you manage it?"

"I said I needed advice about you."

"Oh?"

"Said you could still be dangerous. I insisted they take responsibility."

"That sounds like a genuine request." Munro nodded with approval.

Stephan still grinned. Suddenly he reminded Munro of the days when they had been real partners. He oozed controlled excitement, taking Munro's little pistol from his pocket and tossing it to Munro.

Munro checked. It was loaded.

"There's a captain in charge of the guard," said Stephan. He seemed confident. "No one else of any importance. But they're not stupid. I have told them to be on the alert. When the time comes he'll take my instructions."

"When does the time come?" asked Munro.

"When it's dark," said Stephan.

"It's dark now," Munro pointed out.

"When the guards have supper," said Stephan.

They had their own meal in Stephan's office. Munro ate a little, but Stephan was suddenly very active, searching through his desk. Munro knew most items of value Stephan would carry in his head, but he found a few papers he stuffed in his pocket. He pulled a couple of jackets from a cupboard, and threw one to Munro. They were like a battle-dress.

"Put that on."

"What's the plan?"

"They lock the gate after dark. There's a guard—I'll get rid of him. We'll have only a couple of minutes." He held up a key. He too had a revolver. He turned up the intercom on his desk. They could hear the noise of men talking and laughing. "There's a dining room at the far end of the building." Stephan took a deep breath, grinning, alert. "Ready?"

They moved into the corridor, Stephan going ahead, giving a quick glance up and down, then nodding to Munro. It was all so easy. Munro was nervous about that. But why shouldn't it be easy? Stephan was the most senior man in charge of the unit. He had been able to arrange it. Perhaps that was the nagging doubt in Munro's mind. He had been beguiled by the ease with which Stephan had arranged things in the past. He stayed on guard against the unseen trap.

"Stay here." Stephan left him at the door of the building, in a small porch, vanishing in the dark.

The man at the gate shouted a challenge. Stephan replied. Munro could hear a scrap of conversation. It took longer than he expected. The man seemed to be doubtful about something. Stephan gave a sharp command, and the man could be heard moving off. A minute passed. Munro thought something had gone wrong. There was a wave of noise from a room down the corridor.

The door opened beside him. It was Stephan, fast moving, very silent. He signaled, and Munro followed him out.

They went through the garden. The gate was unlocked. Munro slipped out; Stephan stopped and relocked the gate.

"We'll have to move fast."

"What did you tell the guard?"

"I said I'd stay on guard until he got back."

"Which way?"

"Best get off the road."

They went over rough ground. Clouds came and went over the moon, shadows traveling fast. They fell into a rhythm they had used many times before.

"No transport?" Munro was still suspicious.

"I thought of that," said Stephan, "but it would have kept us on the road. And they could have told which way we went when they found it."

That made sense.

They were some distance from the farmhouse. All seemed to have gone well. No sound of alarm.

"West," said Stephan, "they won't expect that. And we've used that route before."

Munro remembered when they had last used it. The recollection was disturbing. Not that they would go as far as the villages to find a crossing. There was at least one old wooden bridge he knew of over the ravine, and it could not be far away.

Stephan was already moving on. Now he had committed himself, he appeared to blot from his mind anything but the escape. Munro marveled at the man. He was clearly enjoying the adventure, going at a fast lope, giving a quick glance over his shoulder. They were only a hundred yards from the road. It showed in the moonlight, a long thin ribbon, deserted. Stephan turned and gave Munro the thumbs-up signal. "Takes you back," said Stephan. It took Munro back so vividly that his heart thumped.

They had been going about twenty minutes and had covered over a mile when they heard rifle fire. They stopped and listened.

"Sounds like they're missing us," said Munro.

The smile never left Stephan's face.

"Just keep moving," said Munro.

They started up again, the same steady pace, as though there had been no break in an old pattern. They talked as they went, keeping their voices down, for sounds carried on the cold night air.

"Any idea what they'll do?" asked Munro.

"They'll try to find Dejes. He'll still be traveling. So they will report to Tiranë."

Munro was thoughtful. "If it was only me, I don't think they'd be too worried. But you . . . ?" He was doubtful. "What will they think?"

"They'll think you have a gun on me."

"They won't think you've made a run for it?"

Stephan shook his head. "If they had decoded the messages, yes. But we're ahead of them."

Munro hoped he was right. "They won't be happy," he said.

"Don't worry." Once he had admired Stephan for this fearlessness; now he wasn't so sure. Stephan must feel he was immune, immortal. Brave, because nothing could happen to him. Well, Munro had learned a bitter lesson. No one was immune.

They moved in shadow over the rocky plateau. The road came into view. Munro grabbed Stephan and pulled him back. A couple of headlights came towards them, picking out the barren land as the car took the bends. There wasn't much chance of being seen, but they stayed motionless as the lights passed.

Stephan was very still.

"What is it?" asked Munro.

"Dejes," said Stephan softly.

"You said . . ."

"They must have got in touch with him."

The dark shape of the car pulled away from them. "They must have phoned the patrol down the track. Stopped him and sent him back."

They were silent. Instead of having a clear run, there would be patrols alerted and Dejes back on his unit, directing, planning, thinking ahead. He was an astute man.

"It's a long frontier," said Munro. "Any reason why he should guess we're going his way?"

The lights of the car were now pinpoints in the dark. Stephan let it vanish, then he said, "You came by Mesara. If Dejes thinks you've got me prisoner he'll probably expect you to take the same route."

"If he thinks we're working together?" said Munro.

"He could send patrols anywhere."

The car had gone. There was no sound, no movement.

They moved off keeping an eye on the road. The moon passed behind clouds. They went over the uneven surface, taking them into a ravine.

Stephan was ahead, but Munro had sharp eyes in the dark. He saw the figures first. They came up from the ground like shadows. He had his gun in his hand with a speed he thought he had forgotten—he could have shot all three before they moved. But Munro held his fire for a second, and in that second the moon came out, and he saw the men in their black capes, staring at him. They had wide eyes, startled from sleep. All young, and at this moment, alarmed. Munro guessed they had been posted to guard the flock. Part of their flight was guilt.

Stephan greeted them in their dialect. They still looked nervously at Munro. He put his gun away, but they were afraid. Stephan spoke again; one of them mumbled a reply.

"He says the rest of the family are down the track."

"How far?"

Stephan asked. The men shrugged.

"They say, less than a mile."

Munro nodded to the men. "No point in hanging around," he told Stephan.

"They've seen us," said Stephan.

"Can't be helped," said Munro.

"They could give us away."

"They don't have any contact with the locals," said Munro.

"Patrols will ask."

"There's nothing we can do about it," said Munro sharply.

"We could change course."

227

"Keep going," said Munro, "We're a step ahead. Let's stay that way."

Stephan saluted the men cheerfully. They watched as he and Munro hurried on.

"I wonder what they made of that," said Munro.

"I said we were a patrol."

"They believed you?"

"I don't think so."

In a few minutes they saw the lights of fires ahead. It was the nomads' camp.

"There they are," said Stephan. "What do we do? Go around, or straight ahead?"

"Go around."

They were challenged from some distance away. Stephan called back without stopping. The man called again. Stephan didn't reply. They hurried on. The camp straggled on down the edge of the track. A boy watched them from the shadows of a black goat-skin tent.

"What happens if patrols catch up with them?" said Stephan. "How many strangers are in these hills except us?"

There was no answer to that.

The fires were still to be seen burning in the distance when Munro came to a stop. "Hold it," he said. "Just what the doctor ordered."

The track split into two. The main path lay haead; the other, smaller, overgrown, rough, went off at a tangent.

"By my reckoning, it heads for Greece," said Munro.

"Could be," said Stephan. He looked at Munro. "Try it?" he asked. Munro nodded. The unknown had a special fascination for Stephan. He pushed ahead.

They must have walked for over an hour, the path nothing but a goat track. But they saw the steep hills on the other side of a valley getting closer. And that was Greece.

The moon lost some of its light after midnight. Suddenly they were brought up sharply at the edge of the ravine. The drop before them was spectacular; an effective frontier. Not even a goat could make that climb. Stephan nodded to the cliff-face opposite. "There we are," he said, "home and dry." He was pleased with the way things had gone. Munro wondered if he thought of what might lie ahead: did he consider what sort of a reception he'd get? Did he think his charmed life would save him from a bitter accounting? Munro had ceased trying to make sense of the man, but he could think of no one else who would drive along with such energy, such optimism. To follow Stephan was to be caught in the wake of his energy. Munro warned himself not to be beguiled by fantasy. He had suffered for his faith in Stephan before.

They took the path along the top of the ravine, knowing it must ultimately lead to a crossing, or to an easier way down.

The moon had almost faded, and there was a cold sense of dawn in the air, before they found what they were looking for. Stephan pointed. A spur of rock jutted towards Greece. The ravine grew very narrow.

Silhouetted against the dying moon was the outline of a bridge—old, wooden, unkept; but a bridge!

"You were always a lucky devil," said Stephan.

Munro didn't correct him. They went cautiously down the path, and branched with it to the spur.

They stopped as they heard the sound of shots. It was hard to tell where they came from. The ravine confused sounds. There was a dull echo.

"How near?" asked Munro. He was trying to work it out himself.

"A mile," guessed Stephan.

"Greek side?" asked Munro.

"No." Stephan was sure of that. "Behind us. The patrols."

"Closer than one would have thought," said Munro.

There were a couple more shots.

Stephan shrugged. "They shoot to see what happens. They have no idea where we are."

A path had been cut into the side of the rock. An old bridge crossed to the other side, wooden planks bolted with heavy metal rivets. The whole thing was rusting; the planks smashed in places. But it was sound enough.

"Built by prisoners in the time of the Turks," said Stephan. "To last forever." He crossed, with Munro following. It was riveted to rock at the Greek end. The only attempt to put it out of action had been an attack on the planks, but the job was badly done. "For which," said Munro, "we give much thanks." They stepped on to Greek soil with a prayer. Munro stopped. A wall barred their way.

A heap of boulders blocked the track. Barbed wire had been cemented in and out of the barricade. Munro didn't need to test it. He knew there was no way past.

Stephan joined him. He took one look at the obstruction. "Cheaper than patrols," said Munro, "and more reliable."

Stephan scanned the rock face on both sides. "It's a dead end." He went back on to the bridge and looked up. There was no way of climbing the sheer rock. The path they had followed led no further.

"My guess is the Greeks have blocked off all crossings," said Munro.

Stephan shook his head. "Some sheep came across last summer. A shepherd crossed the frontier, to get them back, and the Greeks had a lot of trouble getting him out again. If sheep got through, we can."

"Could have been further up the mountains," said Munro.

"I don't think we should try doubling back," said Stephan.

"Follow the river?" Munro suggested.

Stephan nodded. "Sure to be an easier crossing lower down."

They recrossed the bridge and set off along the top of the ravine.

There were outcrops of rock ahead. From the top they were surprised to see the road. They stopped to watch the lights of a truck go past. It was followed by another.

"The army's up," said Stephan. It didn't appear to disturb him. They hurried on, Munro glad to see that their way curved from the road. They stopped once at the sound of men calling. It was difficult to see in the half light; then a couple of dull uniforms came over a skyline. Munro and Stephan crouched down until they had gone.

"The search is on," said Munro. He was uneasy. Those soldiers had been too close.

Stephan shrugged. "How many miles do they have to cover? And they don't have more than twenty—thirty—men."

"Even thirty men," said Munro.

"Thirty men! With this stretch to cover! We could hide for a week."

"They'd bring up more men."

"We'll be out by dawn," said Stephan.

Munro looked around. Dawn was filtering into the night as it was.

They made good progress; the path became broader.

"We could be near a village," said Stephan.

A red sunrise had come up behind them. They passed a couple of stone outhouses, with signs of animals and men. The ravine grew steeper, narrower, and they could see the Greek side clearly. Barbed wire and iron stakes protected the slopes. The rock face of the frontier was sufficiently formidable.

The path dipped ahead, rounding a few wintry shrubs. About twenty steps further on four soldiers were standing in the shelter of a big rock, leaning back on it, facing the sun, smoking, relaxing; beside them their rifles were propped against the rock. Munro and Stephan were on their bellies instantaneously.

"Four of them?" whispered Stephan.

Munro nodded.

"We could blow them apart before they knew what hit them," said Stephan.

"We don't want to fire unless we have to," said Munro. They had no idea who else might be within gunshot.

"They could be there forever," whispered Stephan. He got impatient quickly. He edged forward. As he moved Munro saw the men coming. He jerked Stephan back. The four men passed less than ten steps away—talking together, rifles hanging over their long, heavy coats. They were regular soldiers; three of them being young, the fourth older, a corporal.

Munro didn't take his eyes off them, his gun in his hand, ready for anything. The four men disappeared—Munro breathed again. He had Stephan pressed to the ground; now he let him go.

"Near thing," said Stephan softly.

They watched the path for a moment; there was no further movement.

"Stay here," said Stephan, "I'll take a look."

"We shouldn't split," said Munro.

"They're looking for you," said Stephan. "If I run into anyone I can talk their language." He got to his feet. "Give me a couple of minutes."

Munro waited a couple of minutes. That was enough time for Stephan to see if the coast was clear. He got up, and moved to the path. There was no sign of Stephan. Munro heard a faint sound behind him. He turned. Two of the soldiers were coming back. They saw him, and for a second they were taken aback, looking at him blankly. Munro knew it was a frail hope, but he gave a casual wave, as he backed away. He had his other hand on his gun.

One of the men called. Munro knew enough of the language. He called back a greeting.

Both soldiers hurried down the path towards him. One of them unslung his gun, and the safety catch came off. Munro stopped and looked at them as though surprised. He had a puzzled smile. The two men shouted at him angrily. Munro said nothing. He looked questioningly at them. This made them angrier, but it also threw them off-guard. The man with the gun was nervous, ready to fire. Munro knew what he had to do, and it had to be done without the sound of a gun.

He hit the first soldier with the full force of his shoulder, and the man went back with a gasp. His rifle hit the ground, and he was almost over the edge of the ravine.

The other man was bewildered for one second, and this was all Munro had prayed for. He snatched the rifle. He didn't see Stephan come up the path behind him, but he felt the revolver in his back. For a split second his mind stopped working. Stephan shouted, "Drop it!" Munro let the gun fall, his brain numb. He heard Stephan whisper, "They're back." Munro looked down the path. The corporal and the other soldier were standing at the bend in the path. The corporal had his gun on Munro.

Stephan shouted. The man understood, and looked uneasy. Stephan shouted again. Munro knew he was giving orders. The corporal hesitated. The soldier on the ground got up unsteadily. Stephan shouted at him. They were still doubtful.

"What's going on?" asked Munro.

"You're my prisoner," Stephan shouted at him. "I'm sending these men for help." He shouted to the corporal again. This time he got a reply. Stephan passed the information on to Munro, digging him with the gun as he did so. "They have a sergeant down the track. I'm sending for him."

Munro wasn't sure Stephan had convinced the men. They pointed at him.

"They want me, do they?" he asked.

"That's it," said Stephan. He gave them another order. This time they moved away. As soon as their backs were turned Stephan fired. The nearest man dropped like a sack. The corporal staggered before he went down. The third man went over with him, but he scrambled to his feet. Stephan fired but the fellow ran like a rabbit. Stephan went after him. He had two more shots, but the man was around the bend in the path.

Munro stood beside the dead men. Stephan joined him. "It won't take him long to get the whole district humming." He took the rifles from the dead men and handed one to Munro. "Could come in handy."

They set off at a fast walk. Munro was aware that he felt ill, and his body was shaking. It was a long time since he had been close to violent death. One gets out of practice. The anonymous enemies had been living a moment ago. It was the vulnerability of men that made Munro tremble. His brain didn't seem to be working too clearly, and he was glad that Stephan had taken over the lead. "We'll get off this track," said Stephan.

They went into the hills. Munro didn't know he was tired, but he collapsed among the rocks, and the sweat ran off him. "I'm getting past this," he said to Stephan.

"We both are," grinned Stephan. "This'll be the last time."

They lay in the hills for an hour, watching the track. A couple of peasants went past, but no one else. There was a chance the fourth soldier had failed to report to his sergeant.

"Or perhaps they guess where we're heading," said Stephan, "and they're going to wait."

"Let's take another look at the ravine," said Munro. They went over the hill and saw the ravine. It didn't look promising. "It might be our only chance," said Munro.

They stood on the edge and looked down.

"Once we're there," said Stephan, "we're rats in a trap."

Munro could see the risk. "Looks like a village ahead," he said.

There were a few huddled buildings on a hillside a couple of miles ahead.

"Let's see," said Stephan. They went on, keeping cover. It was a slow journey. They got in quite close to the village by sticking to the ravine. Then Stephan saw a bridge over the gap. Munro heard him laugh. "You know where that is?"

Munro recognized those few houses. "Try it my way," he said, "let's climb the ravine." He had no desire to see Karlovo again. They went along the ravine, trying to find a way down. They knew it was hopeless long before they gave up the search.

About midday they lay among stumps of hard rocks, alone on the high plateau, harsh country around them. The world was empty. At this altitude, three months of winter froze everything. Only now had the sun a trace of warmth in it. They scanned the area—nothing moved. Their sense of isolation was complete, but they guessed it to be illusory. From where they lay, they could see the bridge. It seemed to Munro like a piece of cheese in a mousetrap. Too tempting to be what it seemed—a simple way to freedom.

"There are two alternatives," said Stephan; "either the village hasn't been put on an alert, or they have an ambush waiting."

"With a patrol of thirty men, they can't cover every-

234

where," said Munro. He peered at the dark huddle of stone cottages. An old woman and a child went into one of the fields. Munro noted this; one saw few children in Karlovo. And then, as if in answer to their question, a man came after them and sent them back. He was in uniform. "Now we know," said Munro. "The question now is, how many are there?"

"Can't be many," said Stephan.

"What do we do? Wait for dark?"

"You know what Dejes is doing now? Cursing at the delay in Tiranë. I guess he's phoned twenty times. He wants help—his patrol isn't big enough! I mustn't be allowed to get out. In Tiranë they won't know why he's so excited. Who is Stephan Aroso? Unless he gets authority from the top, he won't get help."

"Will he get that?"

"Yes. but it will take time, most of today. Then a truck or two of regulars will come up. That's a different cup of tea to your country lads on this patrol. That's why I don't think we should wait."

Munro thought it over. "What do we do? Stroll through? Run for it?"

"A good trick works twice," said Stephan. "I'll take you as my prisoner?"

Munro never liked a gun in his back, not even Stephan's.

"Right," he said, "worth the risk."

They started towards Karlovo, Munro ahead, Stephan following. "Better make it life-like," he said.

Munro couldn't help suspicions clustering in his head. All Stephan needed to do was pull the trigger, and he'd look like a hero to the locals. That would make it easy for him to slip across the bridge. The habit of suspicion was hard to kill.

The bleak walls of the village loomed close. Blank windows watched them over the stony pasture. The place was hushed. "Down the gap between the houses," directed Stephan.

Munro knew this alley-way. Last time Stephan had been in front.

"Turn left."

235

He didn't need the instruction; the bridge lay to his left. Stephan followed. They turned into the village street. There were five soldiers between them and the bridge. Munro almost stopped.

"Keep moving," barked Stephan.

The men heard him. They were talking to a woman in a doorway. Now they turned, watching blankly. Stephan called to them. One of them came towards them. He was a sergeant, gray-jowled, squat, powerful. He shouted to his men; they unslung their rifles. Stephan paid no attention. He let them see he had his gun on Munro. He waved the sergeant aside.

"First doorway on your left," he shouted to Munro. Munro knew the place. It was the corner house where he had spent the night after the visit to the grave. The sergeant shouted angrily, but Stephan ignored him, calling over his head to the men. Munro understood him. He was ordering one man to take over the bridge. They looked at the sergeant uncertainly. He was shaken, unsure. He followed them into the house.

Immediately Stephan began giving his orders. The sergeant hesitated. Stephan lost his temper and shouted at him. He backed out. Munro heard him calling down the telephone.

"I told him to send for instructions."

"Who to?"

"Dejes. Keep him busy. We've got to play this carefully, and quick. I'll handle it as their superior. Once they're doing what I tell them, it will be easy."

"What about Dejes?"

"It'll take him hours. We'll be gone before he gets through."

Munro knew Stephan's optimism of old; he prayed he was right. "Have your gun handy," said Stephan. He took Munro to the sergeant, who was still trying to make the connection. Munro understood enough to know Stephan was telling the sergeant to watch him, and shoot if he had to. Stephan went out. Munro took no chances. He stood opposite the sergeant while the conversation with the operator went on. He could hear Stephan shouting orders. He sounded most authentic; he had established authority over the men.

Munro looked out of the window. He would have gone to the door, but the sergeant waved him back with his gun. He could see Stephan telling the other men what he wanted. He made them obey at the double. He swore at them, threatening punishment. They were used to this. In a couple of minutes Stephan was back. "Going nicely," he said. "Come with me."

"What's the game?" Munro wasn't going to be a puppet on anyone's string.

"Let's see how far we can go . . . while he's busy." Stephan nodded at the sergeant. He indicated with the point of his gun that Munro was to go outside.

The sergeant was unhappy about that. But as they went out, he suddenly began shouting into the phone.

"Time's short," said Stephan, "he's through to someone."

Three of the soldiers were waiting outside. When they saw Stephan they hurried back to work. They were pulling an old cart across the road to seal off the bridge. It was a meaningless task if they'd thought about it; but it suggested efficiency. Stephan headed Munro down the street with a wave of the gun. He stopped to inspect the cart. It had a broken wheel, and took a lot of manhandling. Stephan called the fourth soldier from the bridge. As he did so he caught Munro's eye. They understood each other perfectly. This was the moment.

Munro backed away slightly. Stephan pretended to direct the work at the cart. He shouted for more effort. Then he said in English, "Now!" and Munro turned and ran. He could hear someone coming after him. It had all happened in less than two minutes after leaving the sergeant in the house. Ten seconds earlier and they would have managed it. But not at this moment. The road ahead was under fire; the bridge splattered with bullets. Munro was still running, but Stephan pulled him back. They got the cart between them and the sergeant. He was moving from the doorway with an automatic rifle. If he hadn't been afraid of hitting his own men, he could have got them both.

He shouted, and the four soldiers got out of the way.

237

"Back in the house," called Stephan.

They raced for the doorway. The sergeant had no time to take aim; a burst of fire went over their heads as they threw themselves into the house. Munro noticed the telephone was still off the hook.

They crouched under the window. Munro smashed it with the butt of his gun and fired at the men outside. That took them by surprise. The sergeant yelled, and they scattered. Munro had one more shot at them, then the street was empty. Stephan looked pleased with himself. "Nearly worked," he said.

"No points for a good try," said Munro. He was uneasy when Stephan lacked reality: Munro was never able to divorce himself from danger.

"He must have got through to Dejes." He indicated the phone. Stephan listened to it. "Gone dead." He put back the receiver.

"There's a window overlooking the bridge," said Munro. "We might make it from there."

"The sergeant has an automatic," said Stephan.

"This place is no good to us," said Munro.

"Won't stay a moment more than we have to," said Stephan. "How long before dark?"

Munro squinted up at the sky. "Give it an hour."

Stephan nodded. "Just play holding the fort for an hour. It's going to be easier by night."

He saw someone move in the house opposite and fired. Whoever it was vanished.

Munro moved to the window at the side of the room. From here he could see the approach to the bridge. The cart lay a few feet the other side. He guessed that if he could use it as cover . . . He threw himself against the wall. The window shattered. Bullets swept across the room. Others hit the wall outside.

"You all right?" called Stephan.

"Keep down," said Munro.

Another burst of firing thudded into the wall close by. The sergeant intended to pin them down.

Munro fired back in the general direction of the gunman. All he could do was keep the man from closing in.

238

They heard the sound of a truck coming down the village street, but it stopped out of sight. There was some movement behind the buildings opposite them, then a couple of soldiers ran to the corner beside the bridge. They peered around, then ducked back. Stephan put a shot close to them. They didn't reply, but stayed out of sight.

"Two to guard the bridge," said Stephan. "What happens to the other three?"

The truck started up again and came down the street in bottom gear. It stopped again, still out of sight.

"Army truck," guessed Munro.

"Reinforcements."

They could hear men talking in the house opposite. Vague shapes moved in an upper room. Stephan put a shot through the window. There was a silence, then a short burst of machine-gun fire ripped across their room.

"You were right," said Stephan, "reinforcements."

The machine-gun was angled down at them and sprayed the window. Stephan kept close to the wall, watching from an angle. He fired and a man up the road went down. The machine-gun stopped. In the growing gloom they could see someone dragging him into an alley. They let them do it. A few moments later it was too dark to see.

The phone rang, sounding through the old house. They let it ring for a couple of minutes. Then it stopped. Almost immediately it began to ring again.

"Could be someone returning the sergeant's call," said Munro.

Stephan answered it. "Why hello, Dejes! Nice of you to call . . ." He held the phone out to Munro. "It's for you."

The situation seemed a little bizarre to Munro, but he didn't let it show in his voice. "Where are you, Mr. Dejes?" Then Munro covered the phone. "He's across the road."

Stephan moved to the window. "I didn't think there were two phones in the village."

"Hello," said Munro, "I'm still here."

Dejes was talking. "You understand your situation, Mr. Munro. It is serious. It's also serious for me. That's why I phone you."

"Go ahead," said Munro, "what can we do for each other?"

"We don't wish to detain you. You are in our country by accident. We have confirmed this."

"Oh good," said Munro.

"You have an opportunity to leave," said Dejes.

"You mean I can walk out and cross the bridge?"

"Exactly," said Dejes.

Munro laughed. "But Mr. Dejes, you've got a couple of men around the corner, ready to blow my head off."

"We will recall our people from the street," said Dejes.

"The sergeant has an automatic, and someone brought a machine-gun in that truck."

"We have a machine-gun," admitted Dejes. He was being very patient.

"It seems to me you might want to get rid of me," said Munro.

"What you did was not of your own willing," said Dejes. "You have been exploited by your own people."

"So you found that out," said Munro. "My, my! You've been busy."

"Don't take this lightly, Mr. Munro. You are no use to us. We wish you to go."

"Let me think it over," said Munro.

"Best to be quick," said Dejes. "I don't want this problem. It is embarrassing for me."

"I see your point," said Munro. "The less fuss, then the less trouble you have with your superiors?"

"That is obvious," said Dejes coldly.

Stephan called across the room. "What's his proposition?"

"He says I can go."

"Accept," said Stephan.

Munro turned back to the phone. "You assure me we can walk away unmolested?"

Dejes came back very promptly. "I said *you*, Mr. Munro."

"Not my friend Aroso?"

"Mr. Munro," Dejes sounded strained, "you know that is impossible. He had been working at a high level; he cannot be allowed to take such information out of the country. No one would expect that."

Munro felt one point ought to be clarified. "You're forgetting something. When I get out I'll be able to tell everybody that Stephan is alive, and he's working for you. They won't use the Aroso code anymore."

"That won't be of any importance," said Dejes drily. "Now you must hurry. I will call our men from guarding the bridge. Leave from the door of the house and go immediately across the bridge. You must be alone." Dejes put the phone down. Munro was left standing for a moment, weighing up the implications of the move ahead.

"So I stay," said Stephan thoughtfully.

"Can't let you go," nodded Munro. "Too valuable."

"I take his meaning," said Stephan. "Poor Dejes, he's going to be in trouble. I worked with him. They'll ask how he didn't guess I was still loyal to my own country."

"That's a good question," said Munro. The lack of substance in Stephan's loyalty to anyone was something he didn't like to think about.

"When does this happen?" asked Stephan.

"He's calling the snipers off at this moment." Munro couldn't see an answer. He wanted Stephan out, otherwise he hadn't finished this self-imposed mission. At the same time he wanted to stay alive himself. How far could he trust Dejes? He had only to step into the street to be a target. He might never reach the bridge. "Shot in resisting arrest," or some such jargon. Yet he felt Dejes meant what he said. Just walk away and the problem was solved; the nightmare over.

"I'm hungry," he said. He remembered the food and wine he had eaten in this house. The cupboards were empty, but there was coffee. He began making that.

"When it gets very dark," said Stephan, "how are they going to know if it's you or me leaving the house?"

"Dejes will have thought of that." Munro wasn't worried. He brought Stephan some coffee. Stephan was still on guard at the window. There had been no shooting since the phone call.

Munro sipped his drink. He had one trump card. Dejes

was unwilling to turn the situation into a large-scale incident. His job was to play it down. Authorities were always anxious to gloss over the seamy arrangements they made with traitors; they didn't like to acknowledge agents publicly. Munro guessed Dejes would call in his superiors only if all else failed. And what he wanted was to get him, Munro, out of his hair, to close the Aroso file for good. The phone rang again.

Munro answered.

"What is happening?" It was Dejes.

"I've been thinking it over," Munro told him. "I've decided you are on the level. But one of your men might be trigger-happy."

"Nothing like that." Dejes sounded anxious.

"Stephan is wanted in his own country to answer charges," added Munro.

"That's impossible." Dejes was angry.

"He was responsible for me being in your jails for a year and a half." Munro winked across to Stephan as he spoke. Stephan gave a wry smile.

Dejes was talking. "We know about this. It is old material, Mr. Munro. Not important."

"It's important to me."

"Yes, but . . ."

"Think how I feel about it. I was the sucker who had to suffer so your scheme worked."

"Mr. Munro . . ." pleaded Dejes.

"It's a long time to spend in jail. And the trial was a worry."

"I promise you he will not get away with it," said Dejes.

"You used him last time when Cecil thought he was dead. Perhaps you're going to do that again."

"I promise you."

"I mean, suppose he could convince you that the code message was from me—just to implicate him. Then you'd take him back into the fold."

Dejes cut him off. But a moment later the phone rang again.

"Listen to me, Mr. Munro," said Dejes. "Don't make me

angry. No reasoning will allow me to give safe conduct to anyone but yourself."

"All right. Forget it," said Munro. "But I want to be absolutely sure about my own safety. I want witnesses."

"Witnesses?" Dejes sounded bewildered.

"There's a Greek patrol a mile up the other side. They're a lousy patrol. Don't go out in cold weather. Can you get in touch with them? Get them down to the other end of the bridge. So that when I come out they see me, and they see me walk across. And if anyone shoots me they see it happen, and they can report it."

There was a pause at the other end, then Dejes said, "Why should we do this for you, Mr. Munro?"

"Because if you don't, I'm bloody well staying here and you're going to have a fight on your hands, and some of your men killed, and explaining to do to your people . . . and a big border incident that will mess up your promotion."

Another pause.

"All right, Mr. Munro. Wait until I call you. We may be able to do that, but it will take time."

"I've got lots of that," said Munro.

"Goodbye, Mr. Munro." Dejes was polite, subdued.

Munro guessed he was right about the promotion.

"How are you and Dejes getting on?" asked Stephan.

"Great little guy," said Munro, "liked him from the moment I clapped eyes on him."

It was a long night. Munro made more coffee to keep himself awake. Stephan stayed at the window.

"Sit down," said Munro wearily.

"They could attack," said Stephan. He didn't sound as if he believed it. It was two in the morning when the phone rang again.

"Dejes?" inquired Munro.

"No sir," came back the voice. "Assistant. To say, sir, Officer Dejes can do as you say."

"He's getting someone to come to the bridge?"

"Yes, sir."

"When?"

"Not yet, sir."

Munro thought about that. "Message received. Tell me when it's set up."

Stephan joined him. "When you go. I'll make a break for it out at the back."

"They'll have that covered," said Munro.

"He's got four sides to cover, and they'll be busy with you. That's going to be my chance."

"I don't fancy the odds." Munro was thoughtful.

"I don't fancy the odds myself," said Stephan, "but they aren't going to get any better."

It was nearly dawn. Munro thought Stephan had fallen asleep, when he said, "I could open a window at the back and get up into the hills."

"I thought about that," said Munro, "but they'll keep after you. It's bad this time of year—no food, very cold."

"If I go east it gets easier. I could cross at the head of the ravine."

"I'm sure they know that," said Munro.

Stephan began opening the window. It looked over the plateau they had crossed. He was very quiet, but a man shouted a challenge. Stephan replied in the same tongue, "And the peace of God go with you," but he moved back into the room. Half an hour later, flecks of morning touched the hills.

"You know," said Stephan, "I used to think about you in that prison. It wasn't my idea. But there was no other way. You know how these things are."

"Sure," said Munro. This was the closest to an apology he had ever heard from Stephan. The closest to a conscience. "Think nothing of it."

A pink light crept over the plateau. There was a faint sound of sheep and goats.

"Anything else you'd like to pass on?" said Munro.

Stephan lifted his eyebrows. "Like what?"

"You've been here some time," said Munro. "Anything you'd like Cecil to know?"

"So you *are* working for him," Stephan smiled.

"I wasn't," said Munro, "but I could pick up a bonus at Christmas."

"I have a lot in my head," said Stephan.

"Could be old hat by the time you get back." Munro was matter-of-fact.

"Anyhow it's complicated."

"What did you work at?"

"I had a finger in most pies. I'm going to surprise Cecil."

"I'll bet you are," nodded Munro.

"Any harm I did his organization I can more than balance."

"What harm?" asked Munro.

Stephan shrugged. "Well, naturally they found out one or two things through me."

"Naturally." Munro wondered what in particular. He didn't ask, but Stephan answered. "They identified four of Cecil's agents."

"Identified." That was a euphemism if ever there was one!

"What happened to them."

"One can't be sure," said Stephan, "but I can square the account."

"How?" Munro wondered how Stephan was going to bring four men back to life.

"I know about a dozen of their people in France, Spain, and England."

Munro looked at him impassively. "So you'll be able to identify them in return."

"Among other things," said Stephan.

Munro was sad. It wasn't that Stephan felt so little, as he bartered humanity. More that such promise, such charm, had so little feeling. Munro was almost glad that the trail was going to end for Stephan in this cold, gray village.

"How do you propose to make the break?" asked Munro.

Did Stephan think he was going to run for it? In front of the Albanian guards and a Greek frontier patrol? Had he some fantasy of escape?

The phone rang. "Let's see if he's kept his promise." Munro lifted the phone. It was Dejes. "Are you ready, Mr. Munro?"

"Got my safe conduct?" asked Munro.

"Your witnesses? Look from your door."

245

"I'll take your word for it. What's the drill?"

"The way is clear. You are free to go." Dejes rang off.

Munro believed him. This was no time to play tricks. Dejes had done what he said: he had caught his big fish, the small fry could go. Munro crossed to the door. He still held his gun, but out of sight. This show of caution was the dregs of an old habit. He kicked back the door. The village was empty; the house opposite silent. Even the machine-gun had been pulled out of sight. From somewhere in the distance came the bleating of flocks.

"Watch it," called Stephan.

"Not a thing," said Munro.

Stephan joined him, staying in shadow, peering down the street. The pink light warmed into sunshine.

"If I ran now . . ."

"Think you'd make it?" asked Munro.

Stephan looked at the silent houses. Nothing moved. No one appeared.

He shook his head. "No," he said, "besides I'd mess it up for you. Can't do that again."

"Thanks," said Munro.

But Stephan found it hard to leave the open door, and the morning light.

"He's done you proud," said Stephan. "Look at the reception! They'll see fair play."

"What is it?"

Munro edged into the doorway and looked out. On the far side of the bridge he could see a number of Greek uniforms.

"Albanian soldiers in disguise?" queried Munro.

"You'd check the details on your own grave," said Stephan. "They are Greek."

Munro shouted to the men on the bridge. They called back.

"Greek," said Stephan. "You're safe."

Munro had been sure all along. "This could be your chance," he said. "As I go, slip out the way we came."

Stephan pushed him out. "You're talking to the expert," he said.

Munro stepped into the street. If they were going to

246

shoot him, now would be the time. He moved slowly and deliberately down the street. Not far away, with growing clarity, was the sound of animals.

At the end of the house he caught a glimpse of men crouching, rifles in hand, keeping cover. They didn't move. Munro knew he was a free man. Only then did he realize there were more than Greek soldiers on the other side of the bridge. The first person he saw was Yanni. The fat man was a little behind a squad of soldiers, watching Munro. He didn't move. Beside him was the gaunt figure of Professor Rhodes; the old man was peering restlessly towards the village. Obviously he couldn't see Munro, and turned to enquire impatiently of the girl at his elbow. Munro saw Susan. He had a rush of discordant emotions—tenderness, and anger. A step behind her stood Cecil. This was indeed a reception committee! Munro strode smartly across the bridge. He stopped to look back. Dejes was close to the broken cart. Munro lifted a hand in recognition. Then he was surrounded. The Greek captain saluted him. He began asking questions. Munro found his mind had gone blank. Yanni was pumping his hand. "Thank God, Mr. Munro, thank God."

"Thank you," said Munro. He couldn't think what he had done to inspire such devotion in Yanni.

"Well done," said Cecil. "Quite the most spectacular escape on any of our files."

"I'll send you a report," said Munro. He was saying anything that came into his head, because he didn't want to look at the girl. She was standing with her face against Rhodes, as if she were crying.

"And what about Stephan?" asked Cecil.

Munro looked at him blankly.

"Stephan?" He couldn't think what Cecil was talking about. "Died years ago."

"Come along, old fellow," said Cecil, "it's all over now. All on the same side. You got the coded message, I suppose."

Munro nodded. "It did the trick."

"Then let's not fool about," said Cecil. "It implicated

Stephan, so he's alive. These blokes across there would confirm it."

"Forget him," said Munro. "The heart stopped functioning a long time ago, if, indeed, it ever was alive."

"My dear Munro, it was always like that with Stephan. That's what made him invaluable. Where is he, old fellow? Do hurry up."

Munro indicated the house. "I've just left him."

"If they let you go . . ." began Cecil.

Munro interrupted. "Not a chance! Stephan has the whole of their security locked up in his head."

"He *must* escape!"

"He's thinking about it."

"He knows what will happen if he gets caught?"

"Yes."

"For heaven's sake, Munro," Cecil exploded, "we have to do something. The man must be a mine of information."

"Dejes would agree." Munro nodded to where Dejes stood.

The Greek captain began to get impatient. "Time we go, sir," he said to Cecil.

"Yes, yes, just a moment." Cecil turned to Munro. "How many men does Dejes have?"

"About nine. There are one or two more around the back."

"Only nine?"

"Yes. He didn't want to blow the affair up any bigger. It all reflects badly on him."

Cecil looked at the Greek patrol. There were about thirty. The entire area squad had been mustered.

"Don't try it, Cecil," said Munro.

"There is a tide in the affairs of men," said Cecil.

Munro began to feel he was the only rational being in a sea of insanity. Was Cecil prepared to risk his reputation? For what? A cardboard cut-out Stephan Aroso, who didn't see the implications of his actions? Who took tricks or lost them with cards that were people? Playing a game with no rules? Stephan wasn't a man to save.

"I won't help you," said Munro.

"I understand," said Cecil. "He must be hard to forgive."

248

The noise of the sheep and goats mingled with men shouting and barking dogs. They'd been getting closer since first light. The Sarakatsan tried to avoid villages, but that was difficult at Karlovo. They had slowed a little when they saw uniformed men. Now the first startled sheep and goats hurried across the village street.

"A godsend," breathed Cecil. He called to Rhodes. "Professor! We need your advice. They still have Stephan Aroso. I believe you know him." Cecil sounded like a recruiting sergeant, but he rallied the old man's patriotic interest.

"Of course I do," said Rhodes. "It was his grave . . ."

"He's not dead," said Cecil, "he's a prisoner. In that house. Trying to make a break for it."

"Look, Professor," Munro had to protest, "he's been working for those people. Any trouble he's in . . ."

Cecil interrupted. "He has valuable material for us. If we could get the boy back, instead of letting him fall into their hands . . . Munro knows what their jails are like."

"They won't jail him," said Munro.

"We must get him out," said Rhodes. The old man braced himself. "We can't leave one of our own men."

"Listen Rhodes," Munro found he was shouting, "the man's a traitor . . . He has no loyalty, no conscience— what the hell can you do anyhow? These Greeks aren't going to help you. You want to start a war?"

"Why not?" The old man's head, so recently on a hospital pillow, was back like a horse at the ready. Munro needed an ally. "Don't let these Greeks do anything," he said to Yanni.

Yanni threw up his hands. The Greek captain looked on uncomprehending.

"Just a diversion, a threat. That's all we need," called Cecil. He still hoped for Munro's co-operation. "I won't let the old fellow do anything foolish. I've got no brief for Stephan. We'll just get all we can out of him. He'll answer for what he's done."

Did Cecil think one corruption absolved another? Let them stew in their own juice, thought Munro.

The nomads were streaming through the village.

"Demand his release," said Cecil. And Rhodes stalked down the bridge. Dejes saw him coming. He had some respect for the old man, in spite of the absurd dream-world he lived in.

Cecil chose his moment carefully: Rhodes was about half-way, and the eyes of those on the other side were focused on him. Cecil held his gun aloft and fired into the air.

There was an echoing burst from the house opposite as Stephan snatched at a last straw. He was down the street, and on to the bridge before anyone saw him.

If he could get beyond the old man, use him as cover—no one would gun down *that* symbol of past comradeship. At speed, gun barking, unable to take proper aim, he felt the stone bridge under his feet. The patrol were slow opening up. When they did, it was a ragged volley. Dejes yelled, sensing disaster. The sergeant let off a burst with the machine-gun from the room above, but he feared hitting the civilians.

But someone had a lucky shot. A bullet, deflected from the parapet, grazed Stephan's leg. It was just enough to send him staggering to the wall, but he had plenty of fight left. He always had guts, thought Munro. He pushed himself along, hobbling, using the wall as a man might use a stick, hopping, jumping, limping. Dejes yelled at his men. They swung their rifles around on Stephan. "Get down," shouted Yanni. A volley whistled along the stone-work. Miraculously, nothing touched Rhodes. The old man hesitated. The omnipotence drained from him. He was suddenly a foolish old poet in the middle of a border brawl. He could do nothing to help the young man who grinned, mouth stretched in comedy and pain.

"Get him back," shouted Munro. And when Cecil hesitated he added, "If anything happens to Rhodes I'll see you charged with murder."

Not a charge that would hold, Cecil told himself, but he called to the old man, and the white head came tottering back; stopping, hesitating again, momentarily lost. And as for Stephan—he was going to make it! He went down on one knee, but pulled himself up, took another uncertain

250

step . . . then another. It was willpower that kept him upright. Even when shaken as another shot took him on the shoulder, he stayed walking. The mechanism of survival was strong within. Another lurch against the wall and he was partly covered by Rhodes, dazed in the middle of the path, standing between the wounded man and his executioners, unwittingly shielding him.

And at this flash-point a Greek guard clapped his hand to his arm and saw blood streaming down; looking at his captain in questioning surprise.

This was an insult to be answered. The captain gave an angry order. They were at the ready. This should have been enough to restrain those on the other side. Dejes watched the wounded Stephan. He had come to a swaying stop. Each step was a struggle. Did he need one more bullet to finish him off?

A bullet did come—from a nervous patrolman on the Greek soil. It sparked off a wild burst on either side. In it Stephan stumbled a step, stood upright, and Munro had an insight into what was about to happen. Stephan would reach freedom; would be patched up as a shell of a man; would indeed be a source of information for Cecil or Sir John; would live, or linger this side of the grave he was already supposed to inhabit—and might well put cold fingers of death on those still living.

It would be hard to say, in the mêlée of shots, which bullet finally brought Stephan down. But as he dropped the shooting died, and Munro put his gun back in its hiding-place. He brushed past Rhodes, and took the few steps that Stephan hadn't managed to achieve. He picked him up and carried him back to Greece.

He didn't hear what Cecil said to him. He heard the girl, white-faced, loving, and afraid; but left her unacknowledged and unanswered.

He didn't let anyone help carry the body to the waiting car. For though he had learned exactly what this man had done, some sad bond of brotherhood still meant that Stephan dead was something more than those who walked beside him. Munro put the body in the patrol truck, and the Greek captain saluted and drove off.

Munro had one last duty. He turned and signaled to Dejes. He didn't want the little man to think he had been part of that betrayal. Dejes saw him, and signaled back.

"Have you a car?" Munro asked Yanni.

"At the end of the track," said Yanni.

They walked up the slope ahead of the others.

Cecil had some difficulty helping Rhodes. He was aware that Munro avoided his eye. Cecil was shaken by suspicion. He doubted if anything could ever be proved; but he guessed that Munro, whom he had used to shape the pattern of his intrigue, had taken it upon himself to shape the end.

When he got to the beginning of the track with Susan and Rhodes, the captain and his men were there; but Munro had gone with Yanni. He wasn't at the Professor's villa when they got there. It was later that day they learned that Munro had already caught a flight from Athens.

"I wanted to see him," said Cecil angrily, when he saw Yanni two days later. "Miss Marsh was very upset. She wanted to see him as well."

Yanni shrugged. "He said nothing of either of you."

"What *did* he say?" inquired Cecil.

"Only that it is as much as a man can do to grow older, do what he sees fit to do, and to stay alive."

"What the devil was he on about?"

"I thought he was talking about Stephan . . . but Stephan didn't stay alive. So perhaps he was speaking of himself."

Cecil was not impressed.

Cecil found him on the promenade at Eastbourne. Spring was warm, and splashed with color. Munro was leaning on a rail looking out to sea.

"What do you want?" Munro was very sure of himself.

"I suppose you heard about Sir John," said Cecil.

"They kicked him out," said Munro.

"That's right. For the incident at Karlovo."

"Wrong man for the job anyhow," said Munro.

"I have something for you," said Cecil.

Munro said nothing. Cecil warmed to his task, buoyant, confident.

"It's in a friendly country, so-called. I need a man, a known agent. You've been all over the papers twice in your life. It will be tricky. Interested?"

Munro gave nothing away. Cecil played his next card. "That was a good little team you made last time, you and Susan. I've put you together again. She's good at the business—for a woman. And she'll be able to give you a hand."

Munro still didn't say anything, but they walked away together.